The End of the Innocence

ALESSANDRA TORRE

www.alessandratorre.com

Cover Designer: Miguel Kilantang, Jr.
www.migzworks.com

Editor: Madison Seidler
www.madisonseidler.com

To the women who teach their sons to open doors, respect women, and make us laugh. Thank you.

They say you will never love someone like you love your children. But my love for Brad was so consuming, so boundless. It stretched my universe and took over every breath, heartbeat, and thought. How could I possibly love anyone more? It seemed impossible.

Prologue

Blindfolded. It was how this whole thing started; it was the birth of my sexual awakening, the first loose thread that started the unraveling of my inhibitions. It almost seemed fitting that, in what could be the end of my life, I was, once again, blindfolded.

I woke up in pure blackness, my senses reawakening one by one, slowly reporting grim details of my surroundings. *Sight.* Pure dark, so complete in its entirety that I felt a wave of claustrophobia hit me. *Sound.* Muffled voices, hard tones filled with anger, hate, and—most terrifying of all—glee. The rustle of fabric against my ear as I twisted my head, the sound informing my brain that I was, in fact, blindfolded. *Smell.* A sickly-sweet scent, coming from the blindfold, almost—but not quite—overriding the dirty, masculine stench that reeked in this room. *Taste.* Wet cloth in my mouth, tugging at my skin, keeping my tongue in place, the horrible aftertaste of vomit in my mouth. *Touch.* Hands bound behind my back with rough, scratchy rope. Ankles spread and secured to chair legs beneath me. Sitting upright, utterly secured, my body recognizing, even without sight, the bruises that covered me.

My brain understood everything about the situation at once, bursting into reality in one, horrific instance, like stepping into the harsh sun, painful in its strength. I screamed through the blindfold, my effort producing only a small sound, and strained every muscle, thrashing my body from side to side, trying to free some small part of my body in at least one minor way. The chair rocked, tipped, and in an agonizingly slow motion, tipped backward and crashed to the concrete floor. The impact slammed my head back, and with one painful crack, my body stilled, all senses instantly snuffed.

Chapter 1

Fiancée. It was a role I knew, had been in just a couple of months earlier. But now, back in the title, with Brad De Luca as my future husband, it felt completely different. I woke slowly, pulling myself out of sleep, aided by the warm sear of his skin against my bare back, the sigh of his breath against my hair, the thrust of his pelvis as he let me know he was up in the naughtiest way possible. Yes, I could get used to this. Yes, I could spend the next fifty years of my life waking up in his arms.

I rolled over, putting us face to face, his eyes still closed, his mouth curving into a smile. I studied the thick line of his lashes, the peace on his face, peace that would disappear as soon as his eyes opened, as soon as intensity stole over his features and dominance ruled the beautiful canvas of his face.

Then his eyes opened, and I lost some of my breath. Five minutes later, he took that breath in a completely different way. With my back arched against the sheets, my hands deep in his hair, the glitter of diamond on my finger the only thing respectful and sane about our union.

I dressed for work, pairing a gray suit and cream shirt, and was putting on earrings when Brad came out of the bathroom, wrapped in a towel, steam following him into the room. He stopped short when he saw me, frowning slightly. "Are you wearing that to my father's house?"

I turned away from the mirror, wincing slightly when my earring didn't go the right way through my ear. "No, *sweetie*, I am wearing this for work. That place that I go to during the week?" I looked at my watch. "The place I will be late to if I don't run downstairs and eat." I moved my hand quickly down, but not before my bare finger caught his eye.

"Where's your ring?"

"It's ah, on top of the safe. I figured you could put it inside."

He stepped forward slowly, the scent of soap and masculinity disturbing my senses. "And why would I do that?"

"I don't know ... so it doesn't get stolen?" I smiled sweetly at him and reached for my makeup bag, his iron grip grabbing my wrist before I made it to the pink plastic. I frowned up at him, tugging with my wrist until he finally released me.

"What is this about?" He towered over me in my bare feet, and I struck a defiant pose, looking up at him with all the tenacity I could muster.

"It's about *me* trying to get to work on time."

"I thought you agreed to come to my father's with me."

"Ah ... no. I dropped the subject, and you assumed I agreed."

"This seems suspiciously like something I would attempt." He folded him arms, looking down at me, a frown on his face — a frown that was fighting to keep from breaking into a grin.

"Good. Then you should see the wisdom in it." I reached for the makeup bag again, and he blocked my arm. I threw up my hands. *Fuck the makeup.* Moving around him, I headed to the bathroom.

"Okay, so you don't want to go to my father's. Fine. What's the deal with the ring? You don't like it?" He had the nerve to look almost hurt. Almost. I don't think anything could hurt this man's ego.

I rolled my eyes at him. "I love the ring. Fucking Marilyn Monroe would love that ring. It's not that."

"Okay. It's the office."

"Yes." I set down the toothbrush I was preparing and turned to him. "I am more than a little freaked out by the idea of the office knowing about our engagement. I didn't commit to working for CDB past this semester. Why go through all that when I can just keep it a secret 'til this semester ends?"

"I'm not used to being hidden, Julia."

I groaned inwardly, wanting to be anywhere other than here, having any discussion other than this one. Especially when I was running late. "I am not *hiding* you. I am avoiding lots of questions, discussions, and evil stares. Please, Brad." I clasped my hands in front of me and tried my best puppy-dog stare, one that I had not had much practice in, and I think a sad clown face ended up coming out instead.

He looked at me with a mixture of confusion and amusement, then threw up his hands and left. With a smile, I relaxed, picking up the toothpaste tube.

He was back before I had time to begin brushing. He set the ring box down with a thud on the marble counter next to me. "Wear it." I threw the toothpaste down and turned to him with a retort on my lips. "I'll be in the office around ten. I'll tell my staff, so you can either be the engaged assistant who looks like she's hiding her engagement, or you can be the confident fiancée I know you are. But I am not going to spend the next seven weeks pretending you don't exist when I want to tell everyone the good news." He winked at me, turned on his heel, and left, my retort dying a slow and painful death in my throat. *Ugh.* Great first day of engagery. I had a brief understanding of what it must have been like for Luke. I had been a pretty heavy-handed dictator in that relationship.

I steamed my way through the entire teeth-brushing process, staring at the damn velvet box the entire time. I had absolutely no doubt that Brad would do exactly as he had promised, telling the news to anyone and everyone he met. A small part of me, one that jumped up and down and did the salsa, was happy that he was proud. Proud of me, of our relationship, of our engagement. That he wasn't treating it as a prison sentence. I tried to suffocate the happy part of myself but failed miserably.

I opened up the velvet box and looked at the ring again. It was so heartbreakingly beautiful, and I was terrified of falling in love with it and then one day having to give it up. I picked out the ring and slid it on, my knees weakening a little in the process. I allowed myself a brief, small happy dance in the middle of the bathroom, then put on my game face and headed downstairs.

I entered the kitchen and waved hello to Martha, hoping to grab a bagel and escape without interrogation, but I knew from the way she set down her hand towel and beamed at me, that I wasn't going to get out easily.

"Julia." She held out her arms and came around the island, pulling me into a strong, soft, lavender-scented embrace. "I am so happy for you." She tightened the hug, and I laughed at the sheer strength of it.

I pulled out of the hug. "I'm sorry, is this the same woman who told me to get my ass out of her house, just—what—*two* weeks ago?" I grinned mischievously and shot around her, grabbing an orange and some grapes from a bowl on the counter.

"Nope. That was bitchy Martha. You're part of the family now, so I'll keep her hidden away." She waddled after me. "You're not eating just fruit. Let me fix you something else."

"I can't," I warbled from a mouthful of grapes. "I'm late for work already." She glared at me, and I saw a bit of the Martha I remembered. "I'll eat tonight, whatever you make, I promise!" I called out the last two words as I trotted out the door, pulling it softly, but firmly closed behind me. I stopped short when I saw my Camry, parked to the side of the garage, Brad, on his cell, leaning against it. He saw me and met me halfway, ending the call and holding out my keys, his eyes sweeping over my ring finger.

I snatched the keys from his outstretched hand, stepping up on my tiptoes and giving him a brief kiss. "Thanks."

"My pleasure. I'll call you in a few hours."

I rolled my eyes. "Fine. Good luck this morning. Please don't come back with news of my eminent demise."

He looked wounded. "Baby, I have better negotiation skills than that. At the most, you'll have a few broken kneecaps. At the most."

"Oh, that's hilarious. Really. So funny." I punched his arm and opened the car door. His hand grabbed my arm and caught me as I started to get in.

"Wait." He pressed back, gently, and I stumbled, pressed against the side of the car. I caught a glimpse of his face a second too late, and he kissed me before I could move. The kiss was soft, not the typical De Luca passion-fest, and he added a second one before raising his head and smiling down at me. "I love you."

"Love you, too," I mumbled, not able to take my eyes off the depths of his.

He leaned down, brushing his lips over my neck, then whispered in my ear. "I like seeing you wear the ring."

"You like getting your way."

"That too." He squeezed my waist and held the door, waiting for me to get in before closing it. I started the engine and put the car in reverse, watching him walk around and enter the garage.

Chapter 2

My car grumbled as it moved through downtown, and I reached out with a distracted hand, feeling around the inside of my purse until I found my phone. I dialed Olivia, a quick glance at the clock confirming that Becca's ass would be drooling and snoring right about now.

"About damn time. You can't leave us hanging like that!" Her indignant tone had me smiling, and the nerves between my shoulder blades relaxed slightly.

"Hanging? You knew?"

"Yes, we knew!" she snapped. "That delicious man of yours had a car — a *limo* — pick us both up yesterday afternoon and take us to the jewelry store."

I twisted my mouth. "And you're telling me Becca kept *that* quiet all night long?"

She giggled. "I fed her tequila. With a side of fajitas. And hid her phone. We thought you'd text or call us with the news, but we ended up drinking all night while waiting." The irritation in her voice was probably more from the hangover than the delayed news, but I spoke quickly to cover my tracks.

"I'm sorry, O. Things got … distracting when we made it back home."

"But you said yes."

"Yes, I said yes!" I suddenly realized that my best friends didn't really know my connection to Brad, the fact that I loved him. So much had slid by under their radar. They didn't know about Brad's family, about the situations that had pushed us together faster than normal relationship protocols allowed. I suddenly picked up on the odd tone of Olivia's voice — not exactly enthusiastic — caution lacing her words. "I love him," I said quickly.

"It hasn't been very long, Jules. And you just broke off your last engagement — "

"This is different. Brad isn't Luke."

"You got that right." The words were spoken under her breath, and I didn't know whether to take them as praise or criticism.

I drove in silence for a moment, not sure of what to say, the pressure building as my car neared the office. *I haven't prepared, I don't know what to say to the office, I need to go.*

"Well …" Olivia drawled. "Becca is passed out on my couch. I've got a nine AM class, so I'll leave her here. But we need to celebrate. Los Compadres at six?"

I bit my bottom lip. I love the girls and wanted to share the excitement of my engagement. But I would also need to find out how Brad's meeting with his father went, how his wing of the office responded, share my own stories of whateverthehell was about to happen inside the firm's prestigious walls. I turned on my blinker, pulled up, and got a ticket for the parking garage. "Another night, O. Give Becca a giant hug when she wakes up, and I'll call you guys tomorrow."

"I'd say you only get engaged once, but with your track record …" I heard the screech of hangers as she finished the flat sentence, irritation coating the words.

"Love you, too, Olivia."

"Yeah. And congrats." She made the word sound as non-congratulatory as humanly possible.

"Thanks." I made a face and ended the call. Stuffing the phone into my purse, I pulled into a spot. I took a moment — a head against the headrest, take a deep breath, put a fucking game face on moment — that did absolutely nothing to calm my nerves. Then I, with my big ass rock, opened the car door.

Chapter 3

7:45 a.m.: The doomed walk of the dead through the lobby. I shielded my ring finger with my purse and smiled a brief hello to Ancient Dorothy, bee-lining for the elevators. I rode up alone, taking advantage of the silence to whisper a short prayer — apologizing for any recent sins and praying for compassion.

I was making coffee when the first person noticed the ring. It was hard to miss, sparkling brilliantly under overhead fluorescents, and Beverly, the wing's secretary, pounced on it like a kitten going after catnip. "What is *that*?" She dropped her lunch box in the fridge and grabbed my hand with both of hers, oblivious to the dirty coffee filter I was holding, and I watched in irritation as used grounds flew everywhere, spotting the white tile with black specks. Her squat body was rooted to the ground, and she gripped my hand with a warrior's intensity, her eyes fixated on the ring like it was a steaming hot funnel cake. I tried to gently tug my hand away, but it was like trying to pull Excalibur's sword from the stone.

"I didn't know you were dating anyone!" Beverly's eyes left the stone and focused on me intently. "Did you get back together with your ex?"

"Errr ... No." I smiled, though I think it came off more like a grimace. "This is someone new."

"And you're *already* engaged?" She tilted her head at me, puzzled, and I cursed the day I ever shared a moment of personal discussion with this woman, or any other creature on this floor.

"Yes. It is quite sudden." I looked pointedly at the deflated coffee filter, and she released my hand with a quick, hurried movement.

"Oh my goodness, dear, I am sorry."

I smiled and moved to the trash, dumping the filter and hoping she would leave.

"That is *quite* a ring. What does your fiancé do?" She moved closer, officially entering my personal bubble.

Aw crap. "He's an attorney," I said offhand, washing my hands as noisily as possible, then started opening and closing cabinets, trying to put as many items and sounds between Beverly and me as possible. "I really can't chat, Beverly. I've got to get this coffee on."

"An *attorney*!" She beamed proudly. "Well, I know *lots* of attorneys. You know, I've been here thirteen years, and our cases involve firms from all over the city. He's got to be a new attorney, maybe he interned here. What's his name?"

I filled up the water reservoir, making a face and pointing to my ear, as if the pathetic pressure from the faucet was a gushing flow of Niagara proportions. That didn't work. She waited patiently by the sink, and the minute I turned the faucet off, she spoke. "What's his name?"

Fuck, fuck, fuck, fuck, fuck. I was out of options. "I think you probably know him," I said brightly, adding the water container to the coffee pot, and scooping out fresh grounds. "He works in the East Wing. His name is Brad."

I really didn't want to look at her, didn't want to see whatever expression crossed her face, but my eyes were drawn to her without bidding, as if they had flipped my subconscious the bird and did exactly what they wanted to because *ohmygodthiswasgoingtobetoogoodtomiss.* She tilted her head, probably trying to think what peon in the East Wing was named Brad, because it couldn't possibly be *the* Brad, and I watched with slow horror the moment her mind came up blank and rested on the only possible conclusion.

She stilled, her sturdy body freezing, and teetered a bit, sticking a hand out and grabbing the counter. Her face took on an odd expression, somewhere between smelling something sour and being constipated. It contorted for three long seconds, in which her mouth opened and closed twice, no words coming out. Finally, she swallowed hard and tried again.

"Brad *De Luca*?" Her voice still held a glimmer of hope, a possibility that she might be mistaken, that there was some new guy, some pencil-pushing nerd stuck in a small corner of divorce, who she hadn't yet heard of. Some Brad Smith, or Taylor, or anything other than De Luca. I hated to squash that hope, almost felt a civil duty to lie. Almost.

I finished the damn coffee-making process and pushed START with an almost proud finality. *Made it through that alive.* Then, I turned back to Beverly. "Yes. Brad De Luca. Good, you do know him." We did this weird country line dance shuffle where I tried to get around her, and she unintentionally kept getting in my way, and then I finally escaped, and was halfway out the door when I felt her iron grip on my arm. I turned, pasting a bright smile on my face. "Yes?"

I was yanked backward so hard I think one of my heels partially came off. Unsure, confused Beverly was gone, and in her place was a court marshal of Judge Judy proportions. She shut the kitchen door in a swift motion — *I didn't even know the kitchen had a door* — and stuck both hands on her hips, squaring off to me. "You. Are Engaged. To Brad. De Luca." She spoke slowly, drawing out the sentence excruciatingly, and seemed to physically grow bigger with every word.

"Yes." I tried to maintain a cheerful disposition, but the air in the room was thick, and I was a little worried she might eat me for lunch instead of whatever was in her polka-dotted lunchbox.

"*The* Brad De Luca. The man who thinks it's his God damn calling to screw each and every hot female in a twenty-mile radius? The man who chews and spits out poor little divorcing husbands like it's a blood sport? The man who, in some ridiculous, dotted-line way, is both my and your *boss*?" Her voice rose with every sentence, until I was certain that every person in our wing could hear her shouts. I had never heard the woman yell, much less curse before.

"Ummm … yes?" I was terrified of feeding this fire. The woman had morphed into a Doberman right before my eyes. I was trying to formulate a more intelligent answer when the kitchen door flew open, almost smacking Crazy Beverly in the back. I felt a momentary burst of relief at my rescue, until I saw the individual holding open the door. Sheila. *Oh shit.*

"Beverly! What in God's name has gotten into you! We have *clients* in the lobby, for goodness sake!" Her cultured, dignified tone was as perturbed as I'd ever heard it, and she pierced Beverly with an appalled stare. I expected Beverly to deflate slightly, acknowledge her scorning — to apologize. But she stood firm and met Sheila's stare head-on. She raised a finger, pointing to me. *No. Please no. It's Monday for Christ's sake. Go easy on me.*

"Julia, *tell* her."

I died a little, right there, on the kitchen floor. My distress grew when I heard a click and looked up to see the kitchen door, once again, closed. Sheila now matched Beverly, her hands on her hips, her iron gaze drilled into mine. Beverly had a smug look on her face that I wanted to smack right off.

Chapter 4

"Julia? What's this about?" Sheila's voice was kinder, but firm. She probably thought I had forgotten to order copy paper again.

"Nothing." I smiled brightly, my face beginning to hurt from all of the fakeness. "Beverly had noticed my engagement ring, and I was just sharing with her the good news. That is all."

"Yes. Julia is engaged. Wahoo. Guess to *who*, Sheila?" Beverly's voice had lost its anger and was now evil in intent, almost gleeful at my upcoming demise.

"*This* is what you are standing here yammering about? *Yelling* about!" Sheila threw up her hands in disgust. "Julia, congratulations on your engagement. But we have a business to run, and can't stand here gossiping all day. Beverly, you should know better." She turned, wiping her hands on her pants, and reached for the doorknob.

"Brad. De. Luca," Beverly's voice crowed in the small kitchen, causing Sheila to pause in her exit. She turned, eyes sharp.

"What? What about Brad De Luca?"

"*He* is who Julia is engaged to. Brad De Luca."
Beverly gestured to me with the motion someone
might use to display a flat tire. Disappointed,
irritated. *What are we going to do about this damn
Julia?*

Sheila brought a hand to her forehead, squared her
shoulders, and stood even straighter. "Beverly,
please leave us. There are clients in the lobby, please
attend to them. Also, let Mr. Burge know that I have
Julia, so that he does not wonder where she is. And
don't *ever* raise your voice in this office again. I
don't care what the reason." She spoke quietly,
which scared me even more than Beverly had.

Beverly, somewhat subdued, left the kitchen, and
we were alone. I backed up in nervous anticipation.

"Is this correct, what Beverly said? You are *engaged*
to Brad De Luca?"

"Yes."

"This is a new event?"

"Yes. As of last night." The situation felt eerily
similar to being questioned by police.

She blew out a breath and looked sharply at me, her
wrinkles enhanced by her stern expression. "I may
be confused, but I feel like you and I had a

conversation about Brad. A conversation where I told you his reputation, and warned you not to fall victim to him. You don't want to be like that *other* intern, Julia. This will ruin your reputation, both with this firm and any other."

I bristled slightly. "I'm not sleeping with a firm partner, Sheila. I'm *marrying* him. I think there is a big difference."

Her brows knitted together. "Are you pregnant?"

I physically gasped at that. "What? No!"

She scoffed. "Well, Brad De Luca is not the marrying sort. Not to anyone, much less an intern who he has known less than ... well, I don't know how long you two have been carrying on this secret. But less than two months. If you're *not* pregnant, then why? Why would he settle down?" Her steely gaze left no possibility of evasion.

I shrugged my shoulders. "We're in love." Even to my ears, it sounded weak and pathetic.

She actually laughed at the statement. Then she shook her head and stepped forward, clasping my hands in hers, her tone turning condescending. "Julia. That man doesn't love anyone but himself. I don't know what is going on, or why he would toy with you, but you do not want to marry Brad De Luca. Find a sweet, caring boy who will treat you like the prize you are, and let men like Brad grow old, alone and miserable." She patted my hand, her palm brushing against my ring, and she recoiled at the contact. She dropped my hand and stepped back, opening the door and leaving me alone in the kitchen.

Behind me the coffee pot dinged.

Coffee. That hateful liquid that had *certainly* not been worth the last five minutes of hell. I looked back at the open door, my mind going through the other inhabitants of our wing, envisioning the next eight hours and the additional hell they would bring. It was even worse than I had imagined, an assault of disapproval mixed with a side of haughtiness. It soured whatever good feeling I had, and I hated them for marring my excitement.

I poured Burge a cup and carried it to his office, bringing it on a tray with cream and sugar. I knocked on the door gently, and then pushed it open. He was typing, and looked up at my approach, a smile crossing his face.

"Good morning," I said. "How do you take your coffee?"

"Just black. Thank you." He stood, taking the coffee from the tray and straightened his glasses. "This is your first week of the fall semester, is that correct?"

"Yes, sir. Classes start this Wednesday, so I'll only work on Tuesdays and Thursdays after today."

"What are your plans after graduation?" He sat, gesturing to an empty seat.

"Law school, sir." I sat, clasping my damp hands in front of me, covering my ring with the palm of my other hand.

"Will you go to law school here?"

"Yes. Assuming I am admitted," I said with a smile. It was a decision that Brad and I hadn't discussed. But my plan, all along, had been to stay here. To maintain the roots I had put down and keep my alma mater.

"Right. One of the things on Broward's desks was a form to complete for your professor. It asks about your conduct and work product, and asks for a recommendation letter." He moved the form underneath the desk lamp and squinted at it.

"Yes. That will be crucial to my law school application." My leg shook nervously, and I stilled it, pushing down on the floor with my toe.

"The problem is, I haven't been here. I'll have Sheila complete it and type up something for me to sign." He moved the paper dismissively and was on the verge of saying something else when I shot to my feet.

"Sir. I would really prefer Sheila not complete the form for me." *My conduct?*

He frowned at me over the desk. "Why not?"

Yes, Julia. Why not? "Sheila and I recently had a … disagreement. I worry that she won't be impartial."

His frown remained, etched into his face with the staying power of stone. "I doubt that. Sheila seems very capable, and not one to hold grudges." His blue eyes hardened behind his glasses. "But, I will let you know that I have very little patience for office drama."

The statement, almost comical after the kitchen standoff, hung in the air, my mind unable to conjure a response. I nodded, a ridiculous movement that didn't respond to his comment at all, and stood, picking up the coffee tray and exiting his office. I didn't bother returning it to the kitchen, instead bee-lining for my office and shutting the door. I set the tray on an empty chair and unlocked my computer, trying to focus on anything, everything, but the disaster this day was quickly becoming.

I could physically feel the buzz outside my door. Feel the energy. It fought in the hall and pushed at my closed door. Whispers. Chatter. Gasps and scoffs. The good news is that I wouldn't have to go around and tell each and every person about the engagement. The bad news is that eventually I would have to leave my office.

Chapter 5

Brad pulled up to the guard gate of his family's estate, waving to the guards and waiting while they went through the ridiculous procedure of making sure that he wasn't carrying anything of concern in his trunk or under his car. The iron gates in front of him finally parted, and he pulled in, rounding the curves of the drive until he came to a stop in front of the imposing home.

Oddly, his father opened the door, and Brad glanced around for the staff.

"This needs to be quick, Brad. I have items to attend to."

Brad nodded, meeting his father's eyes and walking past him to the formal living room, which had not changed since his childhood. He stopped next to the massive stone fireplace. His father closed the front door, and the room darkened considerably. With his hands in his pockets, he turned to face his father, who eyed him warily, skipping right to the point. "You mentioned a wrinkle in this situation?" his father prompted.

"Yes. Last night I asked Julia for her hand in marriage. She accepted."

His father's eyes closed briefly, and he took a few slow steps forward and sat in a cream, wing-backed chair, gripping the arms tightly as he leaned back. "Sit."

"I don't have much time. Like you, I have business to attend to." He sat on the chair across from his father and studied him across the space.

His father sighed, a raspy, exasperated sound. "Is this you being stubborn? I'm assuming this Julia you speak of is the intern who has been so troublesome?"

"Yes, that is Julia. And no, I am not being stubborn. I love her."

"I thought you were too intelligent to allow love to dictate your life."

Brad laughed. "It isn't a dictation. You are thinking in terms of power, which this isn't about."

"Isn't it? You've played the only hand that could win this game. And twisted my arm in the process. You've won this match, Brad. But signed yourself up for a lifetime of servitude in the process."

"It's not a lifetime of servitude."

The old man laughed sharply, the quick action causing his chest to clench, and he stifled the outburst, coughing and staring grimly at Brad. "Right. Because you can just divorce, right? My son, the king of destroying marriages, of ripping apart families." He shook his head bitterly. "You disgust me."

Brad stood, his hands clamped in fists. "Because you are my father, and I still respect the head of this family, I won't respond to that with what is in my heart. But know that I find it despicable that, of all of your sons, I would be the one that you find shameful. Thank you for reminding me of why I cut off contact with you."

He strode past the old man's chair and opened the door, the harsh sun filling the room with light.

◆◆◆

Word jumped, like a bloodthirsty flea, from our wing to the rest of the firm, spreading through the East Wing within five minutes of Beverly leaving the kitchen. By the time Brad stepped off the elevator, there was not a person in Clarke, De Luca, & Burge who hadn't received word of the train wreck engagement of the fourth floor. He pushed open the heavy door to the East Wing, and silence fell, cloaking the space with thick, palatable tension. He smiled, welcoming the change and what it meant. *Julia must have told them.* He strode into the lobby, meeting his secretaries' tense greetings with an easy grin.

He certainly wasn't new to disdain, gossip, or disapproval. He was expecting that, but—as he walked through the space—this mood felt different. He settled into his office, leaning back in his desk chair, trying to decipher the atmosphere. It was almost hostile, as if from a swarm of irate, overprotective fathers, instead of faithful and loyal staff. *Fathers*. The oversight hit him squarely, and he sat quickly forward, cursing his lack of attention. Grabbing his phone, he dialed Julia's extension.

♥♥♥

I exhaled with relief when I saw Brad's number light up on my phone's display. *Thank God*. He was here, and for once, I needed his protective, overbearing self. "Hi," I whimpered into the phone.

He ignored the pitiful tone of my greeting, barging right into a question. "What's your father going to think?"

I sat up, my attention refocusing. "My father?"

"Yes. Have you told him?"

"About our engagement?"

"Yes."

"No. I haven't told anyone. Other than Beverly and Sheila, who, I assume, have told everyone within a three-mile radius." I sighed dramatically. "Brad. It's *horrible*. They were so mean to me when they found out."

The infuriated response I expected didn't come. His storm to my rescue, threats to fire everyone, his mandate that 'everyone be nice to Julia' didn't even enter his thought process. The damn man *chuckled*. "Babe. You've *got* to have thicker skin than that."

I frowned into the phone, trying to formulate an appropriate withering response when he spoke again.

"So, you haven't told your father."

"No. I just told you that."

"Okay. Let's go to Centaur for lunch. We can discuss it then. In the meantime, don't tell anyone else."

Like *that* was a remote possibility. "You act like I'm running around waving a big ass sign! I'm the one who wanted to wait to share the news. Speaking of fathers, did yours take the news well?"

There was a brief moment of silence, which definitely wasn't a good sign. "He's fine," Brad bit out. "You are officially out of danger. But he will want to meet you. He didn't say so, but he will. Thanksgiving is soon, so you can meet everyone then."

Meet the entire Magiano line, the family responsible for killing my boss and putting a hit out on my own head? Sounded *super* fun. "I don't know if I can take a lunch. This is Burge's first full day."

"So. I'll tell them I need you for something."

I glanced in the direction of Burge's office. "That's not going to work. Especially now that everyone knows we are together. Just wait and see me after work."

"No."

I frowned. "This is not how our marriage is going to work."

"Our marriage?"

"Yeah. You know, that *thing* after engagement? To have and to hold, and all that?"

"So you *are* planning on marrying me."

I growled into the phone. "I'm hanging up now. I'll see you tonight."

There was a click, and he was gone. I buried my head in my hands.

Chapter 6

Somehow, I made it through the rest of the day. I cringed at every interaction with Burge, waiting for a comment, a question, a statement. But he was purely professional, and I wanted to hug him for that. He also seemed to lack the workaholic gene, and walked out the door at six, another point in his favor. Five minutes after he left, my cell rang, Brad's name displayed on the screen.

"Hey."

"Hey. How much longer are you going to be there?"

I looked at my watch. "Thirty minutes?"

"Great. Want to come to the house and eat?"

"Sure. But I'm not going to stay over; I need to be at home tonight."

He grunted something into the phone. "Just hurry."

I rolled my eyes and ended the call, focusing on my computer screen. I didn't really have anything to do, just wanted to wait for everyone to leave. And, with Burge out of the building, everyone else should soon follow suit.

They did, no one bothering to swing by my office and say goodbye—an oddity, but one I was grateful for. I waited until the wing was silent for a good ten minutes, then gathered up my items and snuck out. I was being weak and cowardly, but I didn't give a damn. I wanted nothing more than to crawl into someone's arms and have a good, long cry.

Seeing Martha opened the dam. She swung open the back door before I even reached it, concern already on her face. "Honey, I can tell from the way you're walking that you're down in the dumps."

I smiled at her, feigning casualness, but that facade lasted only a step or two, and I launched myself into her arms, sniffling. She held me tightly to her chest, patting my back and shushing me, walking us backward into the kitchen. I was distracted for a brief moment and snuck a glance to the stove, seeing fried pork chops sizzling in a skillet. Then she had me on a stool and sat across from me.

"Julia. Last week your life was in danger, and you held yourself together just fine. What is going on?"

I spat out words quickly, jumbling my sentences together in a mush of tears, indignation, and stress, and she had the gall to laugh when I finally took in a big, gasping breath. I swallowed a lump of saliva and glared at her. Brad spoke from behind us. "What's wrong?"

I covered my face quickly, my hands squeezing any tears off the skin, my eyes blinking quickly in an effort to return their appearance to normal. "Nothing."

Martha, damn her, spoke, "Julia's upset because the women at the office were mean to her. About the engagement."

I glared at her fiercely, my back to Brad, and waited for him to join in the laughter fest. Steps were heard on stone, and then he was behind me, wrapping his arms around me and turning me into his chest. He tilted my chin up, looking into my eyes, his own turning troubled when they saw my face. "You're *crying* about this?" His voice was so baffled that I almost laughed, a strangled sob coming out instead. I flung myself into his warmth, body shaking, my sobs now wet and sticky, seeping out of my body in huge waves of emotion. He held me and kissed my head. "Julia, stop crying, please."

"I don't want to go back," I whispered. "Burge knows, he might say something to me, Sheila is going to write me a bad recommendation, and everyone keeps pointing and whispering." A surge of anger hit me, and I pulled back, reaching out punching his hard chest. "This is *your* fault! I didn't want to tell anyone, and now everyone knows!" He caught my fist before it landed another blow and tried to frown at me, the corners of his mouth fighting to turn up.

"Julia. I need you to be strong on this. Fuck the office. I'm getting my own pushback from the staff. We need to be united, a team. The girl I fell in love with doesn't hide in the corner on stuff like this."

Fuck. How could I respond to that? He was right; I was normally good in situations like this. I wasn't an *embracer* of confrontation, but I could hold my own. Why was I hiding in my office? I sighed, leaning back into his arms. He tightened his hold on me, and I closed my eyes, taking a last, delicious moment of feeling sorry for myself. Then I straightened, keeping my arms around him and looked up into his face. "Okay."

He frowned, wiping moisture gently off my cheeks. "You always say that, and I never know what it means."

"Okay. I'll stop being a baby about it."

He grinned, leaning down and brushing his lips against me. "Good." He glanced over at Martha. "Martha, how much longer do you need?"

She shrugged. "It's ready now."

Chapter 7

We ate, just the two of us, at the kitchen table. Martha had fixed a plate and taken it upstairs, her preferred way of dining. Brad drank from his glass of tea and looked at me. "Let's talk about your parents."

I chewed furiously, trying to get the piece of pork chop down my throat before I spoke. "Okay."

"I know next to nothing about them."

I shrugged. "There's not much to know. They're pretty normal."

He smiled wryly at me. "Well, I'm not too familiar with normal. Humor me."

"Okay. Mom's a botanist. She works for a co-op of local farmers, helping to increase their field's production, developing hybrid strains of cotton, that kind of thing. Dad's retired from Gulfstream — he spends most of his time fishing or going to garage sales, a hobby that drives my mother absolutely crazy." I grinned for a moment, forgetting the horror that had been my day. "I should go home more. With school and work … I haven't been home as often as I should. But, now that you'll be driving me crazy, I am sure I'll make the pilgrimage more often."

A look of mock pain crossed his face. "That's mean. Really mean."

"I'm sure your ego can handle it."

His brows knitted as he chewed. "So what exactly are they going to think of me?"

I laughed, covering my food-filled mouth with my hand. "I have absolutely no idea." It sounded terrible, but I wanted this engagement to cause him at least half the discomfort it was causing me.

"I erred in not asking your father for your hand before I proposed."

I shrugged. "He won't care. It's not like he knows whether you are good for me or not. Actually, it probably works in your favor that he doesn't know anything about you."

"I would defend that statement if it wasn't accurate. So, how do you propose we tell them?"

My fork froze. I hadn't actually considered the fact that I would need to tell my parents. Now, it seemed ridiculous that the thought hadn't crossed my mind, especially with all of the questions he had just asked me. "Do we have to tell them *now*?"

"Why would we wait?"

"Ummm ..." I slowly moved my fork the rest of the distance to my mouth, chewing the meat ridiculously slow. I mumbled the next sentence through pork and saliva, hoping that the words wouldn't translate properly. "Because I may not have told them that I broke up with Luke."

"What?" He moved the fork away from my face. "I couldn't understand that through your mastication of food."

I slumped, finished the chewing process and repeated the sentence.

He shook his head in disbelief. "Why not? It's been, what, almost two months? Isn't that the type of thing that comes up in phone calls?"

"My parents raised me to be independent. Ever since I left for college, I haven't been in as close of contact with Mom and Dad. It's not that they aren't interested in my life — they have just encouraged me to spread my wings, live my own life. Luke loved my parents, and Mom really took to him. I guess I've just put off making the call to tell her. I didn't really want to hear her thoughts on the matter, especially once my decision was made." The reminder of Luke's reaction to our breakup — his repeated calls, guilt trips, his insistent to let our relationship go — made me frown. The truth of the matter was, I hadn't really wanted to speak ill of him, to explain in honest terms to my mother the multiple reasons behind my decision. I looked up, meeting Brad's steady gaze. "It hadn't, at the time of the break-up, seemed like urgent, I-must-share-this-right-now news. And now, two months later, I just haven't got around to telling her yet."

He stood, walking over to my bag and rummaging through it, then returned to the table and set my cell in front of me. "Call her. Now."

"Fuck you. I'm not calling her now." I shoved the phone to the side and defiantly scooped up some mashed potatoes.

"If you don't call her now, you'll wait weeks, and then you'll have to explain why you waited so long to tell her the news. My family already knows. When they meet I don't want you stressing out the whole time over whether your mom will find out how long we have been engaged."

My jaw dropped. "When they *meet*? They aren't meeting."

He raised his brows at me as he stood over me, still pushing that damn phone toward me, somehow making the infuriating gesture look sexy. I picked up the iPhone and threw it, the landing making a satisfying crack against stone that caused both pleasure and despair to shoot through me. But at least I wouldn't have to call my mother.

He smirked, which pissed me off even more.

I stood, the heavy chair beneath me not cooperating, and I untangled myself from it until I was beside him — still six infuriating inches too short to meet his gaze full on. "I'm *not* introducing my lovable family to your bloodthirsty vulture nest."

He staggered back, his hand across his heart in mock pain. "Dearest, that is my blood you speak of." He stepped forward again, gripping my waist sternly and bringing me to him. "I'll have to ask you to take that back."

I narrowed my eyes at him and pushed him back, the damn man for once cooperating, releasing my waist and leaning back against the table, our eyes now level. "You plan on us being married and our families not meeting? That's not going to work out. Besides, your family will love my family. Trust me. They're Italian. Being warm and hospitable is second nature to them."

"So are iron suitcases and broken hubcaps!"

He tilted his head at me, a large grin crossing his face. "I think you confused that ... never mind. Let's cross one disastrous bridge at a time. Do you want us to go to your parents, or should I bring them here?"

My body was on the verge of a breakdown — stress, anticipation, and anger all fighting losing battles inside of me. I imagined Brad's huge body in my mother's small kitchen, her Southern hospitality ingrained insistence that we stay with her, my tiny bed, the house hot, her thermostat religiously resting at seventy-eight degrees. Then I imagined my dad here, lost in Brad's huge house, his worn-out suitcase rattling and rolling around the stone floors, him finding a gun when he reached for a toothbrush. Panic started to set in, spots appearing in the air between him and me.

My face must have shown something, for concern lit Brad's face, and he reached forward, pulling me gently to him and hugging me against his chest. I sagged there, my arms stretching around his body to grip him tightly. My cheek pressed against the silk blend of his dress shirt, and I inhaled the scent of him — slight citrus, masculine, ocean, spice. A delicious blend of everything. "Just call them, babe. We don't have to worry about making travel plans yet. Just call them, tell them the news, and then let me talk to them."

I murmured a string of words against his hard chest, the word 'phone' slipping out into the open air. He straightened me, my legs wobbly before finding firm footing, my eyes focusing on him. Then he reached in his pocket and pulled out his cell, handing it to me with a warning look.

"Don't throw it."

I hefted the phone in my hand — his seemed pounds heavier than mine, though that was impossible. Then I sighed, pressed in the digits for my family's home phone, held the phone to my ear, and hoped like hell no one was home.

Chapter 8

I should have prayed instead. The phone didn't ring three times before my mother answered, her voice breathless, as if she had sprinted across the house to answer the call.

"Mom, you sound busy. I can call back." I spun, walking across the kitchen and opening the back door, which lead to the porch.

"What? No no no. This is perfect, sweetie. What number are you calling from? And did you get my message? I called you last week …" Her voice dropped off, and I hoped it was a rhetorical question. I really needed to get in the habit of checking my voicemail more often. Heaven forbid it had been something important.

I closed my eyes tightly, rubbing my temples, and tried to find the right words to get this over with. She spoke on, not waiting for a response. "What's going on with you? Your father is here, but he's in the garage, building something that I'm sure he'll want to bring into the house. I swear, Julia, that man … he would fill my whole home with other people's garbage if I didn't keep him in line." She huffed into the phone, and I could imagine her in the kitchen, fixing dinner with the phone tucked between her neck and shoulder.

"I have some news, but I don't want you to freak out when I tell you." I waited expectantly for reassurance that I knew would never come.

A pause. A stilling of whatever she had been doing that had created noise. "Oh. My. God. What happened? Is it cancer?"

"No! I'm healthy and fine." I spoke quickly, trying to head off her panic attack before it came.

"Well, dammit, Julia. You almost gave me a heart attack. Please don't start a conversation like that; it's terrifying to a woman my age."

I gripped the chair's arms, and fought the urge to rock the damn thing so hard the rockers would break off. "I ended things with Luke. A few months ago. I—"

"What? No you haven't." The relief in her voice, along with the certainty of her tone, caught me off guard.

"I know it seems sudden, but—"

"A few *months* ago? Julia, what are you talking about? Luke is *here*, waiting on your internship to finish up."

I stopped rocking completely, my mouth involuntarily falling open. "What? What do you mean *here*?"

"*Here*, here. He's in the garage with your father right now. He's been here a few days; I put him up in your room."

"WHAT? Are you crazy!"

"Between the two of us, *you* are the one acting crazy." Her voice took on an edge of irritation. "He's almost family. I wasn't going to turn him away when he showed up on Thursday. I left you a message about it then. Besides, we all assumed you'd come home for a visit as soon as your internship wrapped up. When *does* your internship finish? We don't have any details on it, or on your new place." The sound of the mixer started in the background. She seemed to have completely missed the entire focus of this conversation.

I breathed loudly into the phone. "Mom. Get him *out* of there. I broke up with him *months* ago. He is being a crazy stalker; I can't believe he is there!"

"Julia. Stop getting worked up. This is *Luke* we are talking about. He's not a *stalker*. He's the sweetest boy you've ever been with, I can assure you of that."

"Mom, you don't know half the people I've been with, so you can't assure me of anything. Where is Dad? Let me talk to him."

"I am *not* putting your father on so you can spout this nonsense to him. When your internship is finished, come home. We can discuss this then, and you and Luke can work out whatever tiff you are having so we can continue with wedding plans. Trust me, these things blow over, and he has been *such* good company to your father this week."

Wedding plans. God, please tell me she hadn't still been working on those. I had told her to halt all planning for that ill-fated possibility six months ago, when my gut had first told me the wedding might not ever become a reality.

I spoke rapidly into the phone, but my words went unheard, nothing but silence in my ear. She had hung up. I pulled the phone from my ear and gawked at it. I don't know why I was surprised. My mother, the queen of independence, wasn't the type to drag out conversations, especially when she had supper on the stove. I locked the phone screen, trying to work through what had just happened. *Luke.* At my parents' house. Anger boiled with quick fury in my blood, and I stood, whirling around and yanking the heavy door open, stomping into the kitchen a bit dramatically, embracing the anger that flowed with greedy speed throughout me.

Brad turned at my entrance, his plate empty, his eyes locking on his phone and following it as I swung my arms emphatically. "You won't *believe* this shit!" He stood, snagging his phone from my hand and pocketing it, as he grabbed his plate and took it to the sink.

"They aren't happy about the engagement?"

"I didn't even *get* that far! Luke is staying at my parents' house!" His blank look returned my infuriated one. "Luke! My ex-fiancé!

He set down his plate, the sound echoing in the empty kitchen. I expected fire, an outrage to match my own, nostrils flaring, hands clenched, a dramatic show of he-man strength. Instead, he tilted his head slightly, his expression unreadable. "I know you've told me about Luke, but refresh my memory." He walked back to the table, sliding out a chair and sitting down, his face calm and peaceful across from my furious one.

I blew out a long breath, flexing my hands in front of me. "Dated eighteen months, engaged for twelve of those. I ended it about a month or two before you and I met."

"Nice guy?"

"*Was* extremely nice. Quiet, kinda lazy. But when we broke up he went batshit stalker on me — showing up at work and the house, power-calling my cell. That's why I moved in with the guys and quit my other job. I started my internship at CDB, changed my number, and haven't seen him since." I rolled my neck and blew out a breath, willing my heart to slow down. I glanced at him, scowling at his calm expression.

He met my look with an easy confidence, shrugging nonchalantly. "What is it you want me to do?"

"I don't know. Wave your arms about. Scream. Charge up there and forcibly remove him!"

He chuckled at me across the table. "Julia. This relationship between you and him needs to be ended by *you*. Anything I say to him won't resonate. You spent a significant amount of your lives together." He reached over, dragging my chair across the stone floor until it touched his, his strong hands pulling me onto his lap. I sat, in a child's position, curled on his lap, his big arms engulfing me, his breath on my hair. "I've had you for three weeks, and the thought of losing you is unbearable. He had you so much longer than that. I don't blame him one bit for going crazy without you. You need to be kind and gentle, but firm, with him."

I growled against his chest. "I was kind and gentle and firm—when I broke up with him almost three months ago!"

"And drunk."

I winced. "Yes, and I was drunk. But we've talked since, while I've been sober, and I've told him the same thing."

He leaned back, tilting up my chin until my eyes met his. "Why don't we go up to your parents'? I will support you in any way that I can, but the conversation between you two needs to be in private. He's already lost you; his pride doesn't need to suffer, as well."

I narrowed my eyes at him. "He's not a wounded puppy. He's an invader in my childhood home, sleeping on my sheets, and probably going through my shit. I've made my feelings crystal clear by my complete avoidance of him. He's not hanging out at my parents' house thinking we are 'on a break' – he has run out of places to stalk me and is hoping my dear ol' mom and dad will give him a clue as to how he can track me down."

He grinned, a devilish smirk that made me want to yank down his zipper and suck his cock. "You just evaded the Magiano family. Your ex-boyfriend is hardly cause for panic."

I frowned. "You are way too relaxed about this."

He leaned forward, kissing me swiftly, his hands moving as my mouth opened to his, strong fingers circling then gripping my waist, twisting my body until I had no choice but to lift one leg over and straddle him. My worries were lost in his kiss — a soothing connection that turned sexual in a moment, his hands moving brusquely over the top of my shirt, yanking it out of my dress pants and sliding his hands underneath the fabric, the warmth of his touch causing my breath to hitch. I ground against him, feeling him respond underneath me, as he squeezed my breasts, his thumb teasing my nipples through the fabric of my bra.

By the time he laid me back, tugged off my dress pants, and wrapped my thighs around his head, it was decided. He was coming home with me, but I was on my own with Luke. *Damn my weak resolve.*

Chapter 9

We left Friday night, hitting the interstate at six. I called Mom on the way, keeping the conversation brief. I didn't mention the hulk of a man at my side, or my reason for coming. I didn't want to give Luke any benefit of preparation. Then I called Olivia remembering two hours out of town that we had made plans for Saturday night—dinner and a movie—a mini-celebration of my new engagement. Olivia wasn't happy, but understood, her irritation turning to indignation at my mention of Luke's presence. With her blessing to kick ass in hand, I closed the phone and settled into the passenger seat.

I grew up in a town small enough to be close-knit, but large enough to have a Wal-Mart. Located in an unassuming corner of Georgia, too far from any airport, it typically took me seven hours, but Brad's car ate up the drive in six. The drive went almost too quickly for my taste, and my mind was still processing possible outcomes by the time we pulled down the quiet suburban street that had sheltered my upbringing.

It was a half hour after midnight when Brad brought the car to a slow stop next to our mailbox and slid it into park. I leaned over, kissing him gently on the lips. "I'll call you in a bit. You'll find a hotel?"

He grinned at me. "From the looks of my GPS, this town doesn't seem big enough to get lost in. I'll be close by. Call me when you're ready."

I took a deep breath, steeling myself for the upcoming battle. Then I opened the door and stepped out.

♥♥♥

It'd been almost a year since I'd been home. Maybe longer. Long enough that I didn't recognize the new planters on the steps, overflowing with blooms, Mom's green thumb at work. The planters had, no doubt, been Dad's handiwork, that item on the 'to do' list finally attended to. I also noted new white curtains in the window above the kitchen sink. *Wonder when Mom made those?* My childhood home was small, a square block of brick, built in the fifties, back when rooflines and architectural features weren't deemed aesthetically important. But I can't help but love its imperfections. I can't help but think, whenever I step down this cracked drive, that I should come home more. I have so many memories inside these walls. So many moments that shaped my growth, in good ways and bad. I walked down the drive, noticing Luke's truck, and stepped onto the first step of the porch, my eyes adjusting to the dark, seeing the front door stoop and the man who, at almost one in the morning, leaned against it. *Luke.*

Looks were never Luke's problem. His looks were what drew me to him, his looks were what kept me around during the slow times, and his looks had *almost* made me reconsider my decision to leave him. Thick, blond hair that always misbehaved perfectly, a strong jaw, full lips, and pale blue eyes that had always held a hint of anguish. He stood, his hands tucked in the pockets of his faded jeans, a baby blue polo pulled tight over his broad, muscular chest. He said nothing as I wound my way along the entry sidewalk and came to a stop in front of him. Just watched me, his face tight and eyes tortured. He pulled off 'tortured' better than anyone else I knew. And, just like that, the familiar weight of guilt settled around my heart and squeezed.

He had, simply put, not been good enough for me. My over-confident ego had decided I needed someone better — someone more successful, responsible, intelligent. It had been the right choice. But that didn't mean that my heart didn't break a little when I looked at him. Because he had truly, head over heels, loved me. And probably still did. I never worried about Luke looking at another girl, or had any doubt of his feelings for me. I had been his entire world. He stepped forward slightly, hands coming out of his pockets, and I held up a hand. "Luke. Stop. Please sit down."

I wasn't surprised he was awake. Wasn't surprised that he was on the porch, waiting for my arrival. It was why I had had Brad bring me straight here. I knew Luke would be there, ready, hopeful. But validation of that fact, his weight against the porch, where it had probably been for hours? It made it harder. Added another stone to my mountain of guilt.

He obeyed, sinking into the closest rocking chair, his eyes never leaving mine—light blue prisms of hope. I sank into the rocker next to him and propped a foot up on the railing, closing my eyes and trying to sort through the churning wave of emotions. *Of course he obeyed.* He had always behaved, always tried to please my ever-increasing demands. I had been the alpha, he the submissive.

"What are you doing here, Luke?" I turned to look at him—a mistake—the raw look in his eyes nearly tearing me into two.

"I couldn't find you anywhere. I *need* you, Jules; I'm lost without you." He reached out, grasping my arm, his strong fingers caressing the skin before he pulled it, leaning into me. I resisted, dragging my arm away and leaned back in the chair.

Need. Yes, he had always *needed* me. To wake him up in the mornings, so he wouldn't miss work. To remind him to renew his car insurance, file taxes, pay his parking tickets. He needed me to cover his rent when his cash was low, pick him up from the bar when he had drunk too much, and hold him in my arms when he was feeling insecure. He had needed me way too much. It was one of the things that made the guilt that much heavier. I wondered, still worried, how he functioned without me.

And it was crazy. I had a new fiancé, another life, but still the pull of guilt almost washed me closer to him. Almost made me weak enough to say things other than what I needed to say. It was why I had cut all contact two months prior. The guilt at leaving him … it was too hard for me to be firm. Firm seemed to equal 'cruel.' But that was needed. Especially when the game had gotten to this unthinkable stage.

I sighed, trying to form words that would hit home gently. "Luke. It's over. I have avoided you for a reason. You being here at my parents' house — it's invasive. You *have* to move on. You have to forget about me."

"I'll be better. I'll try harder. I won't go out anymore or skip work or —"

"Luke." I stood and faced him, my eyes sharp. *Be strong. Be firm.* "You don't need to change for me. You need to find a girl who loves you just as you are. Stop thinking about a way to get me back. I'm not ever coming back. Ever. I need you to realize that."

"Is this about that guy? The one who dropped you off?" He looked wounded, slumping back in the chair, a bare foot coming up and hitting the porch rail. The glimpse of his foot — it struck some latent chord in me, some reservoir of anger, resentment. He had stayed here *a week*. Gotten comfortable enough in my childhood home to walk around barefoot. Prey on my uninformed parents.

"No. It's about you and me. There was no one else who caused our breakup to happen."

Were my words strong enough? Cruel enough? I wasn't sure, the look in his eyes unchanged. Needy. Wanting. Desperate. I needed to find the aggressor role that I used to so easily command. The one that I had lost mastery of in my new relationship with Brad. I swallowed. Tried again. "Please go inside and pack. I need you to leave. I will pay for you to stay in a hotel for the night, but in the morning you need to head back home. If you ever cared for me, I need you to leave me alone. Move on with your life. I won't — I can't — come back to you. We are done."

He looked at me, my gaze holding despite the shake in my heart, the contact horrific as I watched a piece of the man I once loved die in his eyes. Then he dipped his head, eyes avoiding mine, saving me from seeing any more pain. He nodded, his head down, eyes trained to the ground, foot falling off the railing and landing with a quiet thud onto the porch. "Okay Jules. I'm sorry."

"Me too," I whispered, hoping—as the words fled my mouth—that he hadn't heard them. Worried that they reopened some window to the room I had just locked close. Then I leaned against the porch and crossed my arms, watching him walk inside. The moment the door closed behind him, tears leaked, running down my cheeks with wild abandon. I hated this shit. Hated dealing with him, hated the resurgence of feelings and emotions for a man no longer in my life. This was bullshit, this ache of hurt, not for me, but for him. And the worst thing was that my own ego was creating this tidal wave of pain. I was not that great. He could—and would—do better. Someone who appreciated him. Someone who loved him in the all-consuming way that I loved Brad. I contained the heaves of my chest, guilt wracking my body in silent sobs. I wiped my face, blinking rapidly and took a few deep breaths, willing the ache in my heart to dissolve.

◆◆◆

Luke, as expected, behaved. It took him almost fifteen minutes to emerge. Fifteen minutes when I went through a roller coaster of emotions and fought going inside to see if he was ransacking my room. He finally emerged, a duffel bag in hand. Evidence of my tears gone, I walked him to the driveway, to his faded red truck, every dent and scrape on it familiar to me. We had fucked in the bed of it, the hard metal floor painful to my knees. We'd spent another night inside of it, on a road trip to his parents', both of us too broke for a hotel, the cab colder the later the night had gotten. I stared at the vehicle and tried to will the memories from my mind.

Luke heaved his bag, his muscles easily tossing the black duffel into the bed. Then he turned back to me, holding out his hand.

I stared at it blankly, recognizing that he wasn't reaching for my hand, but waiting for some item. *Right. Hotel money.* I held back a comment and reached into my pocket, pulling out some cash and putting it in his palm.

"So who was that?" he asked suddenly. "The guy who dropped you off."

I met his eyes, willing my voice to be casual, steady. "Someone I'm dating."

He frowned as hurt quickly joined the complicated party of sadness and regret in his eyes. "Wow. That didn't take you long, Jules." He shot me a wry, sarcastic smile. "Went after money, huh? Shocker."

I didn't respond, watching as he climbed in the truck and slammed the door. He stared into my eyes through the windshield, and we stayed like that for a minute; I was unable to move. Then he shook his head, and his truck roared to life.

Eighteen months. One small diamond.

A life path extinguished.

I stood in the empty driveway for a moment, watching the taillights of his truck as it peeled out and down my parents' street. *It was done.* I instinctively knew that he wasn't coming back, that — while he might not disappear completely — he realized that I would not take him back.

I turned to the house, noting the absence of lights and glanced at my watch. 12:53 a.m. My parents hadn't waited up, not a huge surprise given the hour. I called Brad.

"Hey babe." His confident voice sent calming strength through me.

"Hey. Luke just left. How far away are you?"

"A few blocks. You finished quicker than I expected; I haven't gotten us a room yet."

"That's okay. Come pick me up. I'm going to leave my parents a note and make sure the doors are locked, then I'll be out front."

"I'll be there."

There was no doubt Mom would be hurt when she found out I was staying at a hotel, but I'd have to face that battle in the morning. I jotted down a quick note, stated I'd be by around nine, then checked the locks, and headed outside to Brad's car.

Chapter 10

The morning brought with it the hum of an air conditioner, scratchy sheets, and the delicious feeling of having Brad's warm body spooned tightly behind me. I ran my fingers lightly down his forearm before gripping it and tightening it around my body. He groaned behind me, burrowing his face into my neck, his stubble tickling me. He flexed against me, his hard cock ever present against my ass. I opened my eyes, taking in the yellow wallpaper, small television, and cheap coffee pot. I grinned. Brad had taken serious issue with our accommodations, unable to believe that my small hometown didn't have at least a three-star hotel. Sex had been comical—the bed sagging pitifully beneath our weight, creaking and rattling with every thrust. We had finally taken the act to the wall—his strong arms holding me easily as he slid in and out until we were both satisfied. My eyes passed over the plastic clock, widening as they read its red digits. "Shit, Brad, we have to go." I wiggled out of his arms, shooting across the worn carpet and flipping on the bathroom light. Glancing over my shoulder at his still body, I increased my tone. "Brad!" Leaning over the sink, I turned on the water.

♥♥♥

My mother was visible through the front window, her eyes scanning, processing, and reigning hell before we even opened our doors and got out. Any feisty part of my personality had undoubtedly been a product of her genes. I gripped Brad's hand and whispered premature apologies as we climbed the front steps. The door opened, and there she stood.

My mother was beautiful; there was no disputing that. Slim and tall, she had curves where it counted, wrinkles noticeably absent despite her hours in the sun, and bone structure that models would die for. Her eyes skipped right over me and fixated on Brad. "Julia, who is this?"

Here goes nothing. "Mom, this is Brad. Brad, this is my mother," I dutifully recited, squeezing past her and hugging my father, who waited patiently inside. He gripped me tightly, pressing a kiss to my cheek before surveying me approvingly.

"You look good, sweetie. It's nice to have you home." My father, thinning hair carefully combed into place, wearing a sweater from the seventies paired with pressed gray slacks, shook Brad's hand with a friendly smile.

Mother, suddenly remembering her manners, ushered us into the living room, where we sat — me perched nervously on an ottoman, Brad relaxing easily into the couch. We had a moment of peaceful silence before she opened her mouth and flames came out.

"Julia, what's going on? I wake up this morning to a note from you — you stayed *godknowswhere* last night — and then you show up with — no offense — a complete stranger! And Luke is nowhere to be found, his truck gone when I woke up this morning!"

"Debra, calm down." My father interrupted her, reaching over and patting her arm — an action that earned him a glare of Arctic proportions. "Julia just got here. Let her relax for a bit."

"I'm not calming down until I know what in God's name is going on!" She balled her hands into fists and turned to me, eyebrows raised.

I took a deep breath and stood. "Mom. As I said on the phone — I broke up with Luke over two months ago. He shouldn't have been here; he was trying to track me down because I wouldn't return any of his calls. I spoke to him last night and told him to leave, which is why he isn't here this morning. He shouldn't be back again, so please don't respond if he calls you."

My last sentence was too much for my mother, whose mouth opened and closed like a large mouth bass. "*Don't respond*? Julia, *what* has gotten into you?

You can't break up with Luke — the boy is in *love* with you!"

"That's all well and good, but I didn't want to marry him, Mom. And I would hope that you, as a supportive mother, would stand by me in this decision." *That* shut her up, and she closed her eyes briefly, clasping her hands in an effort to remain composed.

Then Brad spoke, and the shit-storm hit a whole new level. "Mr. and Mrs. Campbell, I apologize for the —"

"I'm sorry, but who the *hell* are you, and *why* are you here?" My mother stood, crossing her arms and staring stonily at Brad, intent on steamrolling him into submission. She had no idea who she was up against.

Brad had the nerve to chuckle. "I, Mrs. Campbell, am Julia's fiancé."

My mother gaped, glared at me, glared at Brad, and then stepped forward and grabbed my hand. The ring, its size and brilliance, momentarily stunned her, and I saw a wave of emotions cross her face. I knew what she was thinking: my youth, Brad's age, Luke's absence, her impressionable little daughter standing before her. I gently pulled my hand back before her thought process moved too much further along.

My father stood, joining the party and clapped his hands together. "Well. Now that that's all settled, how about we move to the kitchen for breakfast?"

Chapter 11

My mother hadn't planned on an uninvited breakfast guest; she had expected me, alone, listening to her logical persuasion until Luke returned to his proper place at the table. His cereal, Coco Crisp, stared at me from above the fridge, an adolescent irritation to my already frayed nerves.

Mother scurried, her sneakered feet moving around the kitchen at a frantic pace, the fridge, cupboard, pantry, and then fridge again, all becoming victims to her furious search for something to serve to this man—this much-too-old man who was professing ownership of her daughter. I could feel her nerves; they matched pace with my stress, competing for superiority in the small room. I worriedly met Brad's eyes across the table.

He had sat at the head, following the directive of my mother, but I could feel her disorientation with his seat, a place she normally took. He was, as always, calm and relaxed, and I twisted a napkin under the table as I listened to my father speak with him.

"… it's a Chevy. An Impala. I've been working on it for a few years now, but just recently begun to dedicate proper time to it. Luke …" my father paused, his eyes meeting mine across the table.

"Luke's been helping me these last few days, which is the most I've done to it in a while." He coughed and took a sip of coffee.

My mother approached the table at a sudden pace, setting a plate of cold bagels and assorted cream cheeses in front of us. "I'm sorry for not being better prepared; I normally try to keep appropriate food on hand for guests …" She grimaced, her anguish equally divided over the food choices and the stranger before her, and sat down next to me with a heavy sigh.

"This is wonderful, Mrs. Campbell. He grinned at her, that devastating, gorgeous grin that diminished his fierce features and instantly endeared anyone to his cause. I watched my mother, saw the surprise on her face, and she glanced down quickly, taking a sip of coffee with a shaky hand.

"Mr. De Luca, how long have you been seeing Julia?"

His hand reached out, covering mine, and he gave me a small smile before turning to her. "Two months, give or take. We met through work. My firm had the pleasure of having Julia as an intern."

The emotions showed clearly on her face as the words flitted through her mind. *Two months. My firm. Attorney.* "I see. Julia … reports to you?"

He laughed. "No. I work in family law. Julia was the intern for our corporate law department. We met in passing one day."

Family law. My mother's eyes shuttered slightly at that sentence, and I grinned despite myself. I knew what she was envisioning, bedraggled lawyers carrying worn briefcases to and from court, fighting back child-support cases for broke, deadbeat dads. I was grateful for the table hiding my hands, my ring hidden.

"Two months?" My father's voice came out confused. "Why the rush to get engaged?"

My mother suddenly gasped, clapping a hand over her mouth and looking at me in accusation. "Julia!"

I laughed out loud, knowing what she was thinking, the laugh bubbling out of me and spilling, uncontrollably, onto the table. "God, Mom, I'm not pregnant." Her face watched me suspiciously, traveling from my face to my stomach and then back to my smile. "I swear." I looked at my dad, at his pale face. "Dad, I'm not. We're not getting married until after I graduate in August. We'll be engaged for a year."

That announcement relieved her, and she sank back into the chair. "This ... it's just a lot to take, Julia. I still don't know why you had to go and break it off with Luke. That boy loves you so much."

I met her eyes with a warning look. "Mom, that bridge is so far crossed it is ridiculous. I am in love with Brad. I am marrying Brad. With or without your blessing."

"Oh, for heaven's sake, Julia. Don't be dramatic. Of course you'll have our blessing." She reached over, rubbed my forearm reassuringly, then turned to Brad. "Now, Brad, what does your family think of this? Have they met Julia?"

My world fell apart right there, with her predictable response, and I begged him with my eyes to have the correct answer to her innocent question.

"I am not close with my family," he said casually. "They are aware that I am engaged, and Julia will meet my family at Thanksgiving. That is, of course, if you will allow me to borrow her for that holiday?" He grinned sheepishly, and Mom did her best to respond.

"Well … we wouldn't want to stand in the way of your plans. Certainly, I'd want your family to get a chance to meet her."

"I don't have to, Mom." I looked up, suddenly aware of the potential parachute before me, ignoring the bemused look Brad was sending my way. "I mean, I know you and Dad like to have me here for Thanksgiving …" *Please. Please. Please.*

My flag of distress was ignored by all parties. Mom shrugged, waving her hand casually. "Oh no, Julia. We'll probably spend it with the neighbors anyway. Go. Get to know his family. That's more important, especially with a wedding coming up." Brightness suddenly lit her face. "When is the wedding?"

And with that one thought, Mom fully became Team De Luca. I should have known. My mother, the one who had wanted so badly to plan a fairytale wedding despite Luke's and my limited budget. Fuck the fact that her loyalty to Luke had, moments before, seemed boundless. Fuck the fact that she knew nothing of Brad's family. The wedding was the crack that Brad's easy charisma and my father's support fully broke open. Three stale bagels and two rounds of hugs later, she became fully cemented as our new biggest fan and we were headed back to our world.

One ex-fiancé and family introduction down.

One terrifying Thanksgiving and *whoknowshowmany* of Brad's exes ahead.

Chapter 12

OCTOBER
Days until wedding: 304

I leaned over the bar and scanned the bartenders, trying to catch someone's attention so I could order a drink. It was a futile effort, everyone else seeming to capture their attention easily. I began waving my arms like an idiot, a twenty-dollar bill in my hand.

"Come on." Brad's voice was in my ear, and I turned, my arms still moving. "I've got us a table.

"With a waitress?" I raised my eyebrows, not wanting to lose the headway I may or may not be making in the 'get the bartender's attention' foot race.

"Yes. Come on." He tugged on my waist, his large hands encircling it and pulling. I gave one final look at the oblivious bartenders and then turned to follow him. We moved through the dark club, bodies everywhere, the hum of voices and music creating a blanket of energy.

New York truly was a city that didn't sleep. Two-thirty in the morning, and the club showed no signs of slowing, the energy around us ramping up with each additional song pumping through the speakers. My mind wandered to our hotel room, six skyscrapers over, to the weekend bag already alongside expensive new purchases. Forty-eight hours in this city seemed enough time to spend a fortune and party our asses off.

I grinned down at Brad, who relaxed back on a leather loveseat, a table before him with a chilled bottle on ice. "Looks like you had better luck than me." I carefully navigated around the table until I was settled in next to him on the leather seat.

"Don't be too impressed. I had a little help." His head tilted to the left and I turned, my gaze pulled upward.

Dark blue eyes stared out from a gorgeous face, beautiful lips curving into a smile. A black suit, paired with a black shirt, hid a body that was no doubt perfect. I felt the stranger's hand tug gently on mine, and he leaned over and placed a soft kiss on my knuckles.

"It's a pleasure to meet you, Julia. My name is Marc." He gently returned my hand, and I struggled to speak.

"Nice to meet you." My words came out raspy; I swallowed and tried to regain my composure. Smiling politely at him, I turned back to Brad, a question in my eyes.

He chuckled. "Julia, Marc and I have a long history. He was the prior owner of Saffire, but was generous enough to part with it."

There was a deep laugh behind me, and I turned to see a perfect white smile split Marc's face. "Generous? Your offer gave me little choice, my friend. But you have done very well with it, and I applaud you for that." His eyes twinkled at me. "Have you been to Saffire?"

I blushed. "Yes. It is impressive. You did a wonderful job."

He scowled good-naturedly. "It's taken a few steps upward since my name was on the title. But Rain, this is my baby." He spread his arms to indicate the club. "Unless …" he said with a sly look to Brad, "you intend on adding it to your list of assets."

Brad laughed, curving his arm around my waist. "No, Marc. I don't have the time for anything but this woman right now."

"Yes, I was admiring your ring, it is beautiful," Marc said, his eyes dipping to my left hand. "Congratulations seem to be in order. You must be quite a woman if you tied down this stallion." He sat on the closest chair, his eyes returning to mine, a knowing smile playing over his features.

"More than you know," Brad said, squeezing my side gently and passing me a flute of champagne.

I smiled without comment, taking a sip of the cool bubbly.

A man appeared, bending over to speak rapidly in Marc's ear. His gaze on me, I saw the moment when his eyes changed, urgency darkening their blue depths. He nodded and the man stood, taking a few steps back.

"I apologize, but something needs my attention." Marc stood with an apologetic smile. "Please enjoy the champagne. I should wrap up this issue in the next hour or so. Brad, if you both are interested, I often entertain in the upstairs suite. I would love to share a few drinks with you later."

Brad nodded, reaching out to grasp his hand. "As always, it is great to see you."

I extended my hand, but Marc moved closer, planting a soft kiss on my cheek. "It has been a pleasure," he said softly, the scent of his cologne lingering as he withdrew.

"Thank you for the table."

He flashed that perfect smile and then left, the strange man in his ear, quick words speaking urgently as they disappeared into the crowd. I leaned back into the crook of Brad's arm and sipped the champagne, glancing around the club, a sea of sequins, flirtations, and sexuality.

"What'd you think of Marc?" Brad's eyes held a hint of mischief.

"He's a little intense. Working hard that Rico Suave vibe he's got going on." I took a sip of champagne and looked out at the crowd.

"Did it work?" Brad's voice was low and dangerous, and I turned to see him watching me closely, a hint of a smile playing over his mouth.

"What do you mean?"

"He wants to fuck you," Brad said matter-of-factly, leaning back in the seat and tipping his glass back, his eyes on mine.

"What? No he doesn't."

"I assure you, he does. You didn't see his face when you walked up. How his eyes drank in every inch of you."

I shrugged, fighting the shot of pleasure that traveled through me. "Whatever."

"You don't understand." Brad lowered his voice, moving his mouth to my ear, taking a soft bite of my neck, then playing his tongue lightly over the spot. "It isn't just a desire of his. It is a possibility. One that he recognizes. He is like me, Julia. He goes after what he wants. And he understands that a ring on your finger doesn't exclude him from the party."

My mouth dropped, and I leaned back, putting distance between Brad and myself. "You *told* him? About what we've done?" I narrowed my eyes and Brad laughed.

"Easy, princess. I haven't told him anything. But I've known Marc for over ten years. We have run in similar circles, have shared women several times, sometimes several women." I felt a small bit of jealousy at his words, at their past, which didn't, in any way, include me.

"You've … seen him fuck?"

"Yes." He took a swig of champagne.

"And?"

"And … what?" His eyes danced with humor.

I groaned. "Don't make me spell it out. Is he … good at what he does?" I leaned closer, giving permission, and felt his hand return, sliding around my waist and pulling me tightly to him.

"He is very good at what he does."

"Better than you?"

He shrugged. "Maybe you should find out." His hand grew rougher, squeezing my skin possessively, the change catching me off guard, a sharp intake of arousal stealing all breath from my body.

I bit my lower lip, and stared into the flute of champagne, remembering Marc's lips against my hand, and the intensity of those dark blue eyes. "Well," I said, swirling the flute gently between my fingers, "then maybe we should head upstairs." Then I tilted the glass back, letting the bubbles of champagne pop and slide down my throat.

Chapter 13

An hour later, I straddled Brad's body, and he leaned back into the sectional, his eyes drugged with arousal, watching me, the line of his mouth barely affected by the smile that lay there. He ran his hands freely over the front of my dress, dipping inside my low and loose neckline and cupping each breast in turn. "God, you are beautiful."

I said nothing, only gently moved against him, feeling a slight vibration run through us as the bass rocked a particularly loud note. I could feel the energy of the club, the muted hum of music, of a thousand bodies of barely-contained madness— dancing, kissing, falling in love—underneath us.

"Kiss me," he commanded.

I shook my head with a smile. "No. Keep touching me."

A second hand joined his first, both palms sweeping up and cradling my breasts, the pull of the fabric joined with the rough skin of his palms temptingly perfect. He growled, low in his throat. "Like this?" He squeezed, a little rougher on my nipples, my breath catching.

"Yeah."

"Then kiss me." He bucked up with his hips, throwing me forward, his upper body lifting, his mouth looking for mine, but I turned my head, gave him my neck, giggling when he nipped it.

"Not yet," I whispered. "I'm not going to kiss you until his cock is deep inside of me."

His hands tightened on me, and he groaned my name as he tore at the straps of my dress, pulling the fabric from me, a shiver running through me as my upper body was exposed.

There was a click of a door handle, and my breath caught as I looked up, seeing the black door swing open, a tall suit of gorgeous stepping inside, a phone at his ear, our eyes catching onto and holding each other.

Click. The door shut behind him, and I froze, aware of my bare skin, Brad's mouth making a wet path down my neck, his hands pushing me into place, arching my back as he traveled over my cleavage, flipping his tongue gently over and then sucking my nipple into his mouth. I gasp at the sensation, my eyes still stuck on Marc, and watch as he smiles, ending his call and tossing the cell aside, plastic on granite, a sliding sound fading into nothing as I watch him step forward, down the steps, into the sunken living room, his legs carrying him behind the couch, until he stood in front of me and looked down. "You started without me," he said softly, a bit of accent coating his words. Then Brad did something with his mouth, something on my nipple that made my body squirm, need growing, and I dropped my head back and broke eye contact.

Brad leaned forward, laying me back, his hands replacing his mouth. "Do you want a blindfold?"

"No," I gasped, opening my eyes and propping my body up, meeting his gaze, my stare flicking to the man standing behind Brad, his hands resting on the couch back, his eyes meeting mine. Dark blue fire. A confident smile. So much like Brad in so many ways. It was strange to have my eyes open, knowing the man I was looking at was about to touch me. To fuck me.

There was a soft slap of fabric as Marc removed his jacket and tossed it onto the sofa, fabric hitting leather, his hands unbuttoning and rolling back his sleeves. I watched his hands, avoiding his eyes, my cheeks warming, bashfulness overtaking me.

"Nervous?" His voice was quiet, a tinge of playfulness in their tone.

I looked up, meeting those dark depths. "A little."

"Don't be. I play nicely. Plus," he said, looking over to Brad with a smile, "I'm scared of the big guy."

"As you should be," Brad spoke from underneath me, settled back down on the couch, his eyes on me, his hands running over my skin, over my breasts, rough then soft, perfect patterns that kept my nipples hard and my cunt wet. "She is my everything." I smiled, looking down on him, his mouth tilting up, asking for, then receiving, a kiss. *Damn.* So much for that game plan. But I couldn't stay away from his mouth. It fit too perfectly on my own.

I saw, out of the corner of my eye, the man move. Walked to the bar, fixed a drink, then moved closer. I glanced at him, saw him watching me, his hand moving down for a quick adjustment before he sat next to us on the couch, down a few feet. He reclined back against the leather, taking a slow sip of his drink, the clink of ice cubes registering to my ears. Brad pinched lightly at one of my nipples, drug my attention back to him. I leaned down, gave him a long kiss as his hands roamed me, strong drags of fingers across my skin, possession in every inch, every touch. He lifted up slightly, his hands pushing down my hips as he ground into me, the friction of his arousal causing my eyes to close, a small moan to slip out of me.

"Get on your knees. The ottoman."

I looked back, understanding Brad's directive when I saw the big leather ottoman, one that acted as a coffee table. I slid off him, letting him lean forward and drag the furniture piece over until it was flush with the sofa. He spread his legs slightly and pulled out his dress shirt. Unbuckling his pants, he drug down the zipper. "Your mouth. Come here, baby."

I climbed onto the ottoman, getting on all fours, my hands helping to pull his cock out, everything in the room disappearing as I lowered my mouth to him. I loved to suck his cock. I loved the taste of it. It tasted of need. Of raw, animal want, and never failed to cause a twinge in my stomach, a weight of arousal in my sex. I pushed him down my throat and felt him harden in my mouth.

I was caught off guard when a firm hand closed around my ankle.

Chapter 14

I opened my eyes, my mouth full, and met Brad's eyes. They stared into mine, no hint of a smile, nothing but raw possession in their depths. This is the animal Brad, my favorite side of him, a side I only see in these moments, when he is watching me with another, and every alpha male instinct is on high alert. His mouth moved, curved into a reassuring smile, but his eyes were dark. Aroused. I could feel his level of want in my mouth, hard and ready, his hand settling on the back of my head and pushing down. "Take it all."

I wouldn't. I couldn't. But I took as much as I could, feeling, all the while, the slide of Marc's fingers over my skin, his weight as it settled onto the ottoman behind me. Felt his hands slide up my leg and gently work the ankle strap of my heels, careful fingers working the shoe off. Thud. One hit the floor, my foot released, his hands moving to the other. Thud. Then my feet were bare, free, and his hands were on the move. Sliding up my leg, the doggie-style position giving him a front row view to touch, travel, and then—*gasp*, his tongue caught me off guard—*taste* my skin as he moved up my legs and gripped my ass.

♥♥♥

He wasn't Brad; he couldn't compare, the condom was an additional irritant, but the man could fuck. Holy hell, could he fuck. And from the glimmer in Brad's eyes, he loved my reaction. I laid on my side, on the bed, Marc kneeling between my legs, his cock quick and fast, thinner than Brad's, but hard as a diamond. He played rough, spanking my exposed ass cheek, the first hand laid, ten minutes earlier, light and questioningly, my grin and nod urging him to continue. Now he slapped my skin with aggression, the rough fucks taking me closer and closer to where I needed to be. I looked at Brad, his legs spread, still fully dressed, settled into a chair, his bare cock upright and fisted, his palm slowly stroking its length. Dark playfulness in his eyes. *Why did I ever wear a blindfold?* Jesus, the look in his eyes … I'd get on my knees and scrub the kitchen floor naked if it would bring on that look. An intense heat, possessive and aroused. I cursed any moment that I missed out on it. Just a glance at it, and I was soaked.

Brad stood, his cock at attention, forcing its way through the hang of his button-up shirt. He stepped over, climbing onto the bed and knelt before me, bringing his dick to my mouth, letting me have a taste of it before he sat back on his heels, stroking with his left hand, slowly and purposefully, just inches from my face.

His right hand played over my breasts, squeezing, teasing, then traveling up to my neck, wrapping a firm hand around it, not enough to choke, but enough that I paid attention, my pussy tightening around Marc's cock.

"Fuck Brad, she's gonna make me come." The man swore out the words, his fingers digging into the meat of my butt, one finger stealing over and putting pressure on the pucker of my ass.

"Don't stop, she's close." Brad leaned down, kissed me, deep and hard, his hand on my neck, my eyes stealing a glimpse of his cock. He lifted off my mouth, his hand tightening slightly. "God, you're beautiful." He turned his head to Marc, keeping his eyes on me. "Faster."

Marc obeyed, giving me more, harder. Exactly. What. I …

Fuck.

I took a gasp for air, getting one final look before my world went black, and I came on Marc's cock.

Moments later, I tasted the man's completion — hot and wet in my mouth. Brad finished the job inside of me. With Marc leaving us alone, Brad's hard body above mine, one hand in my hair, his kiss on my lips, I wrapped my legs tightly, felt his shudder, and celebrated one more loosening of my sexual strings.

The blindfold. I didn't need it.

Chapter 15

I blinked, the window coming into focus, the coastline through it showing a mess of skyscrapers and beach umbrellas. Close to home. I turned to find Brad's eyes on me.

"You're awake."

I nodded, covering a yawn. Trying to curl my knees into the plane's seat, I was stopped by the belt. "I'm exhausted."

He smiled. "We didn't get much sleep this weekend. Want to hit bed early?"

"I'll hit my own bed early." I closed my eyes, leaning over until my head rested on his shoulder.

"Stay at my house tonight," he whispered against my hair. I shook my head under his mouth. It was an old argument, one I often lost. "Warm bed. Fresh sheets," he whispered more, furthering his proposition. "Breakfast in the morning. Your clothes pressed and ready."

"Stop." I slapped his chest. "Now let me sleep the last few minutes of this flight."

He growled gently, the sound bringing a smile to my lips, and I settled further into his shoulder.

I won that battle, sleeping that Sunday in my own bed for no other reason than stubbornness. I had to make him wait for something, didn't want to dive into the wife role without the marriage certificate signed. So I picked certain battles, maintained my separate residence, and the days ticked on.

♥♥♥

"Here." Sheila slapped the form on my desk, her tight mouth turning into something someone in Death Valley might consider a smile. I looked from her face to the paper, the word EVALUATION in large letters across the top.

"Oh. Thank you." I smiled up at her, unsure if I should be smiling, terrified to see what fun tidbits she added in the 'Anything else we should know about this intern?' section.

"Sure. And thank you," she said, her words laced with a hint of reluctance. "We've enjoyed having you here. I'm glad to see that Mr. De Luca hasn't been too much of a … distraction."

I relaxed a bit, smiling in parting when her pale suit turned and left the office. My hands were quick the moment the door shut, breathing a sigh of relief when only blank lines filled the available

COMMENTS section. She shouldn't have anything to complain about. Burge's schedule was a far cry from Broward's, our wing had changed gears, adopting normal nine-to-six hours, my attendance perfect despite any attempts by Brad to whisk me off. Burge also enjoyed long lunches, a perk that gave the entire staff the ability to lunch off property, and he'd brought me to court with him a number of times, a development that had me enjoying my job infinitely more. Slowly, the staff seemed to accept me again, forgiving me for the rebellious act of accepting Brad's proposal.

But as the temperature inside the office warmed, the summer heat passed, bringing fall with all its color-changing gusto, each degree cooler reminding me of the looming holiday. *Thanksgiving*. Ominously before us, a family event that guaranteed the Magiano family in full, Italian force. I envisioned bumping elbows with henchmen and spent most nights cursing those damn Pilgrims and their merry feast.

Chapter 16

NOVEMBER
Days until wedding: 283

I knocked gently on the door to Burge's office, his Yankees coffee mug warm in my hand, then pushed on the handle, the door swinging open.

"Julia, please come in." Brad stood behind Burge's desk, leaning over the long expanse, multiple documents spread out in front of them. I paused, surprised to find him there.

"Brad," I said, surprise coming through in my voice. I smiled at Burge. "Good morning, Mr. Burge."

"Good morning, Julia. Please, have a seat. We have some documents that need your signature."

Prenup. This must be it, the moment when I found out how much I would be allotted in the event of our dissolution. I felt a momentary flash of irritation at Burge's involvement in this process. Brad could have easily handled this in his wing, with Rebecca instead of Burge. This wasn't even Burge's area of expertise. I nodded curtly and perched on the edge of the closest chair, fighting to keep the irritation off my face.

"You seem irritated, darling." Brad's amused voice floated over the desk, and I glanced up sharply to meet his eyes.

"I'm not sure what you mean, Mr. De Luca, but I do have *work* to attend to. You need my signature on something?"

"Multiple items, actually." Burge spun the folder around and I stood, stepping forward and picking up a stray pen. I studied the first document, my eyes flitting quickly over it before examining it more closely. It was a stock certificate, for an entity name I was unfamiliar with. I looked up at Brad briefly before moving the certificate aside and looking at the next page.

"Uh, Julia. We need your signature on that," Burge interrupted, gesturing to the initial certificate. I ignored him, flipping through the remaining pages, skipping twenty or thirty signature tags in my examination. Then I looked up at Brad for confirmation.

"You're *giving* me Saffire?"

He grinned. "Well, not all of it. Evelyn has her ownership, as does Janine. But yes, I am signing over my share of the asset, including the real estate, to you."

"Why?"

Burge shifted uncomfortably, and I ignored him, focusing on Brad. He left Burge's side and walked to the front of the desk, leaning against it casually and crossing his arms. "Do you have a moral opposition to owning a strip club?"

"Why give it to me?"

He shrugged. "We're getting married. It doesn't seem like an appropriate asset for a husband to have. And I thought you would enjoy running it. Plus, it might ease any ... concerns you have."

"You mean Alexis." I raised my eyebrows at him.

"Yes. Alexis." He looked pained for a brief moment, the look devastatingly perfect on his strong face.

"We're not getting married for another nine months. Why transfer it now?"

"The process is not one that happens overnight. And I want to fly up there before the wedding. I'd rather do that with your ownership taken care of." He smiled at me, dropping his crossed arms and stepping forward to gently kiss my neck. As he straightened, he paused at my ear, the next words hot on my skin. "Sign the papers."

I shot him a disgruntled look, not appreciating the display of affection in front of my boss. "I'll need some time to review them. Mr. Burge, do you mind if I take a few minutes in my office to look them over?"

The man looked relieved. "Not at all. Just return them to me once they have your signature on them. Certain spots need a notary, so please have Sheila help with that."

I smiled at him, glanced at Brad, and then left, moving quickly to my office. Brad followed, slipping inside and settling into a chair across from my desk. I closed the door tightly.

Brad watched me walk to my chair and open the folder, silence falling over us for a brief moment. "For someone who's receiving a present, you show your gratitude in an odd fashion."

I looked up from the deed I was reviewing. "I'll cover you with kisses once I find the hidden agenda."

He looked wounded. "Because I'm not naturally generous?"

"You are generous with your time, your money, and your cock. This is a business you've spent six years building. I'm your girlfriend."

"Wife."

I shook my head and started to reread the paragraph I'd spent the last two minutes trying to get through. "Not right now. Right now I am your current fuck."

"The sixty grand on your finger says otherwise."

I winced. "Please don't say that. I'm going to hope and pray that is not the case." My eyes caught the diamond, and it sparkled spectacularly.

"You are my fiancée. Don't dismiss it as nothing. What was all the irritation for?"

"What do you mean?" I asked absently as I underlined a sentence in pencil.

"When you came in and saw me with Burge. You seemed irritated at the inconvenience of having to sign something."

I laughed softly. "I thought I was signing a prenup."

Brad leaned forward, interested. "And that irritated you?"

"I wasn't irritated by the prenup, but rather Burge's involvement in the process. I feel that agreement should be something that is kept private, between the two of us."

He nodded thoughtfully and leaned back, playing with his mouth with one hand. "And what terms do you feel acceptable for a prenup?"

I sat back, spinning slightly in my seat to face him fully. "You're the divorce attorney. I assumed that you have some boilerplate contract you've perfected for your personal use."

He stood, walking over to me and leaning over my chair, a hand on each arm, he stared deeply into my eyes. "We're not getting divorced."

I shifted uncomfortably. "Well, not *now*, obviously. But in the future ..."

"No. Never."

"Never?" I squeaked out, the concept so foreign coming from his lips.

"Never," he said, leaning even closer and sealing the promise with his mouth, strong confident movements. He released me, straightening and looking down at me. "There will be no prenup." He tapped on the papers, then turned to leave, the fit of expensive fabric making his exit devastatingly handsome. He paused in the doorway and caught my eyes briefly. "Sign them. You can thank me tonight."

Then he was gone, and I clenched my thighs, hating the traitorous moisture there.

The damn man was … ugh. I took a deep breath and tried to concentrate on the papers before me.

♥♥♥

Thirty minutes later, I signed the documents, my pen moving slowly through the letters, wondering how many more times I would sign my name before Julia Campbell disappeared, kicked to the curb carelessly and taken over by Julia De Luca. I felt as if a part of my life faded with every signature on the documents, a slight dissipation of the broke, ramen-noodle-eating, unpaid parking tickets Julia. With these documents, I became, in my mind, a wealthy woman. I read every line, every addendum, of the documents. They were irrevocable. Despite Brad and my future, Saffire was now seventy percent mine. It was stressful, empowering, and utterly undeserving.

Chapter 17

The meal was to be held at Maria's house. A relief, since she was, apparently, the least violent of Brad's siblings. As Brad's car found its way out of the city and headed to suburbia, I took a deep breath and tried to relax.

I was, in ways, a different woman than three months earlier. While I had stubbornly maintained my crappy dwelling — my clothing, beauty products, and car had all been substantially upgraded. A BMW X5 now adorned my broken driveway, designer clothes weighted down my plywood shelves, and I now enjoyed weekly massages and facials at Le Blanc Spa. I had quickly become accustomed and appreciative of my future life as Mrs. Brad De Luca.

While I didn't necessarily *feel* ready to be Brad's wife, I at least looked, and, for the most part, played the role reasonably well. The BMW turned, rolled along a dirt road, and stopped. We had arrived. *Shit*.

The yard was packed with cars — a sea of mostly black vehicles parked haphazardly across perfect grass. People were everywhere, threading through cars, gathered on the home's porches, or chasing kids across the lawn. It seemed harmless and normal, if not overly crowded. Who had this many family members? I shrugged into my jacket and trudged out of the car.

We made it halfway to the house before we were stopped. There was a loud squeal, a blur of black hair, and Brad was practically tackled to the ground. The tackler was one hundred and thirty pounds of curly hair and loud energy. *Maria.* She finished her hug and turned to me with an ear-splitting grin.

"You must be Julia, the woman who finally tamed my brother." She engulfed me in a hug before I could respond, a strong grip that came with a wave of lilac scent. I laughed, returning the hug and relaxing as she released me. "Now, don't believe all of the awful things you've heard about the boys — only eighty percent of them are true." She laughed, linking her arm through mine and pulling us toward the house. "We're putting the food on now, so let's get you two a plate!"

I had expected tommy guns tucked in corners, fedoras hung on coatracks, and stony faces behind cigar smoke, but everything about her Thanksgiving feast was utterly normal. Just supersized. The men

were huge; food was everywhere, people crammed
in every available hallway, all talking excitedly and
hugging constantly. I expected to blend in with the
madness, but somehow still stuck out, partly due to
Maria dragging me from group to group and
introducing me to everyone. Everyone was friendly,
laughter covered the air, but it wasn't perfect. In the
midst of the familial orgasm, despite the smiles,
hugs, and fawning, it was there — I could feel it.
Coldness. Not to me, but to Brad. Not from the
women, who fawned over him and loaded his plate
sky high, but from the men — a reserved respect that
carried a sea of resentment beneath it.

♦♦♦

I gripped a white china plate tightly and pushed on
a door to the back porch, leaving the warmth of the
kitchen, the fresh air welcome to my nerves, the
breeze taking a layer of stress with it. I moved past a
set of women, their shoulders close together and
words low, girlish giggles reaching my ears as I
moved to the far end of the porch and settled into a
white painted swing. My plate, covered in turkey,
dressing, and three different casseroles, rested on
my lab, and I dug in, scraping fork against china as I
showed the casseroles little mercy. I heard Brad
inside the house, his laugh recognizable above the
din of voices.

I settled back, rocking the swing slowly, looking out
onto the backyard. It was a large yard, with a pool

and children's playground, manicured grass and pavers filling the gaps in between. Azalea bushes lined the outskirts of the yard, almost obscuring a ten-foot iron wall that enclosed the area. I let my eyes wander, picking up discreetly hidden cameras scattered on rooftops and fence corners.

A figure appeared in my peripheral vision, and I dropped my eyes down, making eye contact with a tall, thin man. He moved closer, his eyes studying me, and my mouth automatically turned up in greeting. "Hello."

He nodded at me and removed a toothpick from his mouth. "Good afternoon. You must be Julia."

I nodded hesitantly, my smile wavering slightly as I took in his strong stance and scarred face. Dark eyes that carried no warmth. "Yes. I don't think we've had the pleasure of meeting. You are ..." I attempted to stand, juggling my plate with one hand while extending my free hand out to him.

"Leo." Brad's voice came from behind the man, and I fought a shiver at the tone. It was unlike anything I had ever heard from Brad, a manner that commanded utter respect and, at the same time, carried hatred and disgust.

The man's eyes met mine, and a trace of irritation flicked through them before he composed his face into a mask of veneration. He turned, nodding his head at Brad. "Mr. De Luca."

My hand was still stuck awkwardly out, and the two men stared at each other, oblivious to my social gesture. I sighed noisily and sank back down into the swing, putting the ignored hand to good use and attacking some mac and cheese. I chewed baked deliciousness and watched the men, feeling like a spectator in some ancient art of combat.

Brad had about three inches on the man, and at least eighty pounds of muscle, yet the man seemed unafraid of the fury that radiated from Brad's core. *Leo.* I recognized the name. This was the man who had killed Broward; this was the man who had come to my house in the middle of the night, with my death on his agenda. Brad leaned forward, putting his mouth close to the man's ear and spoke softly. I strained to hear his words, almost falling off the swing in my eavesdrop attempt. I covered the slip by starting to swing, every push of the bench taking me closer, then farther away, then closer to the conversation.

Brad was tense, his jaw flexing, and I saw his hands clench. Leo turned and met my eyes, giving nothing away, his gaze flitting quickly back to Brad. Then they turned as one to me, and I struggled to swallow the broccoli casserole filling my mouth.

"Julia," Brad said quietly. "This is Leo Casando. He is an employee of this family, one who I believe I have spoken of in the past. I apologize for interrupting your earlier introduction, but there was a matter of importance that I needed to discuss with Leo."

Okay. This isn't awkward at all. I nodded to Leo and attempted a smile but failed horribly, the final result being somewhere between a glare and a grimace.

The man started to speak but was silenced by Brad's hand, which gripped his shoulder tightly. "Leo has other business to attend to," Brad said smoothly. He released the man's shoulder and clapped him on the back.

I nodded again and sank back into the swing, watching as Leo turned abruptly and walked away, his gait agitated. Brad sat next to me, the swing creaking slightly and threw an arm casually over my shoulders.

"Is everything okay?" I asked quietly.

Brad shook his head. "He shouldn't have approached you. I'm sure he has been told of our situation, but I just reminded him of it." He leaned over, taking my plate and setting it on the ground. I furrowed my brow.

"What are you doing?"

"Shh …" he said, lifting me up easily and sliding me sideways onto his lap, and nuzzled my neck. "Have I mentioned how much I love it when you smell like fried turkey?"

I laughed despite myself, quieting when the two women next to us glanced over. "Brad, let me up." I pushed against him, and he held me easily down, stealing a kiss before looking into my eyes.

"I want to marry you."

I laughed softly. "We are getting married."

"Sooner. I want my family to recognize you for who you are, my wife." He brushed a bit of hair off my face and studied my eyes. The intensity of his eyes silenced the flippant response in my throat. "Leo and the others, they understand that you are to be left alone, but I won't sleep soundly until you are fully protected. As my wife."

I swallowed, seeing the worry in his eyes. "Brad, I'll be fine." He said nothing, and I ran my hand along his wrist gently. "I need this time, I need to know that I am making the right decision."

He shook his head quickly and let out a small smile. "The right decision is for me to snatch you up quickly, before you realize that you can do better than me."

I tilted my head playfully — mock thinking. "You know … you may be right, Mr. De Luca."

"But no one," he growled, bringing his mouth down to my neck and teasing the curve of it, "will ever love you like I love you."

I said nothing, allowing my soul to swoon as his lips took a slow, lengthy journey up my neck and to my lips. Inside, I fought with my mind as it swooped through endless scenarios that could occur with our future. Then his mouth took mine, and I forgot everything but the sensation of pure, premarital bliss.

Chapter 18

After I polished off some pecan pie we moved—
Brad, Maria and I—a threesome of normal, up a
giant staircase onto a quiet floor and down a plush
hallway. Brad's hand protectively at my back, I
recognized this for what it was—time. Maria gave
me a small smile, kissed Brad gently on the cheek,
and leaned on a large set of double doors.

It was dark inside, and I blinked, trying to adjust to
the light. Dark mahogany lined the walls of my
dream library, a space filled with books of every
shape and size. Other than bookshelves, there was
one fireplace, four chairs, and three men. *The family.*

Maria excused herself, leaving me as the sole vagina
in the room, a ratio that left me distinctly
uncomfortable. I fought the urge to fidget as we
stepped forward.

Beauty. That was the first thing that hit my mind.
The genes that blessed Brad with an impressive
stature, gorgeous features, and mind-numbing sex
appeal hadn't skipped over his siblings. Two dark,
younger versions of Brad, similar in their
devastation, but slightly varied in features, stood
before me, flanking an older man, who stood at our
entrance. He stepped forward, aided by a cane, a

tall man with a shock of white hair and dark skin. He stopped before us and tilted his head at me.

"You must be Julia." A scratchy voice spoke, that despite its tenor, commanded respect. Eyes that studied me carefully.

Unsure of the proper protocol, I stepped forward, extending a hand and shaking his. He had a fierce grip, and grabbed my opposite shoulder as he grasped my hand, locking me into his space, his eyes arresting me. They searched my soul, a desperate invasion that explored every inch, distrust and accusation in their depths. With a jerk, he released my hand, turning away from me and walking carefully back to a leather chair which he sank into, words tumbling from his mouth with a sigh. "Please, sit. I am weary from today's activities."

Brad gestured to a chair and I sat, my legs shaky. He stood beside me, strong and tall. "We can't stay long. We have other obligations."

His father scoffed, an action that turned into a cough, and he stopped for a moment, his face turning red before he let out a series of coughing barks. One of the men beside him stepped forward, concern in his eyes, and the old man waved him off irritably. "Stop that, sit down. Everyone, sit down. Brad, find a chair. I won't have you hovering above me like a damn hawk."

I glanced at Brad, noting his tight face, and watched as he nodded, dragging up a chair, wariness across his features.

"I assume you know the business of this family?" It was a dry question, stated without malice or concern, directed at me.

I nodded, meeting his sharp eyes. "Yes."

"And you find … issue, with this business?" He watched me closely, sitting back in his chair and studying me.

I stared back, my face expressionless. "Issue would be the wrong word. I disagree with your business practices. Issue indicates that I am confrontational in my disapproval."

A slow smile spread over his face, a transformation that brought a hint of the good looks he must have once possessed. "That's an interesting choice of words, Ms. Campbell."

I said nothing, and he glanced briefly at Brad. "What exactly are your intentions with my son?"

"I intend to marry him."

"Yes, I gathered that from my son. The issue is, Ms. Campbell, that marrying Bradley is not quite as simple as happily ever after. Do you love my son?"

I hesitated at the change in his tone, the question rolling harsh off his lips. "Yes."

He leaned forward, fixating me with cold eyes. "Imagine your love for my son, if love *is* what it truly is. Whatever that love is, it won't possibly compare what you will feel for your own children — what I feel for Bradley, as well as my other sons. Your children, whether they are number one or five, will be more precious to you than your own soul. And you, choosing him to marry, to father your children, are putting those future babies in danger. You will never be able to sleep soundly, knowing the evil that waits for them. You will never be able to vacation, or play with them in the park, without worrying about cars driving by, or men who look at you a moment too long. You are not marrying Brad. You are marrying this family, and endangering yourself and your children with that act. You may be scared of me now, child, but I am one family. There are four others, in this city alone, that have us dead center in their targets. You are not, and will not, be safe in this family. You are marrying into a lifetime of fear, and you need to understand that now, before it is too late."

I listened to his words, understanding the reasoning behind them, my thoughts wandering down paths I had not even considered. I had been so worried about being against the Magianos that I had not considered what being part of them would entail.

"I am not marrying Brad for safety. I am marrying him because I am in love."

He leaned back and smiled slightly, a cruel expression on his face. "Let me tell you a story about Bradley. We had a dog, an old mutt that used to sit behind one of our butchers. He would eat the scraps that we threw out each day. And one day we opened the shop to find him inside, his mouth bloody, meat still inside his mouth. I started to kill him, grabbed a meat beater from the counter and went to smash his skull in. But Brad stepped in front of me."

He laughed, looking over at Brad. "The boy was *eleven* years old, and he stepped in front of me, *his father*, to save a dog." He stood, leaning heavily on the cane, the movement slow and pained. "You don't know the Italian way, but disobedience is not acceptable. I told Brad to leave or kill the dog himself. He refused, and stood his ground." He shot Brad a look of disgust. "He defied me over a *dog*, a mutt, an animal not worth mopping the floor with."

He looked into my eyes, stepping forward, speaking slowly. "I used the beater on Brad's skull instead, knocking him unconscious with two blows. He spent four days in the hospital before he woke up.

And his first question when he did?" He closed his eyes briefly. "The dog, he wanted to know about the damn dog!" He finished the statement with a snarl, his finger stabbing the air in Brad's direction to punctuate the sentence.

"We had killed that dog before we even took Bradley to the hospital. Bradley risked himself for a dog—a trash animal he had played with in the alley one day. So yes, he is marrying you, but what does that mean to me?" He straightened and turned, walking carefully, his words tossed over his shoulder to me. "You are worse than a dog, Ms. Campbell. That dog was hungry, eating for his survival. You are eating to get fat, and ruining my son's life with your greedy acceptance of his sacrificial offer. I am not surprised that he is marrying you. I am only surprised that you are stupid and selfish enough to accept." He waved dismissively in my direction and closed the space to the window, leaning heavily on the sill and looking out toward the backyard. "Leave, I am tired."

I stood, anger radiating from me in waves of heat. I felt Brad's hand at my arm, a warning in his touch. "Mr. Magiano, I am *not* marrying into your family. I want *nothing* to do with your family or your way of life. You scorn my decision to endanger my unborn children. I question your role as a father. You think you lead this family? You believe they have respect for you, but I assure you, anyone who respects you is not intelligent enough to distinguish fear from respect. Thank you for your time, it was a pleasure seeing what caused Brad to become the man I fell in love with. Anyone who left this family with some semblance of sanity has my admiration, and he certainly has my love."

He laughed, a hard sound that did nothing but fan my infuriation, frustration swelling in me, mixed with a fear, an awareness of my low standing in this room. He turned, his eyes meeting mine across the room. In unison his two sons rose, twin pillars of gorgeous framing the old man's empty seat. I ignored them, my hands in fists by my side.

The old man spoke slowly, his eyes locked on mine. "For someone who owes me her life, you are a nasty little bitch."

I turned from his face and met the eyes of Brad's brothers, two sets of barely contained anger. *Right back at'cha.* Then I turned, striding to the double doors and shoving on the wood with a burst of anger.

♦♦♦

The doors settled silently behind Julia, and Brad watched them close completely before turning back to his father. "She's not Hillary. My love for her is much stronger than that. And she is *much* stronger than Hillary. You are not going to be able to scare her into submission, or convince her to leave with threats. She will stand up to you."

A small smile creased the lines of his father's face. "I would have thought you would have picked a smarter girl than that, Bradley."

"Stay away from her. And make sure that message travels through the ranks." He stared into one brother's eyes, then the other, both of them shrinking slightly under his stony stare. He turned to leave and was stopped by his father's voice.

"I thought you had her under control, Brad."

He turned to meet his father's eyes.

"You had assured me of her silence, of her loyalty to this family. You expect us to welcome her, to protect her, but she has nothing but disrespect for me and for your family. Why should I trust her to keep her silence?"

"You don't have a choice. You are my father, and she will be my wife. It is done. Last I checked, blood still means *something* in this family." He didn't wait for a response, but turned and left the room, shoving open the double doors without restraint, the heavy wood slamming into the walls with a loud crack.

In unison, the two brothers moved, stepping forward with curses and anger but were stopped with the raised hand of their father. "Let them go." He moved with slow steps back to his chair, settling in with a heavy sigh. "There are other ways to handle this."

Chapter 19

We rode back to the house in silence, my mind flitting through the words of his father, playing on repeat the conversation we had had. My hands threatened to shake, and I squeezed them together. I was not used to confrontation. With Brad, yes. With strangers I didn't know, ones who murdered people without thought, no. It was a new experience, and one I hoped to never experience again.

"Are you okay?" Brad's voice was tight, and I looked over to see his jaw clenched.

"Yeah. You never told me about the dog ... and your father putting you in the hospital."

"It's one of a lot of stories, ones I never want you to have to hear. I'm at peace with them. They made me into the person I am today." He reached over, gripping my hand. "He is right, about your safety."

I ran my free hand over his, watching the muscles in his hand flex. "You mean, from the other families?"

"Yes. It is a small risk, but one that is present. The risk is diminished because of my lack of involvement in family activities. I don't engage in actions that would spark a vendetta. But it is a risk, and the thought of someone hurting you terrifies me." He pulled into the dark drive of the house, pressing the garage door opener and waiting on its movement. He turned to me. "My house is well protected — our security system is the best on the market. But that doesn't protect you the rest of the time. How would you feel about private security? Someone to keep an eye on you when we are apart?"

I shuddered. "No." The words spilled out quickly and with strength. "I don't want anyone following me, or watching me. I need my freedom. I'd rather deal with the risk."

His silence voiced his disapproval, and the car rolled forward, coming to a stop inside the garage. He turned off the engine and turned to me, cupping my face in his hand. He sighed, his eyes searching mine before pulling me to him for a kiss.

I broke the contact, wanting to finish the conversation. "Do you understand? Why I don't want security?"

"Yeah. I wouldn't want it either. But I don't like the thought of you without protection. I want you to start training with Ben."

"Ben? In what, jujitsu?" I raised my eyebrows.

"Yes. Meet with him a few times; he can train you at the house. If you don't think it's worth your time, then you can stop." The concern in his eyes was heartbreaking, unease submerged in dark brown depths.

A close friend of Brad's, Ben didn't strike me as lethal, but I knew martial arts were a major focus in his life. I had met Ben a few weeks after our engagement, and he was a familiar face in the house, taking advantage of Martha's cooking on lasagna night, and often working out with Brad. I liked him, his quiet sense of humor a good fit with Brad's and my outspoken personalities. Newly single, his last relationship had ended badly, the pain still fresh in his eyes when *she* came up. Ben and Brad had met playing baseball, part of a city league that ran for two months every summer. As best I could tell, baseball season was an event they looked forward to all year. Brad had spent a good part of last week in the den, poring over Eastbay catalogs with Ben and ordering custom uniforms, bats, and equipment. They were like kids looking forward to Christmas, our meals now revolving around lineups, schedules, and recruitment of key players.

"It's either Ben or security. Pick one." His mouth was a hard line, and I frowned at the ultimatum. But there was a part of me, a part that I tried to push away, that was shaken by his father's words. They had opened a Pandora's box of insecurity. About my safety, about Brad's intentions, about our future.

I looked away, pressing the button that closed the garage.

"Okay," I said. "I'll start with Ben. See how it goes."

He leaned over and pressed a kiss on my lips. "Thanks, baby."

Then we opened the doors and moved. For now, the conversation was over. But my doubts? Those little black bits of disaster that poison every healthy crevice of your mind? Those ran wild and unattended, setting up house and planning a big party, with all of my insecurities invited.

Chapter 20

DECEMBER
Days until wedding: 236

I folded over the red metallic paper and ran my thumb down the edge of the book, making a crisp line, the only OCD bone in my body was obsessed with perfect wrapping.

"Almost done?"

I turned to look at my mom, smiling when I saw her raised eyebrows. "You're really asking me that question? After twenty-one Christmases of experience?"

"I thought you were bad before. Now, with proper funding, it's become an official addiction."

I bit my lip, keeping my pathetic comeback swallowed. "Think Dad's getting along with Brad?"

"I can't think of anyone your father's ever *not* gotten along with. They'll be fine."

My father, one hour into today's holiday festivities, had shot Brad a look of desperation, one that had been easily received, Brad asking for his assistance with some additional exterior decorations. They had left, Christmas lights and garland on the shopping list. Three hours ago. Three hours during which Martha had made hot chocolate, three batches of sugar cookies, and eight colors of icing. Three hours during which I had called Becca and Olivia, and they had showed up, eggnog in hand. With finals over, my last day at CDB complete, and Christmas just one week away, everyone's spirits were high, and the kitchen and great room buzzed with feminine energy.

Mom and Dad were on day three of their visit, their car heading back to Georgia in the morning. Staying at a hotel in between campus and Brad's home, I had been pleasantly surprised at how naturally they had fit into our lifestyle. Mom hadn't blinked twice at Brad's house, Martha had taken to them both with a friendly ease that had shocked me into silence, and Dad hadn't tried to find a garage sale all weekend.

Friday, I'd taken them both to the office, Mom helping me pack up the drawer-full of items I had accumulated in a little over six months at the firm. It was bittersweet, packing up the pieces of the job that had brought Brad and me together. Once it was done, a small cardboard box holding my belongings, I sealed it with tape and then made my final rounds of the West Wing. Burge was professional, Sheila got a little teary, and the rest of the staff made their polite goodbyes. I had never regained my original standing as beloved intern, not after the news of my engagement broke. But the staff had warmed up considerably over the last two months, and I'd be lying if I said I wouldn't miss, in some small way, that wing of the firm.

"Okay, I've looked through this entire pile, and I can't find a single gift with my name on it," Becca grumbled, looking up from her curious shake of a wrapped present, the evergreen tree and mountain of presents almost swallowing her blonde figure.

"I haven't wrapped yours yet," I mumbled through a mouthful of cookie.

"So … in other words, look for it around Easter," Olivia cracked from the kitchen, where she put the final sprinkled touches on a cookie.

Mom's earlier comment regarding my wrapping addiction was true. Before, I painstakingly wrapped gifts with paper and ribbon, mixing up the landscapes with fun labels. This year I had put Brad's credit card to good use, cleaning out the local Michael's craft store. Half the kitchen table was now covered with ribbons of every shape and size, individual stamp cutters, metallic pens, tiny ornamental garnishes, and enough rolls of paper to cover half of downtown.

"It's six," Martha announced without preamble, glancing at her watch. "You guys planning on eating sugar all night, or should I put something on?"

"Do you feel like cooking?" I glanced over casually. Martha's weekends were traditionally untouchable, a time in which she disappeared from view and did whoknowswhat. The fact that she'd been hanging out with us all afternoon had been shocking on its own, an oddity I had avoided pointing out in fear of scaring her off. "I can call Brad. Have him and Dad grab pizza on their way home."

She shot me a look that, five months earlier, would have melted my bones. "I'm not having him pick up *pizza* when I have a fridge full of cookable food. Let me get something on. But go call him. Tell him it'll be hot in forty-five minutes if he wants to get fed."

I didn't argue, dialing Brad immediately. He and my father returned a half-hour later, bags from Home Depot in hand, and we moved to the dining room and ate, Martha's beef soup and cornbread disappearing amid a flurry of conversation and laughter. Then we headed to the theatre room, my parents agreeing to one movie before they headed back to the hotel.

A Christmas Story won, and I curled against Brad's chest in one of the leather couches, the dark room sending occasional flickers across my parents' faces, two couches over. "Thank you," I whispered to Brad.

He moved his head down, until his mouth was close to my ear, stealing a quick kiss before responding, his voice low, "For what?"

"Everything. Spending time with my parents, my dad."

He turned his head slightly, my eyes looking up and catching his. "Family is important. *Your* family is important."

I didn't know what to say, and pushed up, brushing my lips against his before settling back against his chest, his strong arms wrapping around and squeezing me gently. I felt a moment of sadness at the realization that we would never experience this with his family, with his parents. *Family was important.* But was that only true when the family was a positive force? I didn't know the answer to that question.

Chapter 21

JANUARY
Days until wedding: 197

I blinked rapidly, tried to focus on my professor's voice. Twenty minutes left. Twenty minutes, and then I could hike a half-mile across campus, get in my car, and head to Brad's. Pack a bag and sneak in a nap. Maybe convince Martha to whip up some cookies for our flight.

Hmmm … cookies. Martha's best are plain chocolate chips. Though maybe she could make some peanut butter ones. I like the ones where she puts in chunks of Reese's Cups… Fuck. I closed my notebook quietly and stuffed it into my bag. Law school apps and records had already been sent. Getting a B on next week's exam wouldn't kill me. I knew my strengths. Focusing on a Friday afternoon with Vegas on standby wasn't it. I pushed back my chair and snuck out of class.

We flew commercial, changing planes in Houston and landing in the city of sin at 9:30 p.m. on Friday. Brad was still in work attire and gave Leonard a tired grin as he relieved me of my bag. "Only carry-ons?" Leonard asked, shooting a quick look at the leather duffel Brad carried.

"Yep. This is a quick trip for us. We fly back tomorrow afternoon." He clapped the man on the back, matching strides with him as we headed for the long white car.

"It's good to see you both. And do I hear congratulations are in order?" The older man's eyes twinkled as he opened the door for me, his warm face stretching into a smile.

"Yes, thank you." I grinned, settling down into the dark elegance of the limo, reaching for Brad as he entered, my body naturally falling into the curve of his warmth.

"Have I mentioned how lucky I am?" Brad murmured against my hair, planting a quick kiss on my head.

I shook my head against his chest. "Not recently."

"I am. Very lucky."

I closed my eyes and smiled, relaxing against his warmth.

Twenty minutes later, Leonard pulled down the long curved drive of the Bellagio. Brad's cell rang, and he glanced at the display before answering.

"Janine … Yes. We just reached the casino. We're gonna change, and then we'll head your way." He shot me a quick grin. "She's with me."

I looked out the window while he finished the conversation, watching the building, tourists, and trees come to a slow stop as we pulled into the Bellagio's portico. He ended the call, and we stepped out in unison, twin valets at our doors, offering gloved hands and welcoming smiles.

♥♥♥

"Janine's looking forward to meeting you," Brad called from the closet, where the sound of zippers and hangers combined in reckless harmony.

I shot the mirror a wry look, twisting my hair up and pinning it into place before I reached for mascara. "Likely. I'm sure Janine's less than enthusiastic about my new involvement."

He appeared in the reflection behind me, shirtless, his muscular arms encircling my waist. "Ownership, babe. Not involvement."

"Even more reason for her to hate me. Last time she saw us, I was your weekend piece and topless on a table with one of her strippers."

He laughed, releasing me with a quick squeeze. "Janine's spent a lot more time topless and on a table than you have. That move probably earned you some brownie points. Besides, tonight is more fun than business. I just want you to have a more intense tour of the club, meet the employees, and get a sense of what goes on."

I exhaled a breath, studying my eyes in the mirror. Then I reached for lipstick.

Chapter 22

Alexis leaned forward, critically studying her eyes in the small mirror set into the back of her locker. Her eye makeup was smudged, a bit of black traveling out of its typical territory. She yanked a tissue out of its holder and dabbed at the spot, glancing down at her phone briefly. It sat, silent, in the outer pocket of her purse. As it had all night. She had heard the news, they all had. Brad was in town, and he was bringing *her*. Little Miss Virtuous. A girl who would never, ever, be everything that he would need. But she had known, had seen it from the look in his eyes when he'd been with her. When he had gone upstairs to VIP and watched her with Montana, his expression different than she'd ever seen. He had denied it, had tossed off her concerns without a second thought. But she had known. She could always see her demise before it came. She closed her eyes briefly, thinking of that night. When he had left Miss Virtuous downstairs and went into the office with her.

She closed her eyes and her head fell back, her back arching, body open to him. He reached forward, running his hands possessively down her body, wrapping his hands around her waist. He gave one long thrust, burying himself completely inside her, the depth causing her to gasp in response.

Fucking had always been Brad's strength. The ability to electrify her body and give her exactly what she wanted, when she wanted it. His sexuality was a fire run out of control, stealing the breath and passion of any women who dared to stand too close to the flames. *Fire.* You couldn't control a fire. A fact his new fiancée would learn very, very soon.

◆◆◆

Alexis had loved Brad De Luca from the first moment she saw him. Walking down the plush hallway of the Bellagio, chanting a room number in her head to keep from forgetting it. 2314. 2314. 2314. Her palms were sweaty, a common occurrence at this stage in the game. The unknown was the worst. Not knowing who would be behind the door, what he would expect, how badly he could, possibly would, hurt her body. All she knew, all she needed to concentrate on, was that he was a paycheck, and that she was there to please. Then he opened the door, and everything sane exited her mind.

He opened the door fresh from the shower, the clean scent of soap and male practically knocking her back into the hall. He had buttoned up half of his shirt, the unopened buttons offering her a peek into tan, ripped perfection. Dark brown eyes regarded her carefully, traveling down her body before returning to her face.

She shifted uncomfortably, tugging the hem on her dress slightly before striking a pose against the doorframe.

"May I come in?" she asked, using the husky voice that seemed to appeal to men everywhere.

He was different, taking a step back and studying her silently without speaking, buttoning the remaining buttons on his shirt before beginning with the cufflinks. "Are you lost, or have you been sent by the hotel?"

She ignored the pit in her stomach and grinned breezily, walking past him into the room and reclining onto the couch, her legs on full display, body curved in a way that made every asset count. "You can thank Blake for me." He shut the door and walked over, continuing to work on his sleeves while frowning down on her. He stood close, close enough that his scent invaded her, and she looked up at him, deciphering the expression on his face, one somewhere between irritation and concern. Not the look men typically carried. Greed, arousal, excitement. Those were the looks she created, the reason her new job seemed destined for success.

"How old are you?" He frowned.

"Eighteen." Twenty.

He walked away, entering the suite's small kitchen and opening the fridge. She took the moment to breathe deeply, wiping her hands on the fabric of her dress and willing her confidence to return.

A water bottle, the hotel's brand, drops of condensation dotting its round landscape. He held it out, taking a seat, *not on the couch as she had hoped, but in the chair next to her. She accepted it warily. "Thank you, but I'm not really thirsty."*

"I'd offer you something stronger, but given your age …" He laughed when her eyes regarded his skeptically. "What's your name?"

"Alexis." Sarah Hinkle.

He raised his eyebrows at her answer, speaking in an unhurried manner. "Blake hasn't learned me yet. Once he does, he will realize that I prefer companions of the unpaid variety. That being said, I'm sure you are expected to stay up here for a certain period of time. How about we spend that time talking? Are you hungry?

Gay. The man was gay. She almost laughed as the realization hit her, a burst of relief pouring through her insecure body. She fought to hide the reaction, straightening out of her ridiculous pose and nodding gratefully at him. "A little. Some food would be nice."

Her answer pleased him and he stood, grabbing a room service menu off of the side table and passing it to her. "Great. Look that over. I was going to head out for dinner, but I'll eat here with you. You can head downstairs after that."

He moved to the bar, pouring himself a drink and returned with the phone, pressing an extension and holding it to his ear, shooting her an inquisitive glance.

She quickly skimmed the menu, picking out the least expensive item. "Chicken ceasar salad, dressing on the side. And a Diet Coke, please."

He placed the order, stacking two appetizers, a few side items, and two desserts onto it before ending the call. They sat there, in silence, and she braced herself for whatever was next.

"So … Alexis. What's your real name?" His legs slightly spread, he leaned back in the chair, head relaxed against the headrest, his position as unobtrusive as humanly possible, yet ridiculously tempting as it stretched his pelvis and flat stomach before her, like a clothed buffet just waiting to be devoured.

She hesitated, eyes fighting to stay on his face and then, much to her surprise, her mouth opened, and the truth spilled out.

Fifty minutes later, a white fluffy robe surrounded her — the garment retrieved from a closet and thrust at her by a disgruntled Brad. "Put this on," he had ordered. "Otherwise you'll ruin your dress, and I'll fail miserably at trying to avoid staring at your body." She had smiled slightly, working her way into the robe. She had been wrong. Gay didn't occupy a single corner of this man's universe. She didn't know why he wouldn't touch her, didn't know how — when sexuality reeked from every bone in his body — he managed to converse, laugh, and question her without taking it to the bedroom. She had tried, three times during the meal, to move the evening in that direction, but had been met only with polite resistance. She still knew nothing of the man, of his intentions, history, or relationship status, but he now knew almost everything about her. From her awkward beginnings, to her move to Vegas, to the first few weeks of this new, lucrative job.

He had disapproved, his brows knitting together in concern. "There are plenty of other jobs on the Strip. Waitress, bartend. Anything but this."

He didn't understand. Didn't realize that her sights were set on far more than sweaty encounters with faceless men. She didn't want to slave away for pennies and live in a tiny shithole apartment in North Las Vegas. She wanted the glitz and the glam of the Strip, and to experience it on the arm of a wealthy man. She wanted the easy lifestyle, the limos and the clothes, the stack of credit cards, sparkle of diamonds, confidence of a kept woman. This was her way to get there. With every hotel door that opened, she had one more chance. Maybe this was her chance, he was her Richard Gere, and this was her Pretty Woman *tale.*

"Sexuality is my talent. You wouldn't understand, but this is my best plan." She looked down as she said the words, realizing, too late, that she had scarfed down an easy two thousand calories, inexcusable in her line of work.

"So strip. At least then you have security and guidelines. This work is too dangerous, you have very little control."

He hadn't understood, and the look he shot her at their parting was one of disappointment and worry. And his handsome face, towering over her in the foyer of that luxurious suite, imprinted on her mind for the next three weeks, came to her in the dead of night, when the day was over and she slipped under cheap sheets, ready to sleep away the day's memories. She had left her number, scribbled with a girlish script on a pad of hotel paper. And nightly, she had prayed for a call. But the phone never rang, and as the days passed, the memory faded, until his face no longer came to her when her eyes closed at night.

◆◆◆

Six years later, and she was still checking her phone for his damn call. The irony was not lost on her, and she slammed the locker door shut with more vigor than was necessary. She used to think it was fated, her leaving the escort game to go into stripping, her journey ending at this club, Saffire's gold-encrusted elegance that would later become the property of Brad De Luca. Now, with the club ownership change, it seemed like a cruel joke from whoever was upstairs, life a jerky puppeteer game that had contorted her directly into the hands of Miss Virtuous. She envisioned the young brunette deftly manipulating the puppeteer handles, and her face twisted in anger.

Chapter 23

We pulled up to Saffire, the door opened by a muscular bouncer with a welcoming smile. "Ma'am." He nodded, extending his hand and helping me from the car. Brad appeared and shook his hand, his appearance causing the man's grin to widen exponentially.

"Mr. D. Good to see you, sir. Janine is inside, should I radio her?"

"No, we'll find her. Good to see you, John." He clapped the man on the back, and we made our way through the doors, stepping into the dark club.

Janine found us, striding up with quick efficiency before we even passed through the lobby. She gave Brad a warm hug and turned to me with a smile, extending a hand and shaking mine with a firm grip.

"Brad's told me a lot about you. Welcome. Would you like a tour?"

I nodded, glancing at Brad, who softly placed a hand on my back, assuring me of his presence. Then we moved, Janine starting a steady dialogue that wouldn't pause for forty-five minutes.

Alexis watched them move, a tight group of three, the girl's assets displayed in a dress that screamed expensive. She was softer than Alexis, her chest still natural, a delicate look to her frame. But she had the ass, and that had always been Brad's weakness. She watched with narrowed eyes as the threesome stepped through the backstage doors, disappearing from view. A rough hand on her back had her looking down, into the needy eyes of the businessman she straddled. Smiling down, she ground against his crotch, her need for approval stronger now, more than ever.

♦♦♦

I liked Janine. She was businesslike to the point of being unfriendly, skipping over any fun facts on the tour and rattling off figures, percentages, and problems, a mix of pride and concern in her words. We ended the tour in an upper-level VIP room, seated at a private alcove that looked down upon the club. Janine killed power to a small video camera that looked into the space, and we sat down around a cocktail table.

"When will the changeover take place?" she asked, leaning forward and meeting both of our eyes.

"I've already transferred the stock certificates. Scott Burge, an attorney from my firm, will send over an operating agreement for you to sign. You should receive that this week. Once that is complete, I will be completely out."

She glanced at me guardedly, hesitating before speaking. "Julia, I've never been very good with tact, so I'll come right out with this. Brad and Evelyn have left me alone, occasionally visiting the club and having monthly conference calls to discuss finances. I'm not used to having a boss, and that isn't something I am particularly interested in."

Brad started to speak, and I silenced him, touching his arm lightly. "I plan on having the same level of involvement as Brad. I am not familiar with Saffire and have little to no experience in the business world. Brad says you are an excellent operator, and I trust his judgment. Assuming we continue or improve the current level of revenue, I see no reason to get involved in your business."

Her features relaxed noticeably. "I would appreciate that. Do you have any other questions I can answer while you are here?"

I couldn't think of anything she had missed during the last hour. I shook my head and glanced at Brad to see if he had any thoughts.

He leaned forward, speaking, "I think we're good, Janine. I'll join in on the call next week with Julia, so we can touch base then. Look for that package from our firm."

She nodded, moving quickly to her feet, her eyes already roaming the club. "If that's all, I'd like to get back downstairs."

"We'll stay here and chat for a bit," Brad said, throwing an arm over the back of my chair.

"Just turn back on the security cam when you're done." She gave us both smiles and left, moving at a quick pace, speaking into a mouthpiece as she moved.

I let out a breath, turning to Brad with a smile. "She's nice."

He scoffed. "Did you expect her to be a bitch to her new boss?"

My mouth turned up slightly. "I thought we just clarified that I'm *not* her boss."

"I never treated her like an employee, despite the majority ownership I held. I'm sure you will follow suit."

"You know I will."

Then his eyes changed, from friendly to dark, and I knew, before he even lifted a hand, what was coming.

Chapter 24

I felt the tug on my chair as Brad pulled me close to him. He captured my face in his hands, his eyes examining my features. "I love you so much," he murmured, his eyes moving over and focusing on my lips before he tugged me to him, taking ownership of my mouth with a few soft swipes of his tongue. I opened my lips further, deepening the contact, my hands stealing into his hair. I broke the kiss, pushing my chair back and standing, moving closer to him and spreading his knees with my legs. He slid deeper in the chair, reclining back against the soft leather, gazing up at me with a latent dominance of the nothing-but-trouble variety. I grinned playfully down at him, and slid one strap, then the other, of my dress down, dragging the fabric until my bare breasts were exposed, lit softly by the blue-gray lights of the room.

He groaned softly, a guttural sound, and stared into my eyes, tightening his knees against my legs. "Come here."

I shook my head and knelt, running my hands softly up his dress pants, past his muscular thighs, until I reached his belt. He watched me, his eyes darkening and he leaned forward suddenly, snagging my chin and pulling it up, his eyes grabbing me possessively before kissing me hard, a deep kiss that reclaimed his power before he released me, leaning back and watching me.

"Do you always have to be in control, Mr. De Luca?" I purred the words, unbuckling his belt with one motion, then rubbed my hand over the zipper line, feeling the outline of his cock underneath the fabric, the shape of him hardening under my fingers. He didn't answer, his eyes locked on mine, dark orbs of sexuality. I suddenly needed to see him, needed to have his bare skin in my hand, to feel the throb of what was mine. I looked away from his eyes, focusing, and unbuttoned and unzipped his pants. Then, he was in my hand, an impossibly thick, hard shaft, the skin hot beneath my palm. I stroked it, the firm grip eliciting an intake of Brad's breath.

"Put it in your mouth." The order came through in a drugged tone, desire glowing at me from under heavy eyelids.

I shook my head, increasing the speed of my stroke as I watched him. He frowned slightly, lifting his hips a bit, bringing the nine inches of insanity closer to my face. I spoke, my tone a mixture of dominance and bite. "What is your plan with the girl?"

He sat up slightly, his eyes opening more, and watching me carefully. "What girl?"

"The stripper. The one you fucked last time you were here."

"I thought that didn't bother you."

I hissed. "It didn't bother me *last* time. Things are different now. Are you going to talk to her?"

"I feel like this is a test of some sort ..." he mumbled. His breath hitched a bit as I squeezed his cock, loving the feel of complete stiffness in my hands. "What is you want, Julia?"

I ran my tongue lightly, teasingly, over the top of his head, taking it into my mouth for one brief moment before I pulled off, my hands never pausing in their movement, a quick pace that traveled his entire length with every stroke. "I want you to handle it," I said firmly. "I want her to understand that you will never have sex with her again."

"Never?" I released him, the sudden departure causing his eyes to open and a frown to settle over his features. "I'm joking. Don't stop."

I resumed my movement, my free hand gathering his heavy balls in my hand, squeezing him softly as I stroked his length with a firm hand.

"Come here," he said, sitting up and pulling on my arms.

"No." I fixed him with my sternest look, my hand increasing in speed.

"Julia, come here. I want to talk to you about this without being tongue-tied by your hands on my cock." He pulled harder, his strong arms lifting me easily onto his lap, despite my best attempt at resistance.

Sitting on his lap created a new set of problems. Mainly him, standing at attention against my thighs. I sat sideways on his lap and spread my knees slightly, my hand stealing in between my legs to grab him.

He relented, shifting slightly so I would have better access and turned my face to his. His eyes were troubled, turbulent storms of concern. *For her.* I tried to squash the irritation that rose within me at that realization. "Julia, you've lived a very different life from Alexis. Her relationship with me gives her some financial security."

Whoa. I released his cock and spoke quickly, anger vibrating through my voice. "Your relationship?"

"Don't get bent out of shape at my choice of words. There are things you need to understand, and if you are going to get worked up, I'm not going to be able to explain it to you."

I bit back a retort and waited.

"Despite your emotionally-distant mother and your tiny college budget, you've lived a charmed life compared to Alexis. She's been on her own since she was seventeen. When I first met her, she was working as a prostitute." He tucked a lock of hair behind my ear, his hand stealing behind my neck. "She earns a salary here, one that gives her some semblance of security. She will see our marriage, my departure from her, as an end to that security. She won't understand that my commitment to you doesn't mean an abandonment of her. It will take time, will take her seeing the financial stability continuing, with your name on the paychecks, for her to understand and be okay with it."

I thought for a moment, trying to organize my thoughts. "I don't want her to think, if her salary continues, that it is because you have emotional feelings for her." An unavoidable thought wormed into my mind. "*Do* you have emotional feelings for her?"

He hesitated, a reaction that lit a fire in my psyche. He saw the heat in my eyes and raised a hand. "Wait, let me try to communicate this properly."

I waited, my mouth set.

"You know the story my father told you … about the dog."

I nodded silently.

"I didn't love that dog. I had played with it one day, and if I had never seen it again, I wouldn't have had a second thought about it. But I admired its strength, I felt compassion for its struggle. Sex, for Alexis, is nothing. She has no emotional ties to it. We have fucked, throughout the last five years, out of joint enjoyment. What Alexis yearns for, and needs, is security. I feel compassion for Alexis. I care for her in the sense that I want what is best for her. I felt that I couldn't ignore or stand by when she needed help. I know that she cannot strip forever. I have encouraged her to go to college, had hoped that the small amount she receives in salary will help her to explore other options. You will be my wife; you are my future. I will never jeopardize our relationship in an attempt to comfort Alexis. But please don't ask me to hurt her. Saffire is yours now. If you want to fire her, or cut off her salary, or sell the club altogether, that is your prerogative. But I don't believe that you are the type of woman to treat her in that manner. I will speak to her, and make sure she understands that I am forever and exclusively committed to you. But I'd also like to assure her that I still value her as an individual, and that you will support her job at Saffire as long as she wants to work here."

I leaned back against his chest, my tension releasing slightly as I processed his words. His hand ran lightly up my thigh, gently, slowly moving toward the silk wisp of fabric that comprised my panties. "Are you trying to distract me, Mr. De Luca?" I breathed, my body tightening in anticipation as his second hand joined in, stealing up my stomach until it hit the exposed skin that was my breasts.

"Never," he said, his fingers caressing the silk of my panties, sliding over and over the triangle of fabric, my clit awaking underneath his touch, under the slow, perfect swipes of his fingers. I shifted, tilting my pelvis upward and pushed his hand down, letting out a soft moan when his fingers hit the place where my panties became practically non-existent. He stroked that spot, leaving the thong in place, his thumb strumming a steady rhythm over my clit as his fingers stroked my wetness. I moaned again, pushing on his hand, waiting, needing more. My eyes found his cock, heavy and thick against my leg, and I panted at the sight of glistening moisture at its hard tip.

"You're not going to get this subject to go away with sex," I mumbled, as my mind threw out all reasonable thought processes and prepared to fully enter De Luca worship mode.

"I believe," he whispered in my ear, "that you were the one who brought sex into this conversation."

Then his finger moved, a strong motion that pushed aside my thong and thrust into my sex. I gasped, throwing back my head and pushed greedily down on his hand. A second finger joined the first, and they moved in perfect succession, fully inside and crooking inside of me, delicious swipes that had my eyes rolling back in ecstatic delirium. I reached out my hands, gripping his legs and squeezing, needing some type of grounding solidity to bring me back to reason.

His arms held me still, one wrapped around my pelvis and ending at the wet burial between my legs, the other holding my back tightly against his chest, the forearm hard against my stomach, the hand traveling from breast to breast, squeezing, teasing, and worshipping my tender skin.

My orgasm was coming, my core contracting around his fingers, my body arching against him. "Brad," I gasped, "I need …"

He knew what I needed, and tightened his arms, holding me still, his upper hand turning whisper soft on my nipples as he increased the magic of his lower hand, his fingers taking me over the this-can't-be-fucking-happening mountain, and I fell, in a beautiful, free cascade, a full-body explosion of perfection that had me screaming his name, my words disappearing in the loud club music, my screams turning to moans, until I finally settled on a bed of Brad, my body spent and drunk against his, his fingers maintaining movement inside of me, taking me to a perfect, delirious ending until I collapsed.

Chapter 25

We stayed in that moment, his fingers inside of me, my body heavy on his for a minute. Then, his hands and arms moved, my body curling as they brought me into a fetal position sideways in his lap. I leaned my head back against his arm, my eyes closed and mouth curving into a smile, loving the strength and security in his grip.

I didn't, couldn't, begrudge any woman who wanted Brad. I wanted him for everything — his strength, his weakness, his sexuality, his humor, his ego, his temper, and his security. Maybe she didn't want him. Maybe she gave two shits what Brad De Luca did with his life, maybe she just wanted the salary she got from Saffire, Inc. But I couldn't imagine any woman having, enjoying, and spending any amount of time with Brad and not being head over heels. It was impossible.

I understood what Brad was asking of me. But he was a man. He didn't realize. Everything he told me about her, her struggle, her life — he had intended the words to endear me to her. But they had only made me more wary. For as much as any woman wanted a man, they wanted a Prince Charming even more. For me, Brad was my soul mate. For her, he was a new life wrapped in that love. A way out of her current one.

He didn't want to be cruel. But what is crueler? A slow, painful extinguishing of hope? Or truth—that bitch of life who smacks you into reality?

I knew what I'd want. A quick rip of the Band-Aid, Brad to look square in my face, and to explain reality. *Right*. Who the hell was I kidding? It would devastate me, knock all the life out of my heart in one painful burst. *I was not the one*. It would be a blow I might not recover from. The question was, how would Alexis recover? I worried she wasn't the meek type, the one who'd wallow away on the couch in misery, scarfing down pizzas and rocky road ice cream. No, her recovery was probably of the plotting, sharpen-her-teeth-with-a-knife, stab-you-in-the-back-in-a-dark-alley type. And that scared the hell outta me.

It would do me no good to talk to her. Any news coming from me would be dismissed as skewed, delusional. It would have to come from him. And he seemed reluctant to rip off the damned Band-Aid.

◆◆◆

Alexis glanced up, her eyes on the curved wall of the upstairs VIP section. They were up there, the video feed off, enclosed in a bubble of privacy — their own little secret world. She knew what they were doing. Brad De Luca didn't chit-chat, didn't make polite conversation over martinis and cheese platters. Brad fucked: long, hard, and perfectly. Just the thought of it made her thighs clench tightly around the thirty year old toothpick she was straddling.

Memories flooded through her mind. Brad, whispering words of sex as he fucked her against the wall. Brad, bending her over an upstairs VIP table, his hands and mouth worshipping her from behind before he took her with slow, gentle strokes that increased in speed until she came. Brad, her soul submitting to his dark eyes as she danced for him, the club closed, the shock of his hands as he suddenly stood before her, skimming rough hands over smooth skin, his mouth following his hands. And then she was laid back, hard stage against her back, his mouth, hands, and cock making the night, her worries, her life, disappear in a blur of orgasms and sex.

Soft hands surprised her, taking her out of the memories and she glanced down, seeing pale fingers excitedly traveling up her tight stomach. She shook her head with a smile, pulling the client's hands off her and holding them together above his head, the action causing her breasts to hover inches from his face. She ground softly against him, glancing down and trying to think about anything but Brad De Luca.

◆◆◆

I pushed all thoughts of Alexis out of my mind and focused on the unrelenting cock beneath my body. It lacked social graces, the couth to understand that it was interrupting an in-depth thought process. It wanted only one thing: attention.

I laughed, meeting Brad's eyes, intense and mischievous all at one moment. "You got me all excited," he murmured, pulling me to him and stealing a kiss. "Surely you won't leave him hanging."

I looked out at the club, only lighting and walls a spectator to our alcove. Then I looked down, over the railing, my eyes dancing over sex at every turn. Not actual intercourse, but it was sex all the same, a flowing river of it, invading every pore, molecule, and breath of the downstairs space. An arched body, offering itself, in full glory, on stage. Lips against ears, whispered fantasies dancing between bodies. Spinning flesh, confidence via shot glass, sequins over tans, hands sliding over thighs, gripping ass, grabbing ankles. The sex crept up the walls, invaded the air, moved like invisible smoke upward, slithering into a hypnotic cloud into our room, curling around six feet two inches of sexuality. And underneath my body, legs spread, eyes potent, hardness impressively pushing up from below, was what I craved.

I moved, untangling from his arms and straddled him, sliding my dress upward, over my hips. His hands stopped me. "Let me," he said, taking over the action, his hands drawing out the process, firm fingers teasing as they pulled the dress over my body. The fabric came over my head, and I emerged to find his eyes on mine, intensity in them, his hands traveling slowly back down, a hand taking each breast and cupping them, his thumbs moving over my nipples lightly. "You know, I will never need anything more than you," he said softly. He sat up, a strong hand sliding around my back and lifting me easily, my body now suspended over him, my breasts soft cushions around his mouth. I moaned, his lips finding their way over the soft mounds and peaks of my breasts, hard flicks of his tongue against sensitive places, gentle scrapes of teeth following his soft mouth. His fingers dove back into that wet apex, moving in and out, readying me, moving my body into place until I felt his head. *There.* And he thrust, softly, only the head inside of me. His hand, cupping my ass, carrying my weight, kept me in place as he moved slowly, with short strokes, just his thick head dipping in and out of my folds.

"Brad," I murmured. "Please." Even as I spoke the words, I didn't mean them, didn't want him to stop. It was too perfect, too precise. Enough to enslave, too good to release, but not enough to fully satisfy. I didn't want satisfaction just yet. I wanted this, this incredible yearning met halfway, as a delicious crescendo of tongue and teeth danced across my breasts.

"I mean it, Julia," he groaned, lifting his mouth off me, stubble brushing roughly over my nipples.

Slow. Teasing. Strokes. Not. Far. Enough.

"Please, Brad. I need more," I gasped, gripping his hair, pulling his head back so I could look wildly into his eyes.

He lowered me marginally, his eyes locked in mine, his mouth forming words I didn't understand. "I don't need other woman, or to watch you with other men. What I need, all I need, is this."

He thrust, taking me fully, three rock-my-world strokes before withdrawing, his hand lifting me slightly, resuming his slow, half-inside strokes that left me whimpering in his arms. I was so close, could feel the orgasm coming despite his short strokes, a mounting pleasure that I held on to with determination. And then it swelled, my muscles tightening as one, building intensity that was taking me closer ... closer ....

He stopped, his arms lifting me, my head snapping down, and my eyes flipping open. "What?" I gasped. "Why did you stop?"

"Not yet, Julia." He smiled, his cock taking one quick dip inside of me before withdrawing.

"Not *yet*? I'll come again, trust me." I pushed against his hand, frantic to maintain the momentum that I could feel slipping away.

He ignored me, cupping a breast with his free hand, and taking it into his mouth, his eyes glancing up and meeting my furious ones.

As fucking hot as it looked, his gorgeous face below me, my body in his mouth, my orgasm was waving goodbye, cheerily content with hopping in a minivan and hitchhiking to Cleveland. I gritted my teeth and grabbed his chin, pushing his face up to mine.

"Fuck me," I gritted out. "Now. Hard. Fast. De Luca-style."

He grinned, that sexy, I-fucking-own-you grin and released my ass, dropping me full force on top of my full-time obsession. Gripping me with both hands, he kept me still, and started a full on barrage from underneath. Hard, fast fucks that rammed my body, my core clenched against him, the pleasure erupting with every thrust from below, every hard pelvis hit against my clit. I moaned, over and over, the orgasm pulling a one-eighty and barreling full force toward me with arms extended wide. Harder, faster than it had ever come, my body a time bomb about to explode.

Then I did. Throwing my head back, my feet searching and finding floor, my hands grasping widely for anything to hold on to, I came, a full-body explosion that expelled every emotion I had contained for the last twenty-two years of my life. It was intense, it was incredible, and the best part was looking down on him as I finished, down into that cocky, sexual face that owned me with his eyes.

He thought I owned him. He thought he loved me, that I was enough. But this animal, this sex god who could drive me crazy and steal my heart in the same breath, he would never be fully mine. It was impossible. No one ever owned a god.

I took over control, pushing him back against the chair, digging my heels into the floor and riding his cock, my voice coming out in short bursts, guttural and raw as I took him closer to orgasm. "You say that now, but wait. Wait until you see me on top of another man. Wait 'til his arms are wrapped around my body, his mouth on my tits." I stared into his eyes, watched the dark flash of excitement as his hands traveled over my skin, possessively squeezing. "I'm going to come so hard on his cock, I'm going to fuck him until he explodes all over my sweet little face, and you're going to wonder, baby. You're going to wonder who made me come harder, whose cock I am thinking about next time you fuck me." He groaned and leaned forward, wrapping his arms around me, my breasts tight against his shirt, and came, thrusting into me, over and over, our juices mixing as he fucked me through the orgasm, his breath hot on my neck, his mouth taking mine until we both collapsed, spent and euphoric, on the leather chair.

No, no one ever owned a god. But I was working on taming, fooling him into submission.

Chapter 26

"Are you hungry?"

I considered the question, nodding even as my stomach growled, a sound that triggered a grin on Brad's face. He leaned forward, calling to the front seat. "Leonard, can you call in an order and then swing by Woll's?"

"No." I shoved his shoulder. "Fast food. We're not getting a 'to go' order from Woll's. Besides, it's two a.m., the kitchen is probably closed."

"Fast food?" Brad said dubiously, slinging an arm around my shoulder. With his physique, the man probably hadn't eaten a cheeseburger in years.

"Yes. Fast food. It's called McDonald's. The king of late night." I leaned forward. "Leonard, you know where there's a McDonald's on the way home?"

"Yes ma'am," he said, his eyes smiling at me in the mirror.

"Great." I leaned back and snuggled against Brad.

"So … I get no input."

"Nope," I said cheerfully. "I'm putting my foot down with this one. Besides, you need to learn how to release a little control."

"You know …" he growled in my ear, nipping my ear lobe gently. "I give you one little company and you get all authoritative on me."

"It's McDonald's, Brad. You're overdue."

The line for the drive-through ended up stretching two blocks back—my meal choice being in line with about a hundred other Vegas tourists. We settled in, content on waiting, and I rested my head on Brad's shoulder, watching scores of people walk by at a pace that quadrupled ours. "So, what is your plan for Alexis?"

"I thought we settled this back at Saffire."

"Oh, you mean when you fucked me in the VIP area, and I lost all rational thought processes? No. That didn't settle anything."

"It felt settled."

I tilted my head. "Nope. Not settled. What's the plan?"

He sighed. "I guess I can head over there early afternoon. What time does our plane leave?"

I twisted my mouth, trying to think. "Around six-thirty."

"Then I'll head over to Saffire around three. Talk to her, then swing by and pick you up, and we can head to the airport. Are you sure you don't want to come?"

"As awkward as that'd be, no. Plus, I don't want her to think I'm forcing you to do this."

He frowned down at me as the car rolled forward. "But you are forcing me to do this."

"Moot point, Brad. Moot point." I grinned cheerfully and rolled down the window, watching the metal intercom as we swung to a stop before it.

I ordered for both of us, feeling Brad's irritation as I rattled off an order of mild complexity. I paused, looking up to Leonard, and he passed on his request, the grand total of the order coming to a whopping $21.24. Brad passed me cash, grumbling all the while, and I silenced him with a kiss.

We ate while the car moved, gorging on Big Macs and fries, a strawberry milkshake making mild interruptions into the feast. With tomato juice running down my chin, I closed my eyes in pure bliss, Brad's voice saying something in the background. "What?" I managed through a mouthful of yum, opening my eyes to find him watching me in amusement.

"We can head back through if you need seconds."

I shook my head, setting the burger down and leaning back, my stomach stretched beyond comprehension. "No, I'm good." I cradled my milkshake, taking a long, perfect sip of strawberry ice, the cooling sensation running down my throat in pure bliss. "I didn't see you complaining while you demolished your meal."

He grabbed a napkin and wiped his mouth, grinning at me. "No. No complaints."

I yawned, glancing at my watch. "How far are we from Bellagio?"

"Five minutes. You feel like hitting the casino?"

I arched my brow at him. "Do I *look* like I feel like gambling? I'm three steps away from a cheeseburger coma."

He laughed, scooping an arm around my waist and planting a soft kiss on my cheek. "Fine. I'll forgo a chance to bleed MGM dry and get you into bed."

"Poor you."

He grinned down at me. "You have no idea."

Chapter 27

Sometimes you could see disaster coming, like an erratic wave that kept drawing, drawing, drawing attention to the beach until whoosh a swimmer becomes victim to its grasp.

Alexis was that wave, Brad was that swimmer, and I sat on the beach and watched the whole thing happen.

◆◆◆

I awoke to an empty room, the pillow top absent one impressively large body. Rolling over, I stretched, my arms reaching empty space instead of hard muscle. I frowned, propping up on one elbow and glanced at the clock. 11:13 a.m.

"Good morning, sleeping beauty." Brad strode in the room, rolling up the sleeves on a button-down shirt, looking ridiculously hot with a five-o-clock shadow and dress pants.

"What's all … this?" I gestured sleepily, my hand waving about in an attempt to include his head-to-toe hotness.

"What?" He frowned at me.

"You know what. You. All sexual."

"I was going to hit the tables before heading to Saffire."

"In that?" I sat fully upright.

He tilted his head at me, leaning back against the dresser and crossing his arms. "Yes. What's the problem?"

"You are, in a sense, breaking up with her. Looking hot isn't going to help matters."

"You're being unreasonable. I didn't pack a lot of things, Julia. We came for one night."

I sputtered, moving off of the bed and walking over to him, my new vantage point making the effect only more potent. "Then buy something at the gift shop. A furry sweater, pleated jeans."

"What are you worried about?"

Gee, that gorgeous blonde who's fucked you countless times, the one who probably has an 'I love Brad' poster above her bed? Yeah, I have nothing to be worried about. "Nothing," I mumbled, waving my arms and sighing dramatically. "Go on. I'll be fine here."

He bent, both hands gripping my waist and lifting me easily, my feet and arms flaying out as I struggled. Tossing me onto the bed he leaned over me, his face inches from mine. "Phillipe was going to set up some spa services. I assumed you'd want a massage."

I rolled my eyes, turning my face to the side. "Among other things."

"Want me to take care of you before I go downstairs?"

"No. I'll have Phillipe get me a masseuse that can pull double duty." I rolled over, burying my face in the pillow and trying to blot out the image of Brad's deliciousness in front of a sultry Alexis.

There was a pause, and I felt his presence moving closer. Then his hand brushed my hair aside, and his mouth was in my ear. "Be careful what you wish for, sweetheart. You should know that would only excite me."

I ignored him, ignoring the sweep of his fingertips along the nape of my neck. The trail of his finger down my back in one slow drag. I grinned against the sheet, desire curling in my belly as he dragged the sheet lower, exposing my back to the cool room. I felt his lips, soft broken up with the scruff of his stubble, on my back as he gave me a gentle kiss. Then he was gone, the suite door opening and closing with quiet finality.

Chapter 28

I was in trouble the moment my name was spoken. I was half-asleep, cold cucumber on my eyes, a robe wrapped around my naked body, reclining in one of the suite's soft leather chairs. My hand was held by a spa attendant, the final adjustments being made to my manicure. Two women had transformed my hotel room into a spa, putting soothing tones on the Bose radio, closing the curtains, and dimming the lights to an appropriate level. While I normally would have gotten services in the spa downstairs, this time—given our short timeframe—Brad had arranged the services to be done in our suite. Through the muted sounds of wind and rain, I heard my name and opened my eyes.

He was beautiful in all of the ways that Brad wasn't. Thin where Brad was thick, blond hair where his was black. A tight polo that showed muscular arms, blue eyes that stared confidently out at me from a rugged face. *Yum.* I glanced down, tightening my robe and stood, sliding bare feet into slippers, padding gently across the stone floor 'til I stood in front of him.

"I've set up the table in the bedroom. Are you ready?" the man asked, a hint of California surfer in his tone.

I nodded, and he gestured for the door, holding it open as I moved through into a dim room, lit candles littering the space.

"I'll give you privacy," he spoke from behind me. "Please lie face up on the table. If you need me, just call out. My name is Tyler." I glanced over to him, nodding, my eyes catching the movement of the other attendants, their quiet and respectful departure as they left the suite. Then, the bedroom door closed, and I was alone.

I shed the robe, suddenly too aware of my nakedness, of his presence on the other side of the door. Candles filled the room with lavender and vanilla scents and danced flickering shadows over my skin. I laid on the table, pulling the sheet up to my chest, and then lowered myself until I was flat, my breasts tickled by the soft fabric, my head encased in a soft pillow. I closed my eyes and waited nervously for him to return.

Why was I nervous? Massages, once a foreign treat, had become commonplace in my new life of luxury. My body had been accustomed to strange hands, to men and women alike oiling up my body, to nudity a hairbreadth from gentle touches. I should be calm, relaxed, and ready for a treatment I have had fifty times before. But I wasn't. I was tense. Jittery. Wet. *Why the hell am I wet?* The panicked question flitted through my mind at the same time as I heard him enter.

The sound of the door first. It opened, then soft steps, the pad of feet against carpet, a sound I had to strain to hear. When he spoke, I flinched, my nerves a bundle of live wires. "Do you have any sensitive areas? Or places you'd like me to focus on?" He spoke softly, the husky tone sending a shiver through my body.

Sensitive areas? *A few.* Places I'd like him to focus on? *Yes, please.* "No. Just a normal Swedish massage, please." My voice behaved, coming out casually and unaffected, the right amount of offhand decorating its syllables.

"I understand. Mr. De Luca left very particular instructions," he said the words with a hint of seduction, his sentence causing my eyes to open.

Particular instructions from Brad? That could be worrisome. His earlier threat echoed in my mind. *Be careful what you wish for* … I had wished, hopefully he hadn't granted.

♥♥♥

Brad drove, borrowing Phillipe's sedan, wanting the control of driving and the solitude of an empty car. He had brushed off Julia's concerns over Alexis, but Julia had every reason to be worried. Alexis was not going to take this well. He called her from the road, taking a deep breath in mental preparation as the phone rang.

"I was beginning to think you'd forgotten all about me."

"I'm headed to Saffire now. We need to talk."

"As exciting as that sounds, I'm not working tonight. And there's no way I'm going into Fire on my night off."

He could see this conversation, the direction it was taking, a red blinking sign indicating that his demise was ahead in one decision. He sighed. "Where are you? Can we meet for coffee somewhere?"

She huffed into the phone. "I don't drink *coffee*, Brad. I'm home. Come here. I trust you'll remember the address." The phone beeped, and he looked at the screen, the END CALL message mocking him in its finality.

This was bullshit. Since when did he follow orders from women? Julia was one thing; she managed to boss him around with ease, but Alexis had no hold on his heart. He could turn around and head right back to Julia. To her soft skin and feisty eyes. Skin that was probably being touched eight ways to Sunday right now. He had set her up with Tyler, a masseuse who moonlighted as an escort, his clientele mostly older women married to casino whales. He tried to push the thought of Julia out of his mind, tried to not think of her, naked on a table before Tyler, the man's hands sliding over her oiled body. He moved to the right lane, preparing for the exit that would take him to Alexis's townhome.

Chapter 29

Alexis ended the call, a smile spreading on her face. So, Brad had finally called. She was ready: shaved, moisturized, and naked. She slid a silk robe over toned shoulders, slid her feet into stilettos and fastened them. Unlocking the front door, she positioned herself on the couch, the robe open, in full view of the front door. She closed her eyes and ran a hand softly down her body, lingering over the soft skin, running a finger down her shaved slit, teasing the lips of her sex, feeling moisture as she dipped a finger inside. She sighed deeply, fully opening her legs, spread eagle facing the door, and let her mind take her back to the last time Brad was there.

It had been winter, the cold air bringing a blast of refreshment after the long, hot summer. He had enjoyed his night at Saffire, fought over by the girls, every dancer wanting a shot at his attention. Then, an after party, champagne shared by all, the DJ pumping music through the speakers and turning down the black-lights. Brad had a slew of white-suited chefs take over the kitchen, wheeling in carts full of still-moving lobster. They had all dined, new bottles of bubbly popping every few minutes, eyes starting to shine as the night progressed. And, when the sun started to come up, his limo was put to good use, twelve dancers piling in for a ride home. The car had turned into a sea of sexuality, drunken hands roaming over tan bodies, tops pulled off and bottoms pulled aside. The car sang along to Black Eyed Peas, a sea of naked euphoria. It had emptied slowly — twosomes and threesomes dropped off in the Vegas suburbs. Then it had been just her and him and Lida, a Puerto Rican beauty who had been jockeying for Brad since he bought the club. And they knew, as if by preplanned design, the future of the evening, the limo coming to a stop and all of them spilling out, Brad supporting both of them until they stood, the three of them in her bedroom.

He had stood in front of them, his shirt unbuttoned and untucked, his hair mussed from one too many lap dances. And then they had all feasted, this time not on champagne, but on skin, and somehow, with two of them and one of him, he had made it about them, and they had ended the night entwined as three, their hair spilling over his muscular naked body on her soft bed.

Her body was tightening, responding to her touch, and she was panting by the time the knob turned and the door opened.

◆◆◆

Alexis had texted him, the message coming through as he drove down the suburban highway that led to her neighborhood. The text was short, indicating the door was unlocked and he could come right in. The text should have alerted him, should have warned him of what to expect, but it didn't, and he opened the door to silver stilettos leading to glistening legs,

open and spread for him, her fingers inside her, the
pink of her sex framing her motion, her eyes
opening and meeting his, a heavy gaze that
instantly communicated her need.

Fuck.

He stepped inside and shut the door.

Chapter 30

I let out a quiet breath. Willed my body to loosen, willed my tense muscles to stop telegraphing my stress. Why was this so difficult? Maybe I could blame it on the fact that we were in a bedroom instead of a spa. But more likely it was the tan Adonis whose hands were feeling a little too perfect. *Mr. De Luca left very particular instructions.* Trouble. I was definitely in trouble.

My nervousness melted a little with his movements, confident strokes of sensuality, attending to safe areas: my hands, forearms, and biceps. When he moved higher, I tensed; his hands kneaded me back to butter, his focus on my neck and shoulders. He slid his hands into my hair, used his fingers to massage and release tension. I exhaled, my lips parting slightly, and he traveled, a scent of candlewood and eucalyptus trailing behind him, and ended up at my feet, starting at my soles and working upward.

Ten minutes later I fully relaxed, still on my back, almost asleep, almost convinced that this was a standard service and not some fantasy come true, when his hands started their massage of my upper thighs. The sheet was tucked tightly around my body, and the flow of his hands over and around my thighs created a small puff of wind under the sheet, hitting my bare and waiting sex. It was a reminder, suddenly alerting me that I was, in fact, naked, his hands inches away, nothing but air between them and me. He moved higher, his hands separating, one on each thigh, and he slid them upward, dipping slightly under the sheet before continuing—his hands on top of the sheet.

I breathed easier, having the sheet between us—a barricade of sorts, and one that should keep my sinful thoughts at bay. His hands traveled, two palms across my body and then, I lost my breath.

They moved, in practiced, perfect paths, skimming across my breasts, the sheet underneath his hands only an additional weapon in the game of seduction. My nipples responded, instantly hardening, every light sweep of his hands a throb to my lower half. They swept, twin weapons of passion, down the sides of my stomach, the sheet dragging a little with them, hands moving back and forth, from breast to hip, a delicious sweep that moved a little lower with every pass, my pussy tightening in response, the thin sheet sticking to the moisture between my legs. I fought my pelvis, which, with each stroke of his hand, seemed to tip upward, trying to shorten the length and allow his fingers to reach my sex.

His hands slowed, his strokes shortened, and then, to my utter dismay, stopped.

"Ms. Campbell, if you could flip over, I will start on your back." His voice was professionally calm, an embarrassment, since I was at the point of practically gasping with need.

Flip over? Are you fucking kidding me? "Sure. That's fine." Miraculously, I didn't sound like a wanton slut, barely hanging on to her sanity. I sounded almost, practically, normal.

"Thank you, Ms. Campbell."

I turned over carefully, and he repositioned the sheet, exposing my back.

"You're so tense," he whispered, running his hand down the scoop of my back, his hands fanning out along the curve of my ass.

Shocker. I tried to relax, letting out a breath that ended up sounding like a moan. A sexual moan. *Fuck.*

He massaged, slow circles along my spine before making long swipes of his hands from one side of my back to the other. Traveling up along my back, he moved closer and closer to the sensitive skin along the side of my breasts. He slowed his movements, his fingertips grazing the outer swells of my breasts, my breath hitching despite myself.

Oh my God. I was getting wetter. I was naked, underneath the cool sheet, and could feel the moisture pooling between my legs, threatening to drip from my shaved lips. This was so bad, and I did some kegels, trying desperately to stop my body from reacting to his touch.

This was bad. This was bad in one of those ways where bad was good, and I didn't know if I wanted to be bad, or if I was even being bad if I followed temptation. Temptation was currently running his fingers slowly up my ribcage — my body still facedown. Temptation was now gently tracing the side of my breast, and I let out a moan despite myself.

Chapter 31

While she'd often pretended to know a lot about Brad De Luca, there was only one thing she did know. And that was that he needed, with a primal urge that oversaw any rational thought process, to please a woman. Sex with him was not selfish; it was an extension of his soul, and he showed everything through it. Anger, happiness, love, and compassion. If she needed him, he would be there for her. It was in every ounce of his DNA. Alexis met his eyes and let out a sigh, spreading her fingers and begging with her eyes.

"Alexis." Brad's eyes closed briefly, an insult, and she closed her own eyes in response, dropping back her head and exposing her neck to him. She moaned in response, her legs closing slightly before opening again. He *would* open his eyes, he *would* look at, admire, want her. He had to.

"Alexis, please put on some clothes." There was a tremor in his voice, and she tried not to smile. Yes, she may not know his parents, or his dog's name, or how he liked his steak cooked, but she knew men, and she knew Brad. He would start with fingers, start with making her come, but that would only be the beginning. He would not be able to stop, his arousal at her orgasm making him pliable, vulnerable. She may lose the war, but she would win this battle.

Footsteps, moving closer, and then he stood, between her legs, his scent making her mouth water, a new rush of moisture between her legs. She opened her eyes and moaned, her legs shaking slightly and reached out with one leg, hooking it around his thigh and pulling him closer.

"Alexis—"

"Shhh. Don't say anything, Brad. Just please. Please give me what I need."

♦♦♦

The masseuse's fingers stopped their tease over my back and moved, trailing down the edge of my side, growing more aggressive as they reached the bottom of the sheet, dipping slightly underneath the fabric before gripping it.

Then he spoke, his voice unexpected in the candlelight darkness. "Ms. Campbell, may I remove the sheet?"

I swallowed, trying to bring some moisture to my dry mouth, then spoke, all offhanded casualness gone. "Yes. Please."

He tugged on the sheet drawing it slowly down the length of my lower half, every inch of exposure one more step down the staircase of desire. Then, it was off, my ass and body fully exposed to him, and I heard his breath quicken in the quiet bedroom.

◆◆◆

Brad stared down at the woman, his brain competing wildly with his cock. She moaned beneath him, very near to orgasm, her leg around him, body flushed, fingers slick, hips grinding slightly. If he placed his hand on her chest he'd feel her heart, beating with need; if he slid his hand over hers, replaced her fingers with his, she'd collapse beneath his touch. It would be so easy, so quick, her heat quivering tightly around his fingers, her release perfect. He could do it with his fingers alone. No mouth, no cock. Julia could have her legs wrapped around Tyler right now, his cock inside of her, his mouth on hers. Just the thought of it made him hard, which was a dangerous transition right now. Sarah, or Alexis, or whatever she wanted to be called, didn't regard sex as anything but an act. He could take care of her quickly, reassure her, end this, and then leave.

No. He fought an inner battle with himself, pulling his leg from her, taking several steps away. Then forced his eyes to hers, his voice to strengthen. "What are you trying to do, Sarah?"

"It's Alexis. You know that."

"I didn't come here for this."

She closed her eyes briefly, her fingers continuing their movement. When she spoke, her words were more breath than articulation. "Whether you came for it or not, it is something you will always need."

"No." The strength in his voice caused her to open her eyes. "Sarah, you and I have history, which is why I came to speak to you in person. I will always be your friend, but any sexual relationship is officially over."

"Over." She propped herself up, met his eyes, and spat out the word, disbelief in her tone.

"Yes. *Over.* That's how it has to be."

She exhaled, standing, her long legs accentuated by the heels, and walked across the room until she stood before him. "You and I will *never* be over, Brad. We are cut from the same cloth; we are two sides of the same coin. You and her ... she will never please you in all the ways that you need it."

He placed his hands gently on her shoulders. "Sarah, don't presume to know me because we have fucked in the past. I assure you that I know exactly what I am doing, and Julia is exactly what I need. Don't presume to know anything about her either;

she doesn't deserve that." His voice softened a bit. "Your job at Saffire isn't going anywhere. I just wanted to let you know that I am marrying Julia, and our relationship has to change as a result. Friends are all we can ever be now."

She bristled at his soft tone, crossing her hands over her chest and glaring at him. "I'm not a child, Brad. I don't need you to sugarcoat it. You want to make a huge mistake with your life, go ahead." She turned, grabbing a robe from the couch and shrugged into it.

"I'm sorry you feel that way."

She stopped in front of him, her eyes searching his before she turned away, her shoulders stiff under the red silk. "You can show yourself out," she called over her shoulder.

Chapter 32

May I remove the sheet?

With his question, with my response, I had given more than just permission to remove the sheet. I had opened the door, and I was slightly terrified about what would walk through it.

I lay on my stomach, my head on the pillow, grateful for the hide of my face, the layer of protection it, like my blindfold, gave. He started at my feet, behaving, normal kneading movements that shouldn't have been sexual, shouldn't have made my heart race and my pussy wet. Then he gently lifted and moved, one leg and then the other, spreading my legs slightly, the cold air of the room hitting my folds, alerting me to the fact that I was exposed, open to his eyes. His hands ran along my calves, oiling up my skin, his touch incredible on my tense muscles. I wondered how much he could see, if the moisture glistened between my legs. He worked silently, his touch slow enough to be sensual, practiced enough to be effective. I should have been relaxed, my muscles putty in his hands, but the fight to stay unaffected was only making me more aware. Aware of my open legs, aware of his strong hands, his masculine presence, the fact that I was naked before him. What would I do when it was time to turn over?

He moved closer, his hands sliding over the back of my knees and starting a slow, leisurely knead of my thighs, his large hands running and gripping their whole width, each movement insanely close to *me*, to the spot between my legs that was now soaked.

His hands stopped, releasing me, and he moved, coming around my body, my eyes opening and watching shadows pass until I felt his hands on my opposite side, taking the movement there. I closed my eyes, trying to relax, willing my muscles to loosen. I tried to concentrate on my breathing, tried to think about anything but the ten fingers that were inching their way up my thighs.

A hand touched my back, sliding up the curve of my spine until it reached the back of my neck. I frowned, my eyes opening, trying to understand the placement of the hand, and the location of the masseuse, my bombarded brain confused, then realizing the impossibility of the situation, the impossibility of three hands on one man, and I stiffened, starting to rise, but feeling the hand on my neck keep me down.

"Relax." Brad's voice was in my ear, his hand turning from strong to caressing in moments. "It's me." I obeyed, my body instantly releasing the tension, his presence reassuring to my nervous body. My limbs became loose, and the masseuse's hands continued their perfect manipulation of my thighs. He nuzzled my ear, placing a quick kiss on my neck. "Do you want him to continue, or should I ask him to leave?"

I took a deep breath, knowing the answer before he even finished the question. "Continue."

He chuckled in my ear, his mouth finding my neck again before he straightened. "I'll be here, baby."

Knowing he was there, in the room, in control of the situation, allowed me to fully enjoy Tyler's touch. I inched my legs farther apart, and felt his touch change, the gain of confidence and control with the additional permission. He spread his fingers, the same strokes of my upper thigh now barely brushing my velvet folds, the soft sporadic contact driving me absolutely wild. I had never had so much buildup, so much teasing without fulfillment, and I had an ache that was running out of control. I arched my back, lifting my ass up, reaching, trying to get more, but he kept me at bay, kept his hands on my thighs, the only solace in the occasional brush that seemed almost accidental in its contact.

I heard Brad move, my ears attuned to every sound, the clunk of his watch as he unclipped it and dropped the heavy item on the dresser. His belt, the slide of leather through cloth as he removed it. Leather creaking as he settled into the chair in the corner of the room.

The hands on my body separated, now one on each thigh, and the man moved beyond the professional borders, running gentle hands down the skin of my inner thigh, then a soft hand over my sex, gently passing up and down my lips. I whimpered, holding back a beg, gripping the side of the table and fighting the urge to turn over and demand more.

"Flip over," Brad's voice spoke from the corner.

I complied, moving carefully on the narrow bed, lifting up, my vision suddenly open, my eyes taking in the room. Brad settled comfortably in the chair, one leg up on an ottoman, his dress shirt untucked, possession in his eyes. The masseuse, still fully dressed while I laid there naked, on display for the two men in the room.

"Proceed, Tyler."

I relaxed my head, closing my eyes, and was surprised to feel the silk of the sheet, settling back over my body, my nakedness covered once again. The man spoke respectfully, his voice above me. "Should I continue what I was doing earlier?"

I nodded. "Please." Inside, I was screaming the word, my sub-conscious dragging herself up his thighs, shaking with excitement as she clapped with greedy hands.

It was the same as before, but different, my body so ready, no needy, that every touch was electrified. The knowledge of where Brad was, the possession in his eyes, the knowledge that he was watching, compounded my arousal. The masseuse continued, resuming his movement, his hands caressing as they moved, up and over the swell of my breasts, then back down the side of my stomach. The heat of a hand against a cool sheet, my skin both hating and loving the material, all at the same time. The push and pull of the fabric as his hand moved, brushing against my nipples when he was pressing down along my stomach, tugged at the place where I was wet on his journey upward. Up and down, each swipe seeming to move down, but so teasingly slow I was wondering if it was all in my imagination. The sheet shifted, one hand definitely lower, taking the sheet with it, and I felt cool air slip along one breast, the nipple close to exposure. Up. Down. Closer, but not there. My nipples tender, alive with stimulation. My pussy crying, begging for attention and touch.

Then, his movements were finally long enough, and I felt his hand slide slowly downward until it completely covered my sex.

Brad was watching, but not participating. *Is this cheating? Is this allowed?* Alarm bells rang in my head, but I was unable to listen, a need so great pulsing between my legs, his hand moving slightly as he pulled it away, north along my body, and then back downward. The sheet between us was now soaked, one hand passing aggressively, then softly, then aggressively, down between my legs, the other hand moving back and forth along my breasts, strumming my nipples, my body beginning to arch from his touch. Fuck rules and commitments, anything sane or rational. Brad wasn't going to open my sexual boundaries, send this madness in, and not expect me to fucking enjoy it. I moaned, the sound loud and begged, my lips parting, my eyes opening, and I propped myself up, the sheet falling from my breasts, and stared into the masseuse's eyes.

"I need you to fuck me. Now." I gasped the words, my mouth hanging open, the cold air against erect nipples, his hand cupping me, and one finger moved, swiping under the sheet; he slid it inside of me, and my world went dark.

My arms gave out, and I fell back, arching, a second finger joining the first, and he moved them together, his other hand sliding the sheet farther down, baring my upper half, my body offered to him as I pushed against his hand. He curved his fingers, stroking my g-spot, his other hand worshipping my breasts, now lifting, squeezing and then the additional stimulation of his mouth, hot and wet, sucking and pulling me against his tongue. I reached out, gripping his shirt, my eyes squeezed shut and bucked, my orgasm flooding uncontrolled, an explosion of De Luca proportions. He kept up the movement, my other hand reaching out and finding his shoulder, holding on for dear life as my body let out a final shudder, and then I collapsed on the bed, aftershocks twitching like erratic tics through my body.

My eyes closed, and I heard footsteps travel, latches click, the door open, and then shut. I opened my eyes, turning my head until I could see Brad, at my side, his eyes on my body. I watched him, watched as he placed a hand lightly on my ribcage, running it down my body as he circled the table, his eyes traveling along my skin, an intent, brooding look mixed in with his possessive standard. I murmured, a soft tone of satisfaction that had his eyes looking to mine, the corners of his mouth twitching slightly as he rounded the end of the table and stopped beside me. Bending over, he slid his arms under my body and stood, cradling me to his chest, my body curving, and I instinctively leaned into him, inhaling his scent, one that was 100% Brad, a smile crossing my face when I smelled only him on his shirt and neck. He carried me to the bed, lying me down on the pillow top, my face turning to him as he stood next to the bed, looking down at me.

"Did you enjoy that?"

I nodded, my eyes closing softly, a small smile on my lips. "Why'd he leave?"

He chuckled. "I can bring him back if you'd like. Call and get a later flight."

"What time is it?"

He glanced at the bedside table. "Almost 4:45."

My eyes opened fully, and I pushed off the bed. "Shit! We've got to go."

He pressed me back down, black need in his eyes. "Not yet," he said, unbuttoning his pants. "Not yet."

Chapter 33

Sex with Brad was always different after a threesome. Sometimes it was tender, such as when we were with the Russian girl. Other times it was possessive, as if he was claiming me back, reasserting his dominance with his cock, hands, and mouth. And sometimes it was fire, two souls battling each other, passion and fury in between our bodies, the giant need for each other frenzied in its intensity.

That day, with precious minutes ticking by, I expected it to be fast. But he took his time, laying me back on the bed, his eyes moving slowly over my skin, drinking me in. His hands dropping his pants, then his underwear, until there was nothing but raw, hard cock. Ready for me. Wanting me. He leaned over my body, tasted with teasing kisses, my neck, breasts, the side of my stomach, the curve of my hip. His hands pulled my legs open, and I squirmed as he drug soft lips closer, along the cut where my panties would lie, his eyes catching mine as he lowered his mouth to my sex.

God. I bucked under his mouth. His tongue was a velvet soft flutter over my sensitive clit. I was so aroused. On the edge of everything. He took me to the peak, keeping the rhythm up until I cried his name and clenched my legs. Until I came, my back arching, my hands finding and gripping his thick hair.

He moved up my body, joining me on the bed, his knees pushing my legs apart, his cock settling and thrusting into my hot and ready core.

"Are you mad?" I whispered, staring into his face.

He cocked his head at me, confused.

"At what he was doing … when you came in."

He chuckled, shoved fully in, a place he didn't typically go, the extreme depth of him usually painful. I winced, slapped his chest, warning him with my eyes. "I'm only mad if he was doing something you didn't want. or, if he was making you uncomfortable. From the looks of it, you were very comfortable."

"But you didn't mind just watching?"

"Watching you being pleased?" He shook his head, dragged his hips backward, then gripped my legs and pushed back in. "Seeing your face when you come, your muscles when they clench. The arch of your back at a time when I can focus on it, enjoy it. I lose so many sensations when I fuck you. Your sounds, the flush of your cheeks. Sitting there, watching you come … it was the most beautiful thing I have ever seen. It's not about 'minding.' It's about enjoying." He quickened his thrusts, the movements of his hips, and dropped my legs, returned to my mouth. Then he wrapped his arms underneath me, pulled me to his chest, and rolled us over, our bodies joined as one, until I was astride, and he was below. And then he gave me a brief moment of control, and let me ride him to completion.

Chapter 34

APRIL
Days until wedding: 120

People in danger typically try to put as much distance as possible between them and their attacker. They believe that space equals safety. But they are wrong, and often get hurt as a result. You see, when your enemies are close, when their bodies are pressed flush against yours, at that range they can do very little damage. They need distance to swing a punch, to extend their hands and choke your neck. Distance to reach down and unzip a zipper. The lesson is simple: Dictate your space. Keep your enemies as close as possible until you are ready to give them space. And when you give them that space, use it to destroy them.

I had broken the triangle choke into an acronym for easy memorization. *A. Arm Across.* I move my attacker's arm across his body. *S. Scoot away.* I slide my body away from him, moving him down my chest. *L. Leg over his shoulder.* Creating a noose, which I will use to hang him. *A. Ankle.* I grab my ankle, tucking it under my other leg, tightening the noose. *P. Press.* Press down on his head and squeeze until the air has left his body and he passes out between my legs. After he has gone limp, continued pressure will eventually cause death. *A SLAP.*

Ben had, per Brad's wishes, become my instructor, moving us to the theatre after dinner on Wednesday nights. Brad had the room's seating moved to the attic, blue mats now covering the large space. There, Ben and I would 'roll,' him training me on jujitsu defense tactics created by the Gracie family over the last three decades, tactics designed to allow a smaller individual to defeat a larger one. Ben had grown up in California, trained in their academy for over a decade. Though his instruction would never count in the world of belts and qualifications, it was priceless in the world of my personal safety, a world Brad now seemed obsessed with. I now kept a gun in my SUV, had campus security walk me to my vehicle if night had fallen, and my humble college abode was outfitted with five thousand dollars worth of security cameras, alarms, and monitoring services. I had forbid Brad from placing tracking devices on my car or cell. My stubborn stance on the item had led to a fight, which led to incredible sex, and then another fight, Brad unwilling to drop the subject. But I had stayed firm. A life without freedom wasn't, in my mind, worth living. I didn't ever want my movements tracked, for someone to have a finger on where I was at any moment. There was a level of caution that was necessary and reasonable, then there was a level that was invasive and controlling. Brad was a control freak; it was in every ounce of his DNA. It was important to me that I never be controlled. He could control his work, his clients, his juries, his employees, but not me. So that argument I won, his dark eyes flashing in frustration at the outcome. The jujitsu argument he won, as there was no good reason for me not to have defense abilities.

The sport was a close contact one, most moves requiring limbs to be tangled, bodies pressed in solid contact, faces inches away from each other, breaths commingling as he straddled me, taking aggressive stances that I would try to combat. Ben was often surprised by my aggression, my intent focus on how to best administer pain while in different defensive positions. But his reports back didn't surprise Brad. Brad knew behind my sweet exterior was a need for control, one that often asserted itself during sex, or in other small ways of manipulation. It simmered below my skin, rising to a boil if provoked.

A SLAP. Hopefully, I would never use it.

♥♥♥

"Good. Again."

I released my arms, freeing Ben's neck, and waited for him to stand. "I think I got it."

"You're still holding your breath when you choke me. And you're thinking out the moves. It needs to become second nature to you." He stood, his hands settling to his waist, the dim theatre room lighting putting much of his face into the shadows.

"One more time. Then I've got to take a shower." I didn't know the time, no clock in the room, but it felt late. And I had promised to meet Olivia at the library, both of us facing mid-term finals.

"I'll step in." Brad's voice came from behind my head, and I turned to see him in the doorway, his dress clothes still on, though he had lost his jacket at some point in the evening.

I frowned. "I don't want to mess up your clothes."

He held out a hand, sending a cocky grin down at me. "I'll let a beautiful woman mess up my clothes any day."

"Wrong answer," I grumbled, accepting the hand and yanking it unnecessarily hard when standing.

"I'm sorry, love. I'll let your beautiful ass mess up my clothes any day." He winked at me, stepping backward slightly on the blue mat, until we were at least ten feet apart.

It wasn't about his clothes. I sucked at defending myself against Brad. He was so much bigger, stronger, than Ben. I couldn't fully wrap my arms around his chest, my moves had to be done perfectly in order for my light weight to properly influence and affect his large mass. And I was not, as much as I'd like to admit it, perfect. Far from it. Most days, I felt like I was two steps above mediocre. I was reminded of my lack of proficiency every time Brad stepped onto the mat.

"Go ahead baby." I gestured with my hands. "Give me your best shot."

His best shot ended up forcibly grabbing me, moving me to the floor where he proceeded to pull up my shirt. Took his time groping my chest. I let him enjoy it, putting up a mock struggle until the moment his frisky hand wandered far enough to the right. Then I jumped into action, trapping the arm and rolling, taking it with me to a place that it wasn't meant to go, a place that meant broken bones or disconnected sockets. And for once, my mediocrity didn't interfere, and I heard his hand, the three strong slaps against the mats. I released him, rolling over, his arm snagging me into place, a smile on his face as he stole a quick kiss from me. "Not bad, baby. Not bad."

Chapter 35

Not bad was screaming its way up my shoulder. I winced, taking a break from my textbook and rolled the joint, stretching the limb carefully right and then left, the action catching the attention of Olivia.

"What? What's wrong?"

"Nothing. Just sore."

She snorted, the perturbed sound catching my attention in the quiet library.

"What?"

"That from some crazy sexual acrobats?" She raised an eyebrow at me over the cover of her textbook.

"No. Working out with Ben."

"That is so weird. You rolling around on a mat with Brad's best friend."

"It's not sexual, O. It's self-defense. You should come sometime."

"As you've mentioned a hundred times before. I have Mace. As do you. There's no need for you to be a black belt to boot. And the CIA-level security system he just installed at your house? Was the retinal eye scan not available? Plus, since when does a trophy wife need protection? You gonna get mugged while walking through Neiman Marcus?" She kept her gaze on her book, my attempt to catch her eyes futile.

"I'm not gonna be a trophy wife." I ignored the other attacks, the ground covered ten times before. She didn't know about the attempt on my life eight months before. Didn't know about Brad's family or the hidden threats that would exist for the rest of my life. It was something I would never tell her, along with the side of our sex life that involved strangers and kink. She already had enough reservations about Brad, enough irritation toward the man who had stolen her best friend.

She set down the book, her eyes finally meeting mine. "You're twenty-one. He's thirty-four. You're hot. Driving a BMW. Carrying a hard-working family's second mortgage around on your finger. Probably won't work a day in your life. Nothing about that screams trophy wife?"

I studied her face, the anger in it. Why was she mad? Where was this hostility coming from? Was it too much to ask that she be happy for me? "You're forgetting, in that ridiculous equation of yours, that I love the man."

"No. You're dazzled by him. Without the money, without his man-whore reputation that presents a challenge, you would have dropped him by now. Not run around, letting him orchestrate your every move." She closed her notebook, capping the pen, and stood, sliding the items off the desk and into her book bag, the worn item in sharp contrast to the barely-used Louis Vuitton carryall that slouched carelessly by my tennis shoes.

I stood, fighting to keep my voice low, aware of the attention we were attracting from the others at our table. Pens had stopped scratching, eyes stopped reading, an eavesdropping silence blanketed the entire area. "Don't presume to know how I feel. You have no idea of my feelings, and I shouldn't have to—at every interaction with you—defend my actions and validate my love." I watched with dismay as she bent, hefting her book bag over her shoulder.

"Whatever. Becca's the one who blows sunshine, not me." She pulled out her cell, her fingers moving over the screen, doing godknowswhat as she turned away. "See you later, Jules."

I watched her go, my eyes on her as she moved past the main desk, pressing the buttons for the elevator, waiting for the car, and then stepping on, her head never lifting from her phone, never turning to look, my last glimpse the blue material of her book bag as she stepped onto the car.

I sat, trying to sort out my emotions, trying to understand what just happened, anger brewing amidst the confusion.

"Ouch." The word came from my right, and I glanced over to see brown eyes studying me behind thick glasses, the girl's mouth twisted into a wry grin.

"Yeah," I muttered.

"It *is* a kick ass ring, though." She smiled, dipping her pen in the direction of my hand.

I smiled politely, closing my own textbook with a sigh. *So much for studying.*

♥♥♥

While I planned my future, Rebecca planned my wedding, Olivia cursed my relationship, and arrangements of a completely different nature occurred in the seedy underbelly of the city. Money was exchanged, plans were constructed, and my fate was determined.

For the second time in twelve months, my life was in danger. And just like before, I was completely oblivious.

Chapter 36

"What's going on with your law school application?" Brad's voice came to me through the darkness and I turned, watching the light of the pool reflect off his muscles as he pushed up and out of the water.

I leaned back against the cushion of the pool chaise, my own skin almost dry. We had been swimming almost nightly, the unseasonal heat wave perfectly complemented by laps in the pool. We aimed for dusk, the sunset through the palm trees creating a perfect oasis and a half-hour of darkness before the bugs came out. He cocked an eyebrow at me, waiting for a response as he grabbed a towel off the chair beside me. "I haven't given much thought to it," I responded vaguely.

"You should be giving a lot of thought to it. What's your top choice? We can shoot for admission there."

I shot him an odd look. "My top choice? I was only going to apply to State. It's the only law program nearby."

He shook his head. "State is fine, but we'd be foolish not to use my contacts. Ignore the distance, where do you want to go?"

Where do I want to go? I hadn't even allowed myself to think that way. I was getting married, would spend the next umpteen years of my life in this city. Me trotting off to a strange city for law school didn't seem the prudent thing to do. "Ignore the distance?" I laughed. "Brad, that's easy to say, but you don't mean that."

He stopped in the middle of drying his hair and looked at me. "Julia, this is a huge decision for you. It's three years out of our entire life; we can make arrangements to make it work. Pick your school, and we will work out the rest."

"I don't want to live my first three years as a wife away from my husband. I can go to State. It's no big deal."

He frowned, sitting on the edge of my seat, his eyes locked with mine. "I don't want you to be punished because you decided to marry me. I want you to make the right choices for your career. Do you know what field of law you want to practice?"

More decisions. "No. Not corporate. I died of boredom in the West Wing. Maybe criminal." I reached out and caught his hand, stopping him as he rose. "Being your wife will never be a punishment. I chose to marry you, and living here is part of that choice."

He leaned over, placing a soft kiss on my forehead and then leaned in more, brushing his lips across mine. "Regardless, make a list of your top five choices. State can only take up one spot. I'll see who I know in each alumni base, and Rebecca can start collecting references." He snagged my towel and held out a hand to help me up.

"I can collect my own references."

"She can collect better ones."

♥♥♥

The damn man had the annoying quality of always being right. I assembled my list, bringing it to Rebecca with dread, expecting some bitchy ass comment about adding to her workload. But she held the side of sass, glancing over the paper with a low whistle. "Damn girl, you don't mess around."

"It's my dream list. I didn't say it was realistic." I grinned.

"Give me a few hours. Brad's got enough favors hanging out there that this should be a cinch."

"You've got time. I don't need to send in apps 'til the end of the next month." I prepared to leave, standing and grabbing my bag, but was stopped by her outstretched finger.

She grabbed a pink flower post-it and scribbled something on it, then ripped off the top copy. "This is the next LSAT prep course. With those schools, you're going to need one hell of an LSAT score. I already signed you up last week, per the big man's instructions." She held out the daisy-shaped note, and I took it reluctantly.

"I'm really just happy going to State …" I ventured before she stood up with a start, her chair making a grotesque sound against the stone floor.

"Julia, that man will never forgive himself if you short-change your life because of him. I won't go getting in your business, but trust me. He worries day and night about making you happy. Pick the damn school you want to go to." She cocked a hip and fixed me with a look you might give an unruly child.

"You won't go getting in our business?" The statement was so absurd I literally burst out laughing. I had no doubt the woman probably knew every aspect of our lives, right down to the time of my monthly cycle.

She laughed, then fixed me with a wry smile. "Hey, I'm trying to turn over a new leaf. Now, attend the damn LSAT course and leave me be. I need to find you some references so good that admissions will overlook your paltry three-point-eight GPA."

I didn't even question how she knew my GPA, her investigative skills way too advanced for a mortal like me to ever understand. Screw LSAT prep, I needed to take classes in Rebecca 101.

Chapter 37

MAY
Days until wedding: 108

Rebecca and my mother had taken over wedding preparations. Like, locked me out of the room, forbade me to touch their plans, taken over wedding prep. Which was great, because the details alone were enough to raise my stress level tenfold. I loved the thought of a big wedding, had Pinterested enough images for a hundred weddings, but when it came to organizing it all? Tasting cakes, picking out calligraphy? My chest seized at the sheer enormity. So I turned it over to them, trading hundreds of hours of details with one weekly update. The more money that poured out, the more intricate details and decisions that were added to the spectacle that was becoming our wedding, the less I cared. The more I realized that the details, the window dressing, was unimportant. Important to us was the whispering of words that would tie us together until death did us part. The words mattered, the packaging did not. All it did was dress up the connection—the connection that no one else understood. No one else really got him and me and why we were so perfect for each other. Trying to explain our relationship would involve trying to explain our sex, and no one outside of our world would understand it.

As the days ticked on, my stress began to grow, the thought of my family and friends across the table from bloodthirsty savages too much for my mind to take. And weddings in an Italian family were apparently some type of giant family reunion where everyone was invited and fully expected to rescheduled doctor's appointments and cruises and murders, to drive the five or a hundred or a thousand miles to attend. My family made up twenty-two invitations. Brad's? Ninety-six. On Brad's mother's side of the family, every single invite's RSVP had been returned, all with the box 'Will Attend' firmly checked. On Brad's father's side — the Magiano dynasty — the only response had come from Maria's family and twenty or thirty great aunts and uncles. Total silence from Brad's father, brothers, and cousins. I had cut Rebecca off at that stage of the update, waving my hands wearily and dropping my head heavily on her desk.

"Why were they even invited?" I moaned. "Did Brad know this?"

She looked at me grimly. "Yeah. He said a lack of invitation would be a sign of disrespect. And mentioned something about them showing up out of spite if they weren't invited."

I closed my eyes. Yeah. Dom Magiano seemed to have a thing about being challenged. "So … we have no idea if they are coming."

"Right. And my ass isn't calling them for a follow-up." Her indignant tone broke through my anguish and caused a smile.

"What's Mom think? About his family not RSVPing?"

She shrugged. "I've managed to distract her with other stuff. But just know that there's a chance that six or seven of these gorgeous tables will be empty. Or full. I'm not sure which you'd rather."

"Oh my God," I moaned. "Please stop talking. Is it too late to call this entire thing off?"

She raised her eyebrows at me, pulling out a drawer and lifting a huge, three-ring binder, its seams busting, colored tabs happily dividing plastic sleeves. "And ruin all of my hard work? Puh-lease. This is going to be *the* event of the decade, and that beautiful man in there has already dropped a small fortune on satisfying me and your mother's every whim."

I propped my chin on the desk, looking past her OCD organization and staring into her eyes. "How are you still sane? My head would explode with the decisions, powder versus baby blue, crab cakes versus crab legs …"

She interlaced her fingers and fixed me with a stare. "I'm thirty-two, dating a barely acceptable man who I will probably fuck for another year before I move on to someone marginally better. When, and if, I do ever find someone I want to spend the rest of my life chained to, I'll slap together some crap-ass wedding with a budget that equals two pairs of your ridiculous shoes. I have the opportunity here to plan the wedding of my dreams, with someone else's money, *and* while on the clock. Please, turn into Mariah Carey and have a vow renewal every year so I can make this my full time job." She grinned at me and opened the binder. "Now, let's discuss the seating chart."

Seating. An geometry equation where we tried to keep Campbells from Magianos, Brad's clients and our friends acting as referees via seating clusters, the constant threat of entire empty tables a likely eyesore. The unknowns stacked, like additional cards to an already fragile pyramid. I wanted it all to disappear. Brad's family, even, at times, my own. I almost didn't even want friends at this point, the struggle to please everyone exhausting in its requirement of effort. Olivia and I had, in some way, mended fences — if mending fences meant that we pretended our library argument had never occurred. But any interaction with the girls was still stressful, the pressure to provide a brochure-worthy show of 'life is perfect' just to ensure support of my future life. Support Becca readily gave. Support Olivia dribbled out depending on whoknewwhat. It had all seemed so much easier at Christmas. When the wedding was still so far out, and everyone, including Olivia, had been full of smiles and positivity.

"By the way, you need to go to Franco's and pick out a dress. That should be easy for you, with your penance for shopping."

At her words, I came back to Earth. *A dress*. I could handle that. "Sound good. Do I just stop by there one day after class?"

Dismay flooded her features. "No! You don't just 'stop into' Franco's; this is going to be a full day affair. They need to know your measurements before you arrive, and they will order the best designers and have a fitter there to make adjustments. I'll let them know your favorite champagne and have—"

Nothing was easy anymore. "Oh my God," I groaned. "Please. As few decisions as possible. I'd like to enjoy this. Please call and tell them how indecisive I am. Just have them pull five options, all designed for someone with small boobs. I don't want sequins or beading, or something that looks like Cinderella Barbie would wear. No poufy stuff underneath, or crazy buttons, or glitter. And I don't want to spend over a thousand dollars. I'm wearing this one time." I finished the plea with one long breath outward, looking up to see a disappointed look on Rebecca's face.

"You do realize that you are the worst bride ever. And *cheap*." She said the word as if it was offensive.

I ignored the comment, sitting back in the chair.

"I don't know if Franco even has dresses for less than a grand."

"Then I'll go to David's Bridal."

She wrinkled her nose like I had said a bad word. "Fine. I'll call Franco's. But you know Brad's gonna freak on you if he thinks you are skimping."

I stood, walking around the desk and giving her a hug. "I'll handle the big guy. And I'll go to Franco's on Saturday, just text me whatever time they want me to come in."

"*Try* to enjoy it. You're living every woman's fantasy."

"I am enjoying it. Every bit except when it involves Brad's family. And thank you, you freaking angel, for handling these details." I grinned and headed for the door.

"Later. Oh, and Julia?"

"Yeah?" I turned, one hand on the doorframe, and looked at her.

"You know his birthday is Friday."

My brain closed in a bit. *Friday*. I should have known this, realized—at some point—that a birthday hadn't occurred, that his time clock would be turning one year over. We had been together ten months, I should have asked, should have thought of this by now. "Friday."

"Yeah. You didn't know?"

I walked slowly back into her room and plopped into the closest chair. "No. But thanks for giving me *so* much advance notice."

"Sorry," she chirped, sounding less than apologetic.

I dug my hand into my pocket and pulled out my cell, dialing a number and putting the phone on speakerphone, setting it on Rebecca's desk. She looked at me quizzically and I held up a finger.

"Hello?" Martha's brash voice rang through the speaker.

"Did you know Brad's birthday is Friday?" I demanded, leaning forward so that she could hear me clearly.

"Umm … did you say Friday?" she asked slowly, and I heard the fridge open.

"Yes, Friday," I drawled.

"Okay."

"Okay's not an answer. You did, didn't you?"

"He mighta told me not to mention it. Brad doesn't like birthdays."

I growled, the sound eliciting a laugh from Rebecca. "Anything else he 'mighta' told you not to mention?"

"You ain't married yet, honey. I don't have to open up the treasure trove of secrets 'til you my boss, too."

I grinned at the phone. "So you're gonna start talking then?"

"Probably not."

I rolled my eyes. "Fine, I'll find a way to crack you later. You making dinner?"

"Yep. Baked chicken and potatoes. What time are you gonna be home?"

I checked my watch. "Around six-thirty."

"It'll be ready. Love you."

"You too." I ended the call and looked at Rebecca. "You got dinner plans? You're welcome to come to the house. Martha's baked chicken is deathly."

"Nah. Brad's got me doing research for a case, which means I need to put this fun aside and get some real work done." She grinned at me and moved the gigantic wedding binder to the side.

I leaned back in the chair and stared at the ceiling. "What the hell am I supposed to get him for his birthday?"

◆◆◆

Julia Campbell was not just a job. It was not just money; it was also a joint between families, the rare opportunity to mend a bridge, which had been burned many times before. The Magiano dynasty ruled superior, dominating the other families in this hundred-mile grid of opportunity. A chance to create goodwill with that lead heavyweight was valuable and not something the cooperating family took lightly. The job would need to be done perfectly. So much was at stake.

So proper precautions were made. She was watched, her schedule and habits monitored and recorded. Younger assets were assigned to sit in her classes, trail her along the manicured lawns of campus, and strike up casual conversations alongside her in the library. Their reports back were basic. She ate Chick-fil-A, did not flirt, and rarely went out with friends. After much discussion and strategizing, a plan was decided upon and a date was set. The date became their goal, and a countdown of sorts began, all attention and focus centered on preparation for that day.

Chapter 38

When it all came down to it, there was only one thing to get a man like Brad. A man who had everything, could buy anything, and wanted for nothing. Either a) something he had been deprived of, or b) something he could never get too much of.

I doubted Brad had been deprived of much of anything his entire life. *Love.* He hadn't had enough love; it was something I saw at odd times, times when he cradled my face in his hand, and a flicker of worry went through his eyes. He, at those moments, revealed how terrified he was of losing me. I didn't know how to package love, how to giftwrap that emotion and hand it to Brad. I told him often, as often as I could. But I knew that the more in love he fell, the more afraid he was that I would leave. That I would turn into his mother and choose another reality over this one. I was marrying him. That should be enough of a reassurance.

Hmm … So b) something he could never get too much of. *Sex.* Brad had always been in control of our sexual adventures. It was part of the turn-on for me, the willing handover of my body, unknowing of what he had in store for it. But I wanted something more for his birthday, something other than me, naked and willing, waiting for his command. My mind flickered back to his being deprived. He had been shortchanged of something, for eight months now. Another woman. We had ventured into the water, spending one hot night with a blonde Russian, Brad bringing her multiple orgasms without actually fucking her. He had to miss it, had to miss domination of another woman with his cock, seeing the look in her eyes when he thrust it in, the shock and incredulity as it turned from too much to too perfect.

It was time. Since that night, I had waffled and wish-washed my way back and forth over the line of indecision until my head spun like a drunken coed. But the thought always made me hot, always pushed me over the edge when Brad's head was between my legs or he was buried deep in me. The pleasure he gave me, the incredible heights and depths he brought me to, were too incredible for me not to share — it seemed unfair for me to keep this wealth of sexual knowledge contained solely for my pleasure. When I was with Brad and the Russian, I had loved every minute of the experience, as limited as it was. But to see him *inside* a woman, to see his thrusts and her moans, his hands gripping her skin, his mouth on hers — the thought was almost too intense to process. During sex, I would get snapshot images, entering uninvited into my mind, and my back would involuntarily arch, my orgasm no longer containable, and my world would turn black in a moment of exquisite perfection.

How would I react in that actual situation? When he spread her legs, touched her body? When I saw that look on his face, the look of lust and ownership, the same look that sent me over the edge, the look I strove for, fucked for, and did anything and everything to provoke? How would I take it, and what if he needed more of it?

Would I really be giving him a birthday present? Or was this just one, big, sex-filled test of our relationship?

♥♥♥

I didn't even know how to go about setting up a threesome. It was something I had always had Brad handle, not wanting the awkward chitchat, conversation of limits and desires, the meet and greet. And dealing with a woman seemed even more problematic. If I had to, if every sexual standard Brad and I had in place crashed down, I could walk up to a man and bring up the concept of sex. Men were a given, a single man with a working cock wasn't likely to turn down an offer of no-strings-attached sex. Women were a whole other ballgame. I was a woman who had already been introduced to threesomes, who was familiar with walking into an unknown situation and having a stranger touch me, yet I would still say 'fuck you' if approached by a stranger and propositioned for sex. I couldn't image any woman, other than a prostitute, who would willingly enter into an unknown situation without someone there they were *itrustyouwithmylife* comfortable with. And ... if there was a woman out there who was that down-to-fuck ... I wasn't sure I wanted her anywhere near my man.

I decided to call the only expert I knew, Beverly Franklin, a redheaded bombshell who had popped my sex-party cherry eight months earlier. I locked myself in my office and dialed her number.

When she answered, my opening greeting was awkward, my words tripping out, no good way to introduce myself. There was an initial pause, but then warm sincerity flowed through the phone.

"You're that gorgeous brunette who came with Brad to Masked Innocence! Of course I remember. I've heard you tied that man down with an engagement." The admiration rang clearly through her voice.

"Well, someone had to do it."

She laughed coquettishly. "I missed seeing you at the Christmas party; Brad said you guys went up to Aspen. How was the snow?"

Aspen. The day after my parents left, we locked down the house and flew west, locking ourselves into a chalet and fucking for three days straight before coming home. Snow? I hadn't even noticed.

"It was great, though I hated missing the party. But Beverly, the reason I called is that Brad's birthday is Friday." I explained my predicament, hoping that she didn't take the question the wrong way.

She thought for a moment. "Honestly, Julia, if you're trying to find a single woman yourself, you're probably best going to The Montley House."

I repeated the name, drawing a blank, my naïve mind trying to find something familiar in the words.

She laughed. "Why don't I take you there tonight? It's a place easier shown than explained; plus, they won't accept you without a referral."

I blushed. "That would be great, if it's not too much of an inconvenience."

"It's no trouble at all. Let's meet for drinks first. I need to give you the lay of the land before you make your selection."

We made plans to meet at seven-thirty. I hung up my cell and Googled 'The Montley House,' finding zero results. Any place that successfully hid from the internet could only mean trouble. My stomach flip-flopping, I returned to my files and dove back into work.

♥♥♥

I almost forgot about the damn chicken. I was mid-dial into a call to Brad when I remembered the baked chicken breasts. Martha lightly battered them in flour, mixed with some type of crack, before slow-baking them, and they tasted out-of-this-world amazing. There were few things in life better than her chicken, and I wasn't missing it for anything. I hung up on Brad, his hello cut off by my thumb, and I thought for a moment before dialing him back.

"Yes?"

"Sorry about that, forgot I was getting on the elevator. Martha's making baked chicken tonight."

"I know. I'm on my way home now. Are you leaving the office?"

"Yeah, but I can't stay long. I was just going to grab dinner and then go; I've got plans with the girls."

"Why don't they come by the house for dinner? You know Martha will have plenty."

"I think they have other stuff to do, but I'll ask."

"All right. See you soon. Love you."

"I love you, too, babe." I hung up the phone with a smile, grateful that he hadn't pushed any more. My lies tended to fall into a million pieces at about question three. Anything before that, I held up pretty well. I let out a breath, walking through the plan in my mind. I would go to Brad's house, gorge on Martha's cooking, change into something worthy of a mysterious outing, then go and meet with Beverly. I grinned, embracing the delicious secret. I was, basically, James Bond in stilettos.

Chapter 39

Julia was lying. There was something in their earlier conversation on the phone, something off. And now she was nervous, eating but fidgeting, glancing at the clock too often for practical purposes. Deception was never good, it was an evil snake that planted doubt in the mind of others, and he could feel it stealing over his body. He stood, grabbing his plate and paused on his way to the sink, kissing her neck and flashing her a smile. She flushed, looking down.

He continued to the sink, scraping his plate and glancing at her. "Where are you guys going?"

She hesitated. "Olives. Becca heard it was good."

Yes, Olives *was* good, if you didn't mind paying thirty dollars a drink. A little rich for college student blood. Brad headed to the den, a headache growing.

♥♥♥

I changed, and then changed again, my first outfit looking like a cat burglar's. Frustrated with my lack of knowledge about Montley's, I finally decided on a simple black dress, choosing one that was more daring than conservative, hoping it would fit the vibe of whatever mousetrap Beverly was leading me into. I slid on Jimmy Choos and a cropped leather jacket, then headed downstairs, calling for Brad.

He was in the den, a t-shirt and sweatpants on, baseball playing on the television, and he glanced up at my entrance, his eyes taking in my outfit in one, slow scan. He stood, walking over and stopped before me, his hands on his hips. I looked up at him quizzically. "What?"

"No."

"No? What do you *mean* no?"

"You look way too good." He let his eyes drop, and he trailed a finger along and up my side, the contact causing my breath to hitch, his finger crossing over my breasts and down the dip in my neckline.

I reached out and grabbed his finger, wrapping my hand around it. "Stop. Stop that or else I won't be able to think straight."

"Go change."

"What? I'm not changing! Besides, Olives is fancy, so what's wrong with this?" I looked down at my outfit in dismay, his finger catching my chin and pulling it up until our eyes met. He stared at me for a long moment, his eyes searching mine and I stared back defiantly. He grinned suddenly and pulled me to him, his mouth taking mine, a long kiss that stole my breath. He squeezed my ass as we separated and turned, heading back to the couch and settling in. I stared at him, baffled. "So … the outfit is okay?"

"Yeah. Very … Hot," he drawled, picking up the remote. "You coming back here tonight or staying at your house?" He seemed utterly unconcerned with my response.

"I was gonna stay here," I said slowly.

"Call me if you end up drinking and need a ride." He flashed me a gorgeous smile and leaned forward, watching the game closely.

I turned, checking that I had my phone and headed for the back door, sending one final glance backward at the den.

"Love you, babe," he called as I opened the door and stepped out.

"Love you, too," I said, pulling the door closed and digging for my keys. *Weird.*

♥♥♥

Brad relaxed against the leather couch, listening as Julia's SUV started up, a throaty purr that rumbled past the den on its way out. Wherever she was going, it wasn't to meet the girls, and it probably wasn't Olives. But, when he stared into her eyes, those brown depths that held his heart, he was reminded of who she was, and she was trustworthy. She had never given him any reason not to trust her. And if she needed to lie to him, there was a reason. He'd just have to wait to find out what that was.

Chapter 40

Olives was definitely not my kind of place. Any bar that had a valet was too high-brow for me. I left my car with an acne-covered kid and headed in, gripping my purse and looking for Beverly. It was easy to find her, her shot of red hair sticking out like a flag. I shot a quick smile to the hostess and bee-lined for her, moving through a throng of suits, silks, and perfume until I finally reached her table. She beamed when she saw me, standing and giving me a hug.

"Julia! So glad you made it. Let's move to the back, it's quieter back there." She grabbed my elbow and we hustled, moving to a rear room where the air was lighter and the volume half as loud. Fanning herself, she slid into a small booth and gestured for me to take the opposite seat.

"This is better," I said, grinning at her across the table.

"I know; it's pure madness out there. Everyone packs in like sardines until nine, and then there's not a soul in this place. It makes no sense. I would have started back here, but didn't want you to get lost in that crowd. A young thing like you, those men wouldn't have let you get too far." She winked at me and caught the eye of a server, who stopped by and took our drink order.

"So. Brad's birthday. What kind of girl are you thinking about?"

Well, that was easy. So much for awkward skirting of the issue. It was one of the reasons I had called Beverly. Frank conversation was certainly appreciated. "I'm not really sure. Can you tell me more about The Montley House?"

She leaned forward, her gorgeous face highlighted to perfection with flawless makeup and diamond drop earrings, her blue eyes burning with mischief. "Montley is the underground red-light district for this city, if a red-light district dealt in thousand dollar bills and professional security. They only have seven girls, and they only cater to clients with a personal invite. I'll be your invite. I called Riley and told her who you were and what you were looking for. She'll walk you through the girls they have. Are you wanting more of a submissive or aggressive girl?"

I blew out a breath, considering the choices. "Probably submissive. I don't want a girl who acts beaten; I just don't want one trying to run the show. Brad will want to do that." A thought occurred to me and I frowned. "Every other experience we've had, the other person has been a willing participant. I don't want to force or pressure a girl into this."

Beverly laughed and leaned forward, flashing a playful smile. "Julia, these women are not at Montley because of financial need. They make more in one night than most women make in a year. They are there because they love sex. Not to mention— can you imagine having to force any woman to have sex with Brad? Good lord, Julia. When I first hired him as an attorney, sex was the last thing on my mind. I hired him because I was told he was lethal in the courtroom. But any woman who spends five minutes in that man's presence wants his cock. That's just the way it is. Whomever you pick tonight … trust me, they're going to enjoy every minute of the experience."

She sat back, smiling at the waiter as he set down our drinks, twin martini glasses of sexual confidence.

♥♥♥

I stopped at the second drink, the room a little fuzzy and Beverly getting more beautiful by the second. She knew everything and everyone, and spoke about our lifestyle like it was Wisteria-Lane-normal. It was refreshing, to be able to gasp about the awkwardness of a threesome gone wrong, or giggle when she told me of a sixteen year old kid who somehow snuck into one of her parties.

"I'm telling you, Julia, he stood there for one minute with his mouth hanging open, frozen in his tracks, and then he turned white as a sheet and took off! We probably ruined that boy for life."

"What happened to that girl, the Russian who was there the night of the Masked Innocence party?

"Who, Kate?" She closed her eyes briefly. "When I think about what almost happened in our house, I get sick. That creep who brought her ... the whole point of me agonizing over a guest list is to make sure people like that *don't* end up at our parties. My husband understands that now. Kate lived with us for a few months until we got her citizenship sorted out. Now she works in Customer Service for one of our companies. She's doing well, looks marvelous. Not as pale as she was that night."

Brad walked her around to the far side of the bed, laying her back onto it, her bare skin creamy white against the blood red duvet. He ran his hand down the center of her body, her skin quivering from his touch, and she gasped as his fingers reached the place where her legs met. My gaze felt physically glued to the scene, and I blinked, the intensity of my stare drying out my eyes.

I blushed, hoping the dark bar hid my tell, pushing my memories back. I had handled that experience well, jealousy not a problem, arousal overriding it in one, easy sweep. Would Friday be any different? Kate had been a fumbling, inexperienced partner.

What if this hired vixen blew my sexual attempts away? Reminded Brad of all of the sex and women he was missing out on? But my decision was made. Even if it all led to that, if she was the catalyst to that epiphany, I wanted to know that now; I wanted this breakdown to happen before the wedding, before the joining of our lives was complete. Brad had voiced it, in simple enough terms, when we had discussed a prenup. *We are not getting divorced. Ever.*

I didn't know about a divorce, didn't know any legal contract in which the word 'ever' could really be applied. But it didn't matter what was on paper, or my finger, or filed with the courts. Whether or not our marriage lasted, I would always and forever, madly deeply love the man. My heart was being sewn together with his, each day and night that passed adding threads to the stitch. And our wedding, our exchange of vows, would be the knot tying the whole package together. At that point, it would be too late; my heart would forever be his. No matter how long the marriage lasted.

So this was important. For better or worse, I needed to know if this was something I could handle, and more importantly, if this was something *we* could handle.

Beverly had asked me something, and I looked at her expectant face. "I'm sorry, what was the question?"

"I said it's getting late. Are you ready to head to Montley?"

No, I want to go back home and crawl into bed and run from my insecure fears. "Sure." I nodded. "Let's go."

Chapter 41

Apparently, when you reach a certain level of god-awful money, it comes complete with a driver. A helpful accompaniment in our case, since neither of us was in a condition to drive. The man pulled up in a gray Maybach, and we bundled into the backseat, nervous anticipation causing a shot of adrenaline to shoot through my body.

"Do I need cash?" I whispered to Beverly.

"No, they won't take any money tonight. Riley will handle payment with Brad after the fact. They know we are good for it, otherwise we wouldn't be considered as clients."

"And how much is this all going to cost?"

She shrugged, folding down a mirror and checking her makeup. "If you don't want the girl to stay the night, if she is just there for a few hours … it'll depend a little on the girl, but probably ten, fifteen grand."

Holy fuck. This gift just went way out of my price range. I didn't know what I was expecting, but a five-figure sum wasn't it. I swallowed. Beverly flipped up the mirror and glanced at me. "What's wrong? Is it the money?"

Yes. "Not exactly … I just wasn't expecting …"

She interrupted me with a wave of her hand. "Brad will pay for the girl. That will all be handled by him, and trust me, he won't mind in the slightest. You are giving him permission, which is your present. The cost is a normal expense in his sex life. It won't give him a second's pause." She patted my leg reassuringly. "Breathe, Julia. Get some life back in those beautiful cheeks. We're almost there."

And two minutes later, my face still pasty white, the Maybach slowed, iron gates opened, and we pulled into a cobblestone drive, the gates closing securely behind us.

The doors to the car were opened as soon as it came to a stop, white-gloved men in tuxedos opening the doors with a polite smile. They escorted us to the entrance of a three story Gothic mansion, the brick covered in ivy, oil lanterns flickering light over the brick, twin sentries of illuminations flanking the front door. The white gloves moved past, opening the doors, and we were suddenly in the foyer and asked to take a seat. They gave half-bows, heads moving All-American good looks in unison, then returned to the front, leaving us alone in the grand room.

The three-story foyer stretched before us, the arched windows along the back glowing with views of a blue pool and up-lit palms. I flexed my hands, aware of the dampness of my palms. I could see where the exorbitant fees went. The room's dark floors, large stone columns, and fresh flower arrangements screamed high class, no condom dispensers or neon lights here. The window dressings alone had to have set someone back six figures. From somewhere, the faint scent of cigar smoke lingered. Faintly, I heard the click of heels, moving with brisk efficiency toward us. The staccato was a countdown, and I tensed in anticipation, my nerves high, second-guessing what the hell I was doing here, what I was thinking, what …

The clicks rounded the corner, and then she stood before us.

She was gorgeous; my first introduction to The Montley House, and I was already blown away, slightly insecure at the idea that other women in this house could compare to this statuesque woman. In her late thirties, if I had to guess, the age barely settled on her, her face clear and unlined, large blue eyes intelligently assessing me through thick lashes. Her hair, blue-black tresses, was pulled back and away from her face in a casual bun that somehow seemed perfectly pulled together. A dark purple dress with velvet accents hugged her curves, and she gave Beverly a warm hug and then extended a graceful hand toward me. "Good evening. I don't believe we've had the pleasure of meeting. I'm Riley."

I stood, shaking her hand, impressed by the firm grip and her gracious smile. "I'm Julia. Beverly has spoken very highly of you."

She smiled. "Let's move into the sitting room." She held out a directional hand, and we moved into a round room containing a small seating cluster of two leather chairs and a loveseat, a large fireplace dominating the room. She gestured to the chairs, and I sat, Beverly leaning forward and gently touching my arm.
r
"Julia, why don't I wait for you in the car? Then you can have privacy with Riley."

I hesitated and nodded. "That would be great. Thank you."

She gave me a warm smile and squeezed my arm. "Take your time, I'll catch up on my phone calls." Then she left, and I was alone with Riley. There was a brief moment of silence, a moment where I really wanted to stand up and chase Beverly down, waving my arms dramatically and escape back to the comfort of her car.

"May I offer you anything to drink?"

"No, I am fine. Thank you."

She leaned forward, clasping her hands together and looked into my eyes. "Why don't I tell you a little bit about our house and how it works. We have six girls who can be reserved as singles, doubles, or triples. Our home has several rooms that you can use, or we can send the girls to a location of your choosing. If the girls leave this house, there are several security measures that come into play, so that will be something for you to consider. What kind of experience are you looking for?"

I wet my lips, considering the question. "I was hoping for a threesome scenario, a girl to join me and my fiancé. It would involve sex on her part, she and I pleasing him together, that kind of thing. Nothing involving BDSM, or anything like that." I squeezed my hands nervously and met her eyes.

She smiled. "That is a very common request, and one that any of our girls could satisfy. What kind of man is your fiancé? Sexually, what is his style?"

I blushed, trying to find the correct words to communicate the enigma that is Brad. "Brad is … Brad is a very dominant individual; he likes control. But in the bedroom he is very much a pleaser. He gets off on pleasing a woman, and I think he pulls a lot of his confidence from his sexual abilities." I paused. "Does that make sense?"

"I understand what you are saying perfectly. Let me show you our book of girls." She stood, walking to a low chest, and opening it, pulled out an embossed book. She sat down on the leather loveseat and patted the seat next to her. I moved, settling in next to her, and studied the book, curious about the girls inside.

She skipped the first girl, skimming past a few pages of photos and then stopped, a buxom blonde staring out at me with a playful, open smile. "This is June. I wanted to start with her for a few reasons. One thing for you to consider is her body type. Do you prefer a girl with your body type, or someone different? Many men only go for one type."

With Brad being the town's biggest slut, I didn't have to wonder about his tastes. Hell, he'd been with Beverly, her red hair setting off the generous curves perfectly placed on her forty-year old frame. Alexis, the platinum blonde stripper, with firm muscles and large implants. Stephanie, the brunette bombshell whose framed nude photo had pouted from above Brad's bed, a Marilyn Monroe body complete with a wave of sexuality. Then there was me, different than all of them. The man had one type: female. Nothing else seemed to matter. A terrifying realization—my competition stretching in every direction. "No," I said, shaking my head. "He's open to different types."

"Well then, what are *you* attracted to?" Her voice was so calm; I didn't understand the question at first.

"Me?"

"Yes. This is as much a sexual experience for you as it is for him. Whether or not you plan to play with the girl, I don't want you turned off by the looks of her. Is there a body type you'd prefer?"

I bit my bottom lip, reaching out and turning the pages, glancing at the girls who adorned each page. I had been expecting, coming to this house of sex, to encounter botoxed foreheads, silicone lips, and breasts swelled to unnatural proportions, tattoos and piercings decorating hardened bodies. These girls were nothing like that. They were the fresh-faced natural beauties that adorned Victoria's Secret catalogs, impossible specimens, smooth skin over perfect bone structure, thick hair, soft curves that were either natural, or perfectly enhanced.

Only six girls were in the book, but they managed to cover every spectrum between them. November was exotic, dark hair, green eyes, a mixture of cultures blending perfectly across her skin. January was blonde with light blue eyes, Nordic features, and full, natural breasts. She glowed in her photos, her skin looking velvet soft, light pink nipples that matched soft lips and pink cheeks. June, the first girl Riley had stopped at, was the typical American beauty — tan skin, long legs, blonde hair, and large breasts too perky and perfect to be natural. Her white teeth and sunny smile stretched across three pages, and from some of her poses, she seemed to be double-jointed in multiple ways. August was pure fire, red hair with sexual energy that jumped off the page, pure sass evident in every pose, grin, and wink. April and May were twins, both brunettes, with flawless natural bodies, enough muscle tone to indicate fitness, enough curves to make them every man's wet dream.

I flipped back and forth through the books, getting frustrated with myself, with my lack of decision-making ability. I was stopped by Riley's firm hand placed over mine. "Is it that you like more than one? Or you don't care for any of them?"

I shook my head. "They're all beautiful; they're just all so different. It's hard for me to choose."

"Let me tell you my thoughts. I would suggest either January or May. They are our girls who have spunk, but need leading. If Brad is an alpha male, he will want to direct the situation. You need a girl who will wait for orders, not try and set the pace. I don't want to put you with a submissive, or else there will be no challenge. These girls are a good blend of the qualities I think you need." She studied me, her intelligent eyes watching as I processed her words. I nodded quietly, flipping the pages back and forth between the two girls.

It was hard for me to imagine May without her twin; the two girls fit so well together, their bodies aligned in almost every pose. She was similar to me, her breasts fuller, but our coloring was the same, our faces both holding a trace of Italian heritage. January was different, and I felt pulled more to her, my eyes tracing over the lines of her body, and I had a sudden, perverse question of how her breasts would feel in my hands, the weight of them, so much larger than my own. I blushed and shut the book. "January. Let's go with her."

"Are you sure?"

"Yes. Is she available this Friday?"

"It will depend on the time. Let me check." She stood, moving out of the room, and returned with a small leather book, settling into one of the chairs and opening it up.

"How would ten in the evening work for you? I can put her down for four hours."

How much does four hours cost? "That would be wonderful, though I don't imagine us needing that long."

"And will you come to the house or will you use another location?"

I hesitated. "You had mentioned rules and arrangements if we use somewhere other than this house. Can you go over those?"

"Certainly. Any meetings outside the house require our security to attend. Two men will accompany the girl and wait outside the room. They will need to be in earshot the entire time. That rule is for the girl's safety and is non-negotiable. If, at any point during the evening, the girl feels uncomfortable, or is asked to do something that wasn't discussed in this meeting, she may call for the security detail and leave, and full payment will still be required."

I nodded and ran through the possible locations in my mind. I couldn't see bringing Brad to this house. He would want to be in a situation he had control over. "I'd like to do it at his house." I gave her the address, watching her write it down with perfect penmanship.

"Wonderful. Is that where I should send the bill? It will be couriered."

The bill. My cheapskate innards clenched at the exorbitant possibilities. "Yes, that would be fine."

She closed the book and smiled. "Do you have any questions? I have everything I need."

I shook my head, my breath starting to flow more naturally at the realization that we were done.

Done. And I had survived. "No." I braved a return smile. "Thank you."

She stood, pulling a business card out of the black notebook and passing it to me. I accepted it, rising to my feet, and we moved through the quiet house until we were back in the three-story foyer. A black tuxedo materialized out of the shadows, and a man's hand opened the front door.

Riley nodded to him and extended a hand toward me. "It has been a pleasure. I hope to see you again." I shook her hand, feeling enormously satisfied with myself, for my ability to overcome this daunting obstacle. *I have officially set up a threesome.* It was an unexpected entry to my bucket list. Then I moved through the doorway, stepping into the night and toward the purring Maybach.

♥♥♥

Beverly's driver returned me to valet at Olives, and, five bucks later, I was behind the wheel of my SUV and heading to Brad's. Getting the girl was only one part of the equation; I'd still have to figure out a way to get her into the upstairs guest room without Brad finding out. Ideally, I wanted to come home from dinner and have her waiting and ready in the guest room.

I didn't want her to be in our bedroom. In case the night went awry, in case I couldn't handle the image of him buried deep inside of her, in case this whole thing was a big mistake that I would spend the next ten years trying to forget ... I didn't want our bedroom tainted, didn't want to fall asleep on a bed that she had poisoned. Hopefully that wouldn't be an issue, hopefully it would be sinfully hot, a moment I would replay countless times. But in case, just in case, I was going to have it held in the guest room. I had no issue with tainting that space.

The downstairs was dim and empty, one small light in the kitchen giving off enough juice for me to navigate through to the stairs. I kicked off my heels and jogged up the steps, the sound of running water hitting my ears. I entered the bedroom, dropping my purse and shoes on a chair, and stripping as I walked, leaving my clothes as they fell, a trail of dress, bra, and panties, I was naked as I pulled on the handle, hot steam contrasting with the cool feel of tile beneath my feet. Brad was in the shower, his gorgeous profile gently muted by fogged glass, his head tilted back under the spray.

I pulled the door wider, steam billowing out, the jets in full motion, and he turned at my approach, his mouth stretching into a full grin, his hand reaching out and capturing me, tugging me inside and against him in one smooth motion. "My baby," he murmured, his arms wrapping around my waist, his mouth lowering to mine, a breathless, heady kiss that captured my mouth, his tongue teasing and claiming my own. The door swung shut and instantly fogged back up as his hands and mouth reminded me of where I belonged.

Chapter 42

In an empty office in Brad's wing, I sealed the final
envelope by hand, my tongue sweeping over the
seal before I pressed it closed. Four envelopes, four
applications. Four life paths sitting in the palm of
my hand. I could dissolve them all so easily, drop
them harmlessly in the wastebasket. Mailing them
was planting seeds, setting myself up for an
impossible decision that I would never be able to
make. I had selected the schools carefully, ignoring
Brad's directive that I choose schools selfishly. We
were getting married, joining our lives. I couldn't
make this big of a decision without considering him.

I was applying locally, to the school I had always
assumed I would attend, my prior financial
situation requiring me to attend an in-state public
school with a strong financial aid package. Envelope
Two was for University of Florida, a school that was
close enough for me to return home on the
weekends, a short flight or long drive away.
Envelope Three was a stretch, the prestigious
program at Dartmouth, a school unlikely to accept
me, but one Brad had insisted I attempt. It had been
his alma mater, and he seemed confident that his
recommendation letter would hold the weight my
average application needed. Envelope Four was
another stretch — Stanford Law. Another completely
selfish application, a school I could never afford,

one that was too far away, nestled in the cliffs of the California coastline. But it was a school I had always wanted to attend, so I had painstakingly completed the application, hating every stroke I made of the pen.

I stood, tucking the envelopes under my arm, and walked to the elevators, headed to the mailroom to send off my four potential destinies. I pressed the down button and waited, hefting the envelopes in my hand, sudden stress weighing on me. I wouldn't get in. I couldn't get in. I wasn't qualified, didn't have the pedigree or prestigious undergrad diploma. But what if I did? What if I was accepted to all four? How would that affect our lives? I made a decision, on impulse, dividing the stack in two and pushing the Dartmouth and Stanford envelopes into the closest trashcan, weeks of Rebecca's hard work crushed in two firm shoves. It was a rash decision, made against all sane thought processes. But so was my agreeing to fly out to Vegas with Brad four days after meeting him. So was marrying into the worst family in town. And with that shove? With that dump of those two way-too-heavy envelopes? I felt so much lighter. I could physically breathe again. The elevators opened and I stepped on, a happier, saner woman. It was a good decision. My decision. The elevators started their descent.

Chapter 43

Friday night came way too fast, the flurry of details occupying too much of my mind, so much that I couldn't properly prepare, couldn't properly dissect my conflicting emotions, my confusion over my feelings. When we fucked—when he had his hands and cock on me—it felt too good, he knew too much. How to touch, how to tease, how far to take me before delivering what I needed. It was unfair for me to hoard all that sexual pleasure, for me to covet his talents and deprive another woman from feeling that. I would envision him with someone else, his hands sliding and touching, curving and trailing, his body above, cock within, mouth upon. The thought was so graphic, so physically arousing that I would instantly buck, my back arching, mind exploding, pushed over the edge and into the star-filled epiphany that was my orgasm. It never failed to send me *there*, never failed to arouse and excite, the fantasy incredible in its utter lack of jealousy and possessiveness. How different would reality be? Or was it the aftermath I should be considering? The doubts, insecurities? How much of a role would they play?

The evening had arrived, and I would know soon enough what harm my actions would bring. I watched Brad over the curve of my wineglass and wondered.

He had not mentioned his birthday once, and I had given strict instructions to both Martha and Rebecca to not clue him into the fact that I was aware of it. I had acted oblivious, following Brad's lead when he suggested we go to Centaur for dinner. Dressed in a short dress and heels, my sexiest bra and panty set underneath, I had manipulated our time slightly so that it would fit with my plans. Now we waited on our steaks, him leaned casually back in his seat, his eyes watching me. I fought a smile and set down my glass. "Stop studying me."

"I can't help it. You're breathtaking."

I leaned forward and captured his hand, raising it to my lips and kissing his palm lightly. "I bet you say that to all the girls," I said playfully. He shook his head and cupped his hand, cradling my face before leaning forward and brushing his lips over mine.

There was a soft cough, and we turned to see our plated feast, served apologetically by a blushing twenty-something blonde. "Thank you." I said, eyeing the steak. As much as my stomach wanted to dive in head first, I didn't want to lug around a full stomach while naked next to January. I cut the steak in half and moved toward the lobster. There was no need to waste good food. I glanced at my watch. 9:30.

"Shit." I widened my eyes in what I hoped was a plausible expression of dismay.

"What?"

"I never dropped my civics paper off. It's due tonight."

"Is it finished?" Brad brought a fresh piece of lobster to his mouth.

"Yeah. I finished it last week, which is why I haven't even thought about it. When we leave here, can we swing by the house and grab it? If we drive over to campus, it'll only take five minutes for me to run it inside the Economics building and put it under my professor's door."

He feigned irritation. "God, that sounds inconvenient. I didn't sign on for all this when I decided to date a younger woman."

"*When* you decided? You've been dating younger women for seven years." I grinned at him. "Besides, I'll withhold dessert if you are responsible for me getting anything other than an A in that class."

He shot me a devious look. "I could just *take* my dessert."

"Au contraire. I'm ninety-nine percent sure that's illegal in this country."

He scoffed. "Trust me, by the time I'm done, you'll be begging me to violate every part of you."

I rolled my eyes. "You overestimate your abilities, Mr. De Luca. And you *are* taking me on my 'younger woman' errand. It's part of the fiancé obligation."

His mouth twitched. "I'll take you on your errand, but *only* because you look so beautiful, and because I can't seem to tell you no."

"Then you, Mr. De Luca. Better dig in. I plan on you needing a lot of energy tonight." I watched his mouth curve, his fork move, and that delicious mouth open. My mind went crazy with thoughts of the evening, and I watched Brad signal for our waitress.

♥♥♥

There was, of course, no civics paper. Brad idled in the driveway, and I took the side entrance, leaving the lights off inside and walking through to the back, where I opened the doors to the large porch. Three porch chairs were occupied; their inhabitants rose at my presence. A girl moved forward, smiling briefly, and extended her hand. "January."

She looked as devastatingly beautiful as her photos, no trick photography or Photoshop used to enhance her looks. I smiled, wondering if my nervous appraisal showed. "I'm Julia. Please come in."

We moved as a group, two men, close in size to Brad, flanking the woman, their eyes moving everywhere, sizing up me and the situation in seconds. I led them upstairs and gestured toward the guest room. "If you would, please wait here, and we will be back in about a half-hour. Your security can sit outside the door; there are chairs in the bedroom that they can use. I left instructions in the room." January nodded and one of the men spoke.

"I'm going to need to see ID for both you and Mr. De Luca."

Right, ID. Riley had mentioned that, for the safety of the girl, proof of our identity would be required and would be documented. I left them in the hall and moved to the bedroom, closing the door and going to the closet, my fingers moving rapidly across the safe's dial until it was open and our passports were in my hand. I locked the safe and returned, passing over the identification. "Here are our passports. Riley said you will return them after the event?"

He nodded, passing them to his partner, who reviewed them with a small penlight, then pocketed them.

I glanced downstairs, worried about the time we were taking. "We'll be back shortly. Please don't take this the wrong way, but there are cameras throughout the house, and an alarm will trip if anyone exits or enters. You'll know when we return because the alarm will sound briefly, and I will turn on all of the lights."

The man on the left grinned at me. "I understand and appreciate the information. We take no offense."

I nodded to them and to the girl, then headed back downstairs, snagging my school bag on the way and arming the alarm before returning to Brad's car.

I had chosen the diversion carefully, picking an errand that would take enough time for our food to settle, but one that would not leave Riley's staff in the house unattended for too long of a period. I had worried about that detail of the plan, but Beverly had been quick to assure me of their trustworthiness. She had used The Montley House almost a dozen times, regarded every interaction a perfect transaction, and seemed to have boundless faith in every employee of The House.

My stomach was tight, a knot of rolling emotions as Brad's car rumbled back from campus, his face calm, his hand reaching across the center console and holding my own. I forced my fingers to be loose, normal, as his thumb ran gently across my palm.

My other hand moved, reaching into my purse and wrapping around my phone. I could change my mind. Text and cancel this entire thing. January and the two protectors would leave, Brad and I would return, and we would go upstairs and have solo, break-the-bed sex. That would be enough. We were enough. We had proved that, again and again, with night after night of incredible makemytoescurl fucking. The threesomes, the parties, those were fairy dust sprinkled on the magic that we were, a way to remind us of the incredibleness of what we share.

Then Brad turned down Estate Drive, which led home. *Home.* Amazing that I already thought of it in that way. In four short months it would be. I would haul in boxes and hangers and picture frames, and it would go from his to ours. The Estate Drive sign meant time was up, and I couldn't possibly text anyone, cancel anything now. I needed to put on my game face and stop being insecure. I hadn't started dating this man, hadn't agreed to marry this man, without being confident of my sexual ability. And now, with the blonde waiting upstairs, I had the opportunity to give him the best birthday present of his life. I allowed excitement in, the nervous anticipation turning into arousal, and grinned, the expression hidden in the dark car. I reached for the door handle as he put the car in park.

Chapter 44

Brad smiled. It had been a good birthday. No mess, no fuss, no drama. A great dinner at Centaur with the woman who had stolen his heart. And now, home. Before, it had been simply a house, a place where he bedded women, ate Martha's cooking, and slept. Now, with Julia's light and warmth and messy adorableness, it had become more. He had begged, bribed, and seduced—all in an attempt to get her to move in. But she had stubbornly resisted, returning most nights to the hovel she called a home. And every night she slept away from him, he worried. He unlocked the door, disengaging the alarm, and felt the presence of her pass behind him, her hands flicking on lights as her heels clicked through the kitchen.

She moved perfectly, his eyes following her steps, the curves of her body underneath her dress, her shapely legs on perfect display atop sexy heels. He locked the door and caught up to her as she rounded the corner, heading for the stairs.

"Whoa," he whispered into her neck, inhaling the scent of her as his hands wrapped around her waist and traveled up the front of her dress. His mouth nuzzled her neck and planted soft kisses on her fragrant skin.

"Brad," she whispered, spinning from him and walking backward toward the stairs. "You can finish that upstairs."

"I can't wait that long," he said gruffly, catching her hand and pulling her tightly to him. He lowered his mouth to hers, silencing her response, his hands tugging on the straps of her dress quickly, the material following the path of the straps, her lace-covered breasts quickly exposed to his hands. She groaned, her chest heaving once underneath his mouth, her hands pushing on his chest.

"Stop," she said breathlessly, pulling up her dress until her perfect breasts were once again hidden. "Just wait a sec. I need something from upstairs."

Before he could formulate a response, she was gone, the flash of red soles moving quicker than humanly possible up the staircase. He followed closely, his eyes on the curve of her ass. He grinned, reaching a hand up to grab her when he reached the landing and everything stopped at the sight of two men.

♥♥♥

I heard Brad behind me, getting closer, and I could tell you without looking that he would be reaching for me, intent on getting his hands on some part of my body. I felt triumphant when I reached the top landing untouched, and moved toward the guest room, my smile acknowledging the men that sat outside the door. Brad's voice stopped me instantly, his tone one I had never heard from him. "Julia. Go to Martha's." I froze mid-step and turned to him.

His eyes were not on me, but on the two suits, the large bodyguards who flanked either side of the guest room door, seated in the two casual chairs that typically occupied the sitting area of the guest room. I instantly understood his concern and cursed my own lack of foresight. The two men rose at Brad's tone, their stance one of combative preparation.

I moved three steps, until I stood in front of Brad and blocked his line of sight. His eyes flickered to me briefly, clouds of worry. "Brad, it's okay. I called them here. They are fine." My words took a moment to register, his eyes watching them instead of me, but then confusion crossed his handsome face, and his eyes met mine again.

I smiled, placing my hands gently on his chest and kissed his cheek. "Relax," I whispered. Then I turned, stepping through the men and to the guest room, where I swung the door open wide for Brad's eyes.

The room was dim but not dark, a big enough room that the bed was set back against a far wall, the lit candles revealing enough: glowing skin, blonde hair, porcelain features – the package lounged atop a cream duvet. Brad's frame relaxed a fraction, and he glanced at the men with new understanding, then his gaze settled on my face, a look of confusion affecting his features in an adorable way I had never seen.

"Happy birthday," I whispered and walked ahead of him, into the dark room, unzipping my dress as I walked.

Chapter 45

There was a click, and I turned to see Brad shut the door, his eyes slowly sweeping over me, surveying the bed, his eyes dark and unreadable. Then they returned to me, and he moved only one step forward, his hands pulling off his jacket, tossing it aside, then moving to his belt, the slow, deliberate unbuckling of leather causing my breath to hitch.

A million thoughts ran through my head. *What do I do? Do I get on the bed with her? Approach him? Sit in the chair?*

"Turn around." Brad stepped closer, his eyes on mine, the pull of his stare too great to break, and I turned my back to him slowly, hating to break the eye contact.

His hand swept down my bare back, pulling my zipper farther, to the place I couldn't take it, his hands spreading the dress over my shoulders and letting it fall to the floor. "Keep the heels on," he muttered.

"Do you want me to watch?" I said the words softly, looking over my shoulder at him. I was almost afraid of the answer. Afraid because even I didn't even know what I wanted. I glanced at the girl still on the bed, her body stretched, on her side, expression quiet, eyes open. Watching. Our eyes met and she smiled. A friendly, reassuring expression. *It will be okay. Trust me.*

He shook his head. "I'm not ever, as long as I live, going to have an orgasm without your hand on my cock, your mouth on my lips. If you want to bring in another girl, that is fine. But you are not watching. I'm not settling for second best when you are here." He ran his hand down my back, his hand leaving my skin for a moment before coming back to my ass with one, firm slap, the sensation catching me off guard, and I jumped, turning my head to him, caught off guard by the dark yet playful look in his eyes. "Now get on the bed before you are the death of me."

I smiled shyly at the girl as I climbed upon the bed, her long limbs rolling over as she crawled to her knees, making room. She reached out a tentative hand, running it softly over my skin, the touch so foreign, so soft and delicate. "You are beautiful," she whispered, her hand trailing over and across my back and down my arm.

"So are you."

There was the metal sound of a buckle, and I turned to see Brad unzipping his pants, his shirt removed, his weight joining us on the bed as he knee-walked forward, settling back into pillows, sliding in between us. "Come here, baby," he said. "Straddle me."

I did, my ass settling into the hard bridge of his stomach, his head tilting up to look into my eyes. "You didn't need to do this."

"I wanted to," I said softly, running my hands up the hard muscles of his chest.

"I get off pleasing you, watching you pleased. Another girl … I don't want this if you don't enjoy it."

"I want to try it. We can discuss the rest later."

"Just look at me if you are uncomfortable. I'll know. I'll stop." His hand played with the small of my back before curving down and squeezing my ass. "You nervous?"

I laughed, the question releasing some of my tension. "A little."

"Don't be. This is just like the others." He sat up slightly, his arms wrapping around my waist, his mouth laying a kiss against my neck. "It's about you and pleasure."

I pushed him down, not liking where this was going. "No. This is about your birthday, and rocking your old man world."

He laughed, letting me push him, settling back against the pillows. "Easy, baby. You can't call me an old man on my birthday. And," he said, his voice darkening, "you're doing a lot of ordering around considering it's my birthday. Kiss me."

I pursed my lips, shot him a look I knew he loved, one that spat fire and conceded defeat, and leaned back down, caught off guard when he captured my hands and pulled them together behind me, his large hand easily pinning them to my back.

"What's her name?" he asked, his mouth inches from mine.

"January."

"January, pull out my cock, please."

Chapter 46

I squirmed slightly, caught off guard by his directive, his hand tight on my wrists, keeping me in place. I felt her move, heard the rustle of fabric, the buck of Brad underneath me as he lifted his ass to assist her. He kissed me, his free hand firm on the back of my head, his tongue making a statement that was both strong and needy.

He pulled on my wrists, sitting up with me, my ass sliding down, bumping against her hand and his cock. "Hop off." He released my wrists, moving his hands to my breasts and pushing them into his mouth, taking one frantic taste of them before moving me off.

"Show her," he said. "Show her how you suck my cock."

I knelt on the other side of his body, admiring the thick lay of his cock on his stomach, her hand sliding up and down his thighs. I glanced up, watching her kneel across from me, her blue eyes down, glued to Brad, and I felt a moment of pride as I reached forward, gently lifting and taking his semi-hard cock into my mouth, feeling it stiffen as I sucked, my throat closing, my eyes watering slightly as I took as much of him as I could. I worked his shaft with my hand, sucking hard, watching as January moved a hand forward, running her hands over his balls, then leaned forward, taking them in her mouth.

I felt Brad's hand on my hair, gathering it up in his fist, pushing and pulling it gently, his eyes on mine, his mouth opening slightly as he scowled with concentration, watching his cock as it slid in and out of my mouth. He was so hard, so slick and thick in my mouth, and I watched his eyes close briefly as I took him as far down as I could. "Jesus, baby," he groaned. "You are so perfect."

I drug slowly off his cock, meeting January's eyes, and she took over, her mouth smoothly picking up where mine had left off. Brad's hand, still in my hair, tugged gently, and I looked over, letting him pull me up his body until I was tucked into his arm, his mouth on mine, his other hand taking a tour of my chest, squeezing and pulling each breast in turn, his hands a little rough in their journey. My mouth gasped against his as he slapped each breast slightly, the arm underneath me shifting as he slid his left hand lower, until it cupped my ass, his fingers splaying over and teasing my pussy, the sensitive skin of my taint, and my ass. I moaned, pushing against his hand, wanting more, my mouth pulling off his as I lifted my head and watched her, watching the strange girl take his cock with skill. I could see how hard he was, see the light pink dart of her tongue, the hot interior of her mouth, the veins on his cock—

Fuck.

My eyes closed, two of Brad's fingers sliding into me, one in the hot, tight hole of my ass, one in my wet cunt, the curve of his grip absolutely perfect, his second hand sliding down from my breasts and rubbing gently over my clit. Oh my God. It was incredible, having both of his hands stimulating me, his mouth on my neck, my eyes fighting to open, wanting to take in more of the experience, the arousal of watching him pleasured more than I expected.

I could feel the tightening in my stomach, the clench of my muscles that warned me an orgasm was coming. "Brad, I can't …" I closed my eyes, felt the nips of his teeth on my neck, the vibration of his throat when he growled.

"Come for me. Come for me while she sucks my cock."

I couldn't stop it; my hands gripped his arm like it was a safety bar, holding on tightly when my back arched, when the orgasm ripped through me like an out of control wind. I cursed his name, a string of obscenities pouring out of me as pleasure blossomed, his fingers softening perfectly as my body surrendered to the perfect peak and then fell into the pit of sensitivity. Then, my clit was left alone entirely, his mouth feasting on my neck as he did nothing but pulse his fingers inside of me, my ass clenching around him, the orgasm drawn further out, so much so that I wonder if I had two back-to-back.

Then I sunk, a mess of wanton pleasure in his arms, curled over, my face against his chest, his hands moving me into place without me even knowing it, the girl helping to slide my leg over his stomach until I was back, straddling him, this time him gripping my face in his hands, his face inches away, and he stared into my eyes.

I wanted to close my eyes, too weak with bliss to focus, but he held me firm, arrested me with his stare. I felt strange hands, delicate and soft, *hers*, running down the pucker of my ass, and then his cock, so fucking hard, was at my sex, and she was pushing it in, putting it into place.

Brad went wild.

I loved him fucking me from underneath. Loved the jack hammer of his cock as I did nothing, and he went eight kinds of crazy, the animalistic hunger of his fucks incredibly hot, adding fuel to an already blazing fire, my body loving the barrage on my cunt, the nonstop friction, the push and pull against my g-spot and deep in, quick out, deep in, quick out that drove me over the brink of orgasm in less than a minute.

I came hard, my entire body seizing, squeezing, the delicate push of her finger against my ass sending me straight into holy fuckville territory. It was long, it was insane, it was beautiful, staring into Brad's eyes, his mouth whispering words I could barely hear but knew by heart. "I love you. You crazy sexual beauty. I love every fucking inch of you. I love watching you. I love seeing you in this way. You are mine, you dirty, kinky woman."

Then I shoved off, amazed I still had strength in my body. I rolled off him and lay spent, my limbs useless, my heart pounding. "Fuck her," I moaned. "Please."

"On your knees," Brad ordered, the girl sliding over and assuming the position, her perfect ass bent over before him, my view of the *damn she's hot* scene enough to give me a moment's hesitation. But he moved her, turning her toward me, so that her face was skimming my stomach, her hot breath moving fluidly over my skin. He was positioned behind her, facing me, his eyes on mine, dark possession and arousal in his gaze, a condom package in hand, raised to his mouth for easy opening. Also in his eyes—a question. An 'are you ready for this?' inquiry. I nodded once, my eyes glued to his. He studied me for a second before he ripped the foil package open.

Chapter 47

There had been a moment, when Brad had ordered her to her knees, when I was already two orgasms down, and she hadn't even been touched, that I felt bad for this woman. That I felt like we were using her, not respecting her properly. All of that left my mind when he moved inside of her. Didn't thrust, didn't shove. He took his time—let her adjust. One long, slow movement of his body forward. Her head dropped back, away from my body, and she let out a sound. Something in between a moan and a groan, a satisfied sound, which made me smile, my spent body reviving. Yes, I knew. I knew exactly what that felt like. The chemical reaction of his cock that was somehow, impossibly, different than any other man's. She wasn't getting him bare. She wasn't getting the full force of Brad De Luca. But even sheathed with latex, his cock was incredible. Then he started moving, started fucking, his hands falling to her ass, gripping, squeezing. He leaned slightly forward, gripped her skin, stared into my eyes and moved.

I got it. I got why he did this. I didn't think I'd ever need it the way he did, our threesomes his assurance that I was *beyond* satisfied. He didn't want just satisfaction from me. He wanted my mind ripped three ways from Sunday, wanted my body to peak and fall fifteen times in one night. Wanted me to feel raw animalism alongside heart-stopping passion. Wanted me to feel beautiful, sexual. Wanted me to open every padlocked closet in my fantasy palace and explore whatever treats I locked away. He would never be satisfied with ordinary, would never want just part of my heart, part of my body. He wanted every barrier stripped, every veil lifted, until he and I were fucking intertwined, my pleasure giving him his pleasure, his pleasure giving me mine.

I got it. The feeling that suddenly swelled through me. It was insanity in the form of raving, passionate lust. I felt competitive and jealous and sexual, all rolled into one. I knew, as I stared into his eyes, as he swept a greedy, ravenous stare over my body, that he wanted me. He was eating my body with his gaze, his fucks increasing in tempo, the girl's cries mounting as he stopped being gentle and started being Brad.

"Fuck yourself," he gritted out. "With your fingers. Let me see you. Let me see inside you."

I rolled over and moved back, until I was before them. I spread my legs, dipped a finger, then two, inside my mouth, Brad's eyes darkening as I sucked them. Not lightly, not with ladylike daintiness. I sucked my fingers and wanted his cock. I drug my wet fingers down, his stare following, the muscles on his chest and shoulders standing to attention as he drilled into her, and I spread my lips and let him see the extent of my arousal, the extent of my want.

She was close. I could hear the change in her cries, the slap of Brad's balls, each thrust spanking her clit, his rapid-fire motion taking her quickly up the hill of orgasm. My eyes left Brad's, watching her face, her expression. She met my gaze, her own almost frantic. Gone was the cool and collected vixen who waited on this bed, candles illuminating her perfect skin. Right then she was a current of *whatthefuckishappening*, an identity I knew well, her eyes glazing over as she lost all rational thought and exploded. My fingers stopped fucking around, stopped their teasing ways. They found their way to my sex and dove inside.

♥♥♥

I thought I knew Julia but I didn't. There was so much I had yet to discover, yet to unearth. We hadn't talked about this, hadn't talked about bringing another woman into the bedroom. I didn't need it. It didn't feed my competitive fire. I didn't need to know that I was the best every woman out there has had. I only needed to be *her* best, only needed to learn every inch of *her* body and the way to light it on fire.

But did *she* need a girl? Did she have the same competitive fight that I carried? Did it get her off to see me fuck another woman? If so, I would bang away. Fuck this blonde when the woman I wanted was spread open before me, her fingers where my mouth or cock should be, her chest heaving with intensity that I was not causing.

My fear was that it was not for her. My fear was that she was doing this for me, thinking that this is something I needed, I wanted. My fear was that she hated this, and I was killing a piece of her sexual fire with every stroke into this stranger. I gave one final thrust and pulled out, squeezing the girl's ass and gently rolling her aside, bending forward until my mouth was on Julia, and I was tasting her sweet pussy. Her fingers moved for my mouth, her body bucked up and I grabbed her, held her down and used my tongue to tease the hell out of my future wife.

God, I loved this woman.

♥♥♥

Brad took me to a third high, my barriers to orgasm weak, each peak making the next one easier, my body a tight coil of arousal. January's mouth covered my breasts, her firm tongue playing against my nipples, her teeth gentle when she grazed them across my skin. I reached a hand out, brushed it over her breasts, their weight heavy. They moved so differently than mine. They hung when she bent over, bounced when she got fucked. I tentatively squeezed one, and she smiled, moved closer for easier access. Kissed me softly as I explored her upper half.

Then I came, and everything went black.

♥♥♥

A fight of tongues. Both of us greedy for more. Of his shaft, of his head, the small bit of pre-cum that leaked from his tip. Occasionally our mouths would meet, join for a moment of playful fun, then return, our hands also on him. Stroking. Eyes begging. On our knees on the soft carpet before him.

His never left mine. Dark intensity. Fierce arousal. They stayed on me until his thighs clenched, his abs tightened, his hand found the back of my head and pulled me foremost on his cock. I dove, sucking hard, using my hand and staring up into his face. Then his mouth moved, my name as a groan on his lips and his eyes lidded shut.

I love watching him come.

I took what I could, and January's tongue chimed in, helping me drain him dry. Then he lifted us, one by one, to our feet.

"We'll leave you the room," he said. "Take as long as you need, the attached bath and shower is yours if you need it."

She didn't linger, and a few minutes later, with our passports back in the safe, the men and January gone, Brad closed the door to our bedroom, and fixed me with a look. A look I knew, yet still questioned.

"Get on the bed," he growled.

I didn't move fast enough, and he lifted me up, carrying me in four large strides to the bed where he tossed me, the robe I had thrown on tangling in my limbs, and I fought the silk and looked into his mischievous eyes. "What, you didn't like your present?"

"That wasn't my present," he said, bending over me, his mouth nuzzling the silk robe open, his hands untying the sash and spreading it, bites and kisses running down the length of my torso as he climbed atop the bed, my legs opening before him. "This. This will be my present."

I didn't know what man considered two hours of driving me wild a present, but I could tell you this—

I wasn't ever letting him go.

Chapter 48

I rolled over in the soft bed, pushing through expensive sheets until I felt hot skin. No matter what the temperature in the room, Brad's skin was always fever hot. I pulled myself closer, wrapping my chilly body around the curve of his back, his body turning at my touch, his arm reaching out to pull me tightly against him. I felt his lips against my hair as he pressed a soft kiss on my head.

"Good morning," he said, his voice scratchy.

"Morning," I murmured with a smile, loving the cocoon of sheets, blankets, and Brad, the blackout shades keeping the master bedroom dark despite the sunshine outside.

"That might have been the best birthday ever," he said, his hands gripping my waist and sliding me easily up his body until his lips could reach mine.

"Might have?" I scoffed.

His mouth curved and his dark eyes smiled at me. "Definitely was. Happy?"

"Certainly, Mr. De Luca. Though I'm not sure if you will be so appreciative when you get the bill." I widened my eyes dramatically and grinned at him.

He pulled me to him, kissing me softly in between words. "You are. Worth. Every. Penny. Seeing you with her, the look you get in your eyes …" his voice trailed off as his eyes studied me. "You will be the death of me," he whispered. "I am completely and totally at your mercy."

"Impossible." I moved on top of him, straddling his width. "You always have the upper hand with us."

His gaze moved, drinking my naked body in, his hands following the path of his eyes, caressing and fondling. "No," he said. "But I take my power when I can. And right now, I see a prime opportunity."

It was a prime opportunity, my body already naked, my soul craving some one-on-one time with Brad's delicious body. He devoured me with his mouth, claimed me with his cock, and made it all sensual with his hands. A half-hour later, I fell back asleep, a happy and thoroughly satisfied woman.

My cell rang, loudly and incessantly in the dark room. I reached out with a hand, groping blindly until I found and tapped the screen, silencing the call. There was thirty seconds of peace and quiet, then it began again. I ignored it, rolling over and pulling a pillow over my head, the damn thing finally ending its shrill ring. I relaxed, slipping back into sleep.

"Julia." I kept my eyes closed and body still, playing dead, willing him to give up and go away.

"Julia, wake up." There was a rustle of fabric, and suddenly light. The pillow was yanked from my grasp and a phone replaced it, pressed against my exposed ear.

"Julia, are you there?" *Rebecca.* I opened my eyes to find Brad's amused face above me, his hand holding the phone to my ear. I mumbled some form of greeting.

"Julia, you're supposed to be at Franco's in thirty minutes. Do you *know* what it took to get you in last minute? You've got to get your ass up and over there, pronto. Becca and Olivia are already on their way. Don't *make* me show up at Brad's." I sat up, taking the phone from him and shooting him an irritated look.

"Stop screaming. I have time." I swayed on my way to the closet, the right side now reserved for me, my new wardrobe holding its own alongside Brad's expensive clothes. I yanked open a drawer and pulled out a pair of jeans, grateful that we had showered after sex last night.

"Oh my Lord, if you're not early, you're late. It's Franco's, and you're picking out your wedding dress. Most girls would have already been in their lobby, orgasming in their silk panties by now."

"Been there, done that this morning."

She blew a noisy breath into the phone. "Ugh, that is my boss you are talking about. Please spare me the juicy details of your scandalous sex life."

"Fine. But don't say shit like 'orgasming in silk panties.' It's creepy."

She paused. "Point taken. Now get your ass to Franco's and pick out something that will make me green with envy."

I grinned, hopping into the jeans and flipping through hangers until I found a tank top. "I'll try my best. I'll text you a pic of the winner."

We said our goodbyes, and I returned to the room, grabbing my purse and cell and heading downstairs, finding Brad in the kitchen with

Martha. I handed him his cell and gave her a quick hug.

"You got time for breakfast?" she asked.

"No, I'm late as it is." I grabbed an apple.

"The girls meeting you there?" he asked.

"Yep. We'll probably grab lunch afterward."

There was a rap at the back door, and we turned as a group, a broad-shouldered blond opening the door. Ben. I flashed him a smile and then studied Brad, noticing his matching attire. "What are you guys up to?"

"Hitting the batting cages. Season starts in three weeks." Brad clapped Ben on the back, flashing me a smile.

"No wonder you were so enthusiastic about me going to Franco's."

"According to Rebecca, this is supposed to be something you enjoy, so don't give me hell."

"It is. Enjoy hitting; I'll catch up with you guys later." I hugged Ben and gave Brad a kiss, waving to Martha, and heading out the door. Ahead of me waited Franco's, with its expensive array of designer whites, lace, and beading. The prospect of the perfect dress, mimosas, and the girls got my feet moving and SUV in gear. That, and the risk of death that awaited from Rebecca if I didn't arrive at Franco's on time.

Chapter 49

Secrets. They lay like a force field between my friends and me. What had started as one then led to two, eventually piling into a mountain-sized pile of deceit that I drug around with me on every interaction with them. The threesomes, Brad owning a strip club, Brad's family, their involvement in Broward's death, me owning a strip club, the attempt on my life. The secrets fought amongst themselves, battling for exposure whenever I was with the girls. A casual outing for drinks became a cocktail of inner turmoil. How close could friends be when there was so much unsaid?

Brad had never sworn me to secrecy, or asked that I kept things from the girls. But I knew what would happen if I told them. Judgment. Judgment of my morals, Brad, and me. Questioning of our relationship and how it would ever work. I didn't need that. I didn't need or want to explain my life and my choices. So I chose the suitcase of secrets and their belief that I lived a perfect, normal existence. Yes, there was now distance between us, but at least we were still friends. At least they were somewhat supportive of my relationship.

♦♦♦

"It's absolutely gorgeous, Jules. Totally you." Becca beamed at me over the rim of her Diet Coke, her blonde hair shining in the afternoon sun.

"It's true. I think it really fits you," Olivia added, settling back in her chair.

We sat on the outside deck at Cucumbers, a trendy sushi restaurant downtown, the table covered with sushi rolls, edamame shells, and chopsticks. Franco's had actually been fun, Becca and Olivia running interference between me and the snobby saleswomen, and I had known instantly when pulling on Dress Number Three, that I had found the one I wanted. It was there, in the chandeliered, plush dressing room of Franco's, with Becca and Olivia grinning behind me, looking in the mirror, that I felt it. Excitement. I had always been excited about marrying Brad, but it had been the marriage that I had looked forward to, not the act of getting married. The wedding had been a byproduct, one that — due to Brad's family — I had been dreading. But there, in that dress, seeing my reflection, I felt a quiver of breathless anticipation. I allowed it, allowed visions of walking down the aisle, feeling the strength of his hand sliding a ring on my finger, words spoken, rice thrown, cake and music and toasts and dancing. And for that moment, that brief, fairytale moment, I was naively happy about the wedding.

"Earth to Julia." Becca snapped her fingers in my face, and I scowled, pushing her hand aside and grabbing my chopsticks. "Did you hear what I said? I sent in my app to NYU."

Olivia rolled her eyes. "That's not an application. That's a reservation for a donation. Has your dad already stroked the check?"

Becca sputtered out a few expletives, causing Olivia and I to burst out laughing. I grabbed a napkin, passing it to Becca, and she wiped her mouth, shooting Olivia a dirty look.

"Have you decided? That's your first choice?" I asked Becca, fighting to keep a smile off of my face.

"Pretty much." She shrugged. "I like New York. I'm applying to UCLA also; I always wanted to be a California girl."

Olivia snorted. "That's smart. Choose your schools based on shopping and beaches."

"Do I detect a bit of bitterness in your tone?" Becca asked, sharply raising an eyebrow.

"I'm still undecided," I said brightly, trying to interrupt the incoming argument.

"Undecided? I assumed you'd stay here with me." Olivia's eyes honed in on me, all thoughts of over-privileged Becca forgotten.

"So did I, but Brad is pushing me to apply at other schools." I inwardly winced, hating how the statement came out. Olivia pounced on it like a rabid dog.

"Who cares what Brad wants. What do you want?"

I shot her an irritated look. "I'm a grown woman, O. That's what I'm trying to figure out. What I want."

"This is bullshit, him pushing you into what he wants."

I stared at her. "What are you *talking* about? He wants me to make the same choice I would if I was single. He doesn't want my law school decision to be affected by our marriage. Because of his money and connections, I can look at schools I never would have been able to go to. And you're trying to turn it into a negative? What the fuck?"

Becca started to chime in, to voice her support, but Olivia held up a hand. "Becca, stay out of this. Julia, I just don't like how everything seems like it revolves around Brad."

I bit back a laugh at the ridiculousness of that statement. Wasn't that what marriage was all about? Pushing aside single life to start a new life together? It would be ridiculous not to include him in this thought process, seeing the effect my law school would have on our marriage.

I had no intention of having one of *those* marriages—two people who cohabited the same house but otherwise lived separate lives. Brad had become my best friend, the person who I shared my thoughts, dreams, and life with. He had, in the process, overshadowed Olivia. Her hostility, resistance to anything Brad-related? She tried to hide it. Times like that morning had actually succeeded, playing the role of supportive friend well. But I could feel the tension, worried over the chips and cracks that were forming in our bond. I never realized, in falling in love, that I might lose a friend in the process. She just didn't realize the depth of emotion I had for him. No one did. We were surrounded by casual love, which found our singular focus bothersome. Now, almost nine months into our engagement, her snide comments were wearing my nerves raw. I had started to reach the stage of not caring, of indifference. I loved Olivia, had spent almost four years as her best friend. But our friendship, our connection, paled in comparison to what Brad and I had. And if she couldn't handle the change in my life, then how strong was that friendship? I met her critical look squarely.

"I'm sorry you don't understand my relationship," I said tartly.

It was Becca's turn to play peacemaker, and she jumped in with a cheery smile only to be cut off by Olivia.

"You weren't like this with Luke. Or with any of your boyfriends for that matter. We never see you anymore."

"Really? You're using *Luke* as a positive example? I'm treating this relationship differently because it is different. I'm sorry I don't go to parties anymore or stumble in and out of clubs with you and Becca. But don't blame Brad for that. My life is changing; I'm getting married."

She stared at me fiercely, the sushi forgotten, fire in her brown eyes. "You're making a mistake."

She may have been right, but not for the reasons she thought. Brad and I had our share of problems, but they all started and ended with the Magiano family, not with us.

Chapter 50

JULY
Days until the wedding: 33

I waited at the light, my turn signal on, Becca's voice whining through my vehicle's speakers. "Come tonight … please. Your college career is about to be *over*. You have an obligation to party with me one last time before graduation."

The light turned green. "You're only calling me because Olivia has plans."

"Wrong. Olivia's coming and bringing that lacrosse player guy."

I raised my brow. "What guy?"

"She didn't tell you? Some guy she met in class. Be grateful, she won't shut up about him to me. How's Brad?"

"Good." I don't elaborate; there's no need. Becca's attention span won't last long enough to care.

"So, are you coming? They're closing the whole block off, and each house is gonna have a different drinking challenge."

"Sounds brutal."

She scoffed. "Oh please. You were chugging beers with the best of us a year ago. Now, come on … bring Brad if you want."

Brad. I tried to picture him, his hands on his hips, a glowering look on his face as drunken idiots sloshed him with beer. I giggled. "How about just dinner? I can meet you at seven or eight?"

She sighed. "I guess … if you want to miss out on the fun. But I miss drunk Julia."

I put the car in park, glancing at my watch. "I have to go. Call O, see if she wants to grab dinner with us. I'll call you in a few hours."

"Fine."

I ended the call and turned off the car, grabbing my purse and heading for the restaurant.

I took the seat across from Maria, her smile warm as she beamed at me behind the curve of a large ceramic teacup. We didn't waste time, ordering a variety of appetizers, deciding upon sharing them in place of a full meal. And, after a half-hour of conversation, I could see why Brad's eyes shone when he spoke of his sister. She was, as ancient as the word was, delightful. Bubbly and energetic, there was not an ounce of haughtiness or reserve in her manner. I could not fathom how she came from the stoic evil that was her father.

"How are the wedding RSVPs coming along? Will there be a large turn out?" She tossed out the question innocently, spearing an olive and popping it into her mouth.

I swallowed a sigh, pasting a smile on my face. "I'm not really sure. We're still waiting on a group of RSVPs from your family."

She frowned, her eyes drinking me in with the same insight that Brad possessed. "My father's group?"

"Yeah."

She gave me a tight smile. "It's a wedding. Italians view weddings on the same level as Easter. It'd be sacrilegious not to attend. I'm sure they will get over any ill feelings and show their support. Besides, the gossip mill has been buzzing about you. It was pretty much expected that Brad would never remarry."

"Why is that?"

She shrugged. "He seemed to enjoy his life as a bachelor. And his marriage with Hillary seemed so … unnatural. He just never seemed to fall into the role of husband well. It was like he was a wild horse, unhappy about being broken." She shot me a crooked grin. "He is completely different with you. He seems so at peace, happy. I am so excited for you both." She reached across the table and gripped my arm, her face shining with genuine affection. "I know you've got to be less than enthusiastic about joining our family, but I am so happy to have you in Brad's life. I hope you can overlook my bloodlines, and we can become friends."

I blushed, hating the fact that my emotions regarding the Magianos were so transparent. "I'd like that. Brad adores you, for good reason."

"He was always the best member of our family. Which," she added, "is why the boys have always been so hard on him. I'm proud of him for separating from the family."

"Are you estranged as well?" It was a dangerous question to ask, but she seemed to be an open book in regards to discussing the family business.

She laughed, leaning forward and lowering her voice. "Being female places me in a completely different position in the family. From the moment my sex was discovered, I was a non-issue, a body to be ignored. I was never included in the business, handed off to nannies once Mother left. There has been no point to me disowning the family; it would be a dramatic act that would be regarded as attention-seeking and childish." She shrugged, and I saw a moment of vulnerability that matched a side of Brad. They were both still, even as adults, missing the love and approval of their mother. She continued speaking, her gaze regaining confidence. "We have a strong support system through the women in the family. I am a part of that. We, as women, don't often have much control over the men who our hearts pick. It is difficult to be married to the men in this family, to be a small part of what they do. We need each other, and for that aspect of the family, I am grateful." She smiled, the expression not reaching her eyes.

I played with the straw of my drink. "Your father … when I met him … he mentioned the danger that faces me from other families. Is that a real concern?"

She glanced down, silent for a moment. Then she looked up, and I saw Brad's strength in her eyes. "The same thing I hate about our family, the strength and brutality of its members, I appreciate when it comes to my safety. In the Italian crime culture, women and children are protected, off limits. We are supposed to be untouchable. But that rule applies more to inner-family violence than wars between families. The threat to our lives is present, and concerns me more as a mother than as an individual. I am fighting to keep my sons safe, but worry constantly. My boys, they see the family business as glamorous, my brothers as role models. In that way, we are never really safe." She shot me a sympathetic look. "But it is a world I grew up in. I didn't have a choice but to accept the danger, to do what I can to protect my family. For you, it must be difficult. I can only tell you that Brad has more strength than all of them combined. His strength will help to keep you safe."

Then the waitress arrived, and our conversation switched to lighter subjects. We moved through the appetizers, discussing unimportant topics, and I fought to keep my voice light and face relaxed. But inside, I felt weighted down by her words, the tug of them pulling me into a place of doubts and fears.

Chapter 51

Groan. I loved the sound when it rumbled out of his chest. I lifted up my ass, then set it back down, my hands gripping the back of the couch, the scrape of his shadow against my neck as he buried his face in my shoulder and breathed my name. "Fuck me, baby."

My knees sunk deeper into the leather as I moved, the muted sounds of baseball disappearing as my senses abandoned their notice of anything but this.

Heat. Hot as it thrust in and out of me.
Bite. His hands on my ass set the pace. Pushing and pulling me off his cock.
Scrape. Every turn of his head, his five o'clock shadow burned its way over my ear, my neck, my chest, his gentle mouth following its path.
Sigh. The sounds of my love as he got closer.
Whispers. Orders. Grunts. Worships.
Explosion. I broke in his arms, his hands moving from my ass as he wrapped them around my body and hugged me to his chest, his hips taking over the motion, carrying me as I fell apart, waves of pleasure that stretched out as I heard the change in his voice and knew that he was following suit.

Tumble. Both of us sideways, stretched out on the couch, my back turned to the television, spooned against his chest, his hand in my hair, eyes on my face.

"I love you," he whispered.

And in that moment, with graduation and finals and my family and his, wedding plans stacking up mountains of stress around us... nothing else mattered.

This.

Us.

It was all that mattered.

Chapter 52

AUGUST
Days until graduation: 5
Days until wedding: 11

Dress. Simple and elegant, with a long train that made me feel glamorous.
Ring. Two-point-five carats of perfection in Brad's custom setting, small diamonds off-setting the large stone.
Something Borrowed. Brad's mother's earrings—emeralds and diamonds shining from my earlobes.
Something Blue. Pale blue lace panties that matched my bra. Humorously virginal in their innocence and delicate structure.
Something Old. My husband, who would certainly be in attendance. Oops, shit. Ignore my adolescent humor. Hmmm … something old. My practically vintage Jimmy Choos, bought at an estate sale Brad and I stumbled upon when driving through his neighborhood one day.
Something New. Everything else. My mind spun with the exorbitant bill this wedding must be racking up. Brad had forbid Rebecca to share any details with me regarding cost, but my eyes could easily pick up the details:

- *Two wedding planners.*
- *The diamond-encrusted ballroom at Fleur De Lis, the only location in town big enough to hold our enormous guest list, while still providing charm and elegance.*
- *A four-tiered wedding cake with custom Tiffany & Co Bride and Groom figurines.*
- *A twelve-piece orchestra for the wedding, two bands for the reception.*
- *A five-course plated dinner with wine pairings for over three hundred guests.*
- *Custom invitations, many sent by tuxedoed courier, to the elite of the elite in the city.*
- *The Favors – mini bottles of Dom Perignon accompanied by gold-leaf boxes of chocolate-covered strawberries.*

It had wandered into the land of ridiculous, an opulent show of wealth that would be performed for individuals I barely knew. It would have been, if you subtracted Brad's family from the equation, my dream wedding. Instead, it felt like I was anchoring myself to Dom Magiano, forever tying my life to his, a partnership with Satan sealed with a kiss and a platinum setting.

Everything had become a countdown, my graduation one small blip in the jewel-encrusted timeline leading up the big day. Little did we know, I would never walk down that rose-covered aisle, that Lohengrin's wedding march would start, the couture-clad guests would turn, and be met by an empty aisle, no bride in sight. It would be a countdown to disappointment.

◆◆◆

Mom and Dad arrived again, their car loaded to the gills with whoknewwhat, checking back into the Holiday Inn that had held them at Christmas. In between classes and studying, I spent as much time as possible with them. I shopped with Mom, picking out bathing suits and cover-ups for my honeymoon, the location of which only he and Rebecca knew. In the evening, I took walks with Dad through downtown, ducking into odd shops and ice cream parlors, while he did little talking, and I chattered away.

It was refreshing to have a final act in the role of daughter, before the title of wife put me fully in the role of grown up. I sucked up their love, their proud smiles and congratulatory words, and pretended, for a few days, that I wasn't hiding a hundred secrets under the gorgeous sweep of my wedding gown.

Still, it loomed. The wedding day, the church divided. The thirty-nine wedding invites that still had outstanding RSVPS. A possible collision of suited gangsters and country bumpkins. I dreaded the casual conversations over finger food, the progression into drinking and dancing, the drinking which would loosen tongues, incite tempers, the potential for violence increasing in the midst of elegance. If something could go wrong, it would. There were too many hidden bombs for one not to explode.

Chapter 53

AUGUST
Graduation day
Days until wedding: 6

I changed upstairs, selecting simple clothing to wear underneath the robes, and was aware, while pulling on a camisole, that I was exhausted, the last five days of double duty between my parents and finals taking its toll on me. Rebecca had become a full-time stalker, bombarding me constantly with wedding details and reminders. Her follow-through had no bounds — if I was in the shower, using the restroom, or studying for finals, she was there, with a question or demand — just the sight of her causing me anxiety.

I had, during the last week, escaped when I could, to the theatre room with Ben or to the pool or bedroom with Brad. They had both been quiet, allowing me to work out my frustration in silence. Or, in the case of Brad, with moans and gasps.

I picked up pearls, looping them around my neck, watching my face in the mirror, willing my tight face to relax. Wondering, as I did, what was going on downstairs. What my mother was saying to

Brad, what pitfalls he was no doubt dodging with ease.

Dealing with the men in my life was so much easier. They were all behaving, content in their roles. It was the women who were being difficult. My mother and Rebecca, who had, after getting along perfectly for eleven months, suddenly found something to argue about. Rebecca, who was now bitching about my mother, bitching about the caterers, bitching about everything and everyone to anyone in earshot. Olivia, who seemed increasingly pissed that I was getting married at all, and Becca, whose sole goal was suddenly the need to create a synchronized dance routine for the wedding party to enter with — a burst of passionate creativity that *no one* else was on board with.

Somehow, in this last week, the wedding, the joining of our souls, had become about everyone else. Maybe it had been building that way for a while. Maybe that was how everyone's weddings were . But now, on graduation day, the wedding still six days away, I was ready for everyone to leave. For my parents to pack their bags and head back to Georgia, for Rebecca to return to her office at the firm, for Olivia to get over herself and accept my marriage. Oh, and for Becca to stop breaking into improvised dance numbers, complete with jazz hands and cheery-ass smiles.

I closed the bedroom door, and took a deep breath, willing peace into my body. I lifted the heavy robe, sliding into it and buttoning the front clasps. I pulled on my cords, blue ropes that signified my ranking on the Dean's List. Then the cap was put on, the archaic indicator of graduation, not improved or fashionized in the last three decades. I smiled in the mirror, an image of peace and academia, proof that reflections could be far from the truth.

There was a knock on the door and my mother's voice, muffled, came through. "Sweetheart, Becca and Olivia just pulled in."

"Okay, I'm coming," I called out. Grabbing my purse, I pasted a smile on my face and opened the door.

♥♥♥

Graduation. I could feel the sweat underneath my knees. The guy to my right twitched his knee in a way that made my chair vibrate, and I fought the urge to reach over and still it. It had been almost three hours, and I had reached a new low in the possible levels of boredom. There were four thousand names, four thousand souls packed into this civic center, four thousand bored, fidgety coeds who were regretting the decision to attend this event. The announcer's voice droned on and more black robes crossed the stage. No streakers, no somersaults across the stage. Nothing to break up the monotony.

Then, the voice stopped, my ears perking up at the silence, an audible sigh of relief rolling through the audience. I reached for my diploma, noting that freedom was close, the president making only a brief closing statement before concluding the event. Celebration. We threw our caps, a sea of black rising and then raining down. Then, pure bedlam erupted. Everyone moving in different directions, anxious for release, tripping over folding chairs and climbing over rows in a mad rush for the door. My cell rang, vibrating against my side, but the crush of bodies didn't allow me to stop and reach for it. The room was too loud anyway. I needed to get outside and then I could check my phone.

When I finally escaped, my feet hitting concrete, the summer heat and humidity caused my clothes to stick against my skin, sweat dripping down my lower back. I moved with the crowd, headed for the parking lot, looking for and finding Brad and my parents under the shade of a large palm tree. His eyes were scanning, worry on his face, and I waved to catch his eye.

"Hey," I said, swept into a hug by his strong arms.

"There are too many people. You should have answered your phone."

"I couldn't," I said tartly. "It was too loud and crowded in there." I hugged my parents, posing for two quick photos before insisting that we leave, my body becoming a full-time sweat machine. I texted Becca and Olivia, and we headed for the house.

♥♥♥

Finally. I lay back in the sun. I was wrong. There was still goodness in this world. Maybe walking across that stage actually helped. Accepting that diploma, which now lay somewhere on the floorboard of Brad's car, the proof that I had accomplished something. Closed one piece of my life. Lifted a layer of stress from my shoulders.

All I knew was that I felt great. A paper plate beside me, the remnants of a steak and a gnawed cob of corn, some of Martha's potato salad sharing space with a speck of lemon pie. Olivia and I had swapped out turns manning the blender, churning out margaritas and daiquiris, the combination of iced alcohol and good food comforting in my stomach. From behind me I heard a snore that was most definitely my father's, his and Mom's chaise lounges set up in the shade. I grinned, twitching my toes to the reggae that Becca had chosen to play, and felt the last of my stress, for a few peaceful hours, lift away.

One more week. Then the wedding would be over, my family would leave, and I could relax with Brad, content in marital bliss, all cares and concerns gone, sunscreen application and sexual satisfaction my only obligations.

Chapter 54

10:00 p.m. I sat in my room, the smell of cardboard mingling with the stale air of a room half empty, a sea of open boxes surrounding me. I had sent my parents to the hotel three hours earlier, the rehearsal concluding with brisk efficiency, our choice to forego a traditional follow-up dinner a decision I greatly appreciated. Now, alone, I had turned off the radio and packed in silence, appreciating the peace and quiet. Fold, wrap, pack. This year had been so crazy, changing my life in so many ways. I searched my soul for doubts or uneasiness about the life-changing step I was about to take. But I had complete faith in my decision. The Magiano threat to my life was what had accelerated our relationship, caused the premature engagement. At that moment, when I had accepted Brad's proposal, I knew I loved him. I knew no man would ever be able to compete, to compare, with him. But I didn't know if I was making the right decision. I didn't know if our initial infatuation would have legs, if a foundation could be built to support a lifetime of commitment. I had needed this year. Needed to find my place in the relationship, needed to know Brad would yield control at times, respect my opinion, allow me to maintain my identity in the face of his strength.

He had amazed me, challenging me when I needed it, knowing instinctively when to push and when to pull. With every day, I was more secure in my decision. There was nothing I wanted more than to walk down that aisle and become Brad's wife. And soon, it would happen. Brad, Holy Matrimony, and me.

I pulled out a Sharpie, labeling the cardboard box in front of me with neat block writing. *Yearbooks.* I was close to being done, only three or four boxes left. My DVDs, my accessories, and an assortment of crap that I should probably be throwing away, instead of carefully packing in cardboard boxes, bound for a shelf in Brad's garage.

I stretched, listening to the quiet of the house. The air conditioner, an ancient oversized unit that had wheezed and moaned its way through the summer coughed, raspy air expelled through its vents. That, and the noises of my own movement were the only sounds in the house. The boys had, in typical Friday fashion, gone out, Alex, and then Zach, stopping by my room, hugging me awkwardly before departing. They had been invited to the wedding but were not attending, both inventing a creative excuse that was completely unnecessary. I was secretly pleased they were hitting the bars tonight. The alternative would have placed them on our couch, weed smoke curling through the air followed by thumping bass, then unannounced guests. There would be music and laughter and arguments, and no chance for me to have a clear thought or good night's sleep.

I could have just stayed at Brad's. Packed my meager belongings and then drove over. But I wanted this night, this goodbye to my old life. Plus, I was a traditionalist—at least when it came to this. The day of our wedding, Brad would not see me until I walked down the aisle. It was a sticking point that irritated our photographer, Brad, and Rebecca, but I held firm. We needed every bit of good karma surrounding this union. And I would only be married once. I wanted the anticipation and impact of Brad seeing me in my dress.

I heard my phone ring and stood, deftly navigating through piles of clothes until I got to the bedside table and picked up my phone, Brad's number showing up on the screen.

"Hey baby." I smiled as I spoke.

"Hey, my beautiful bride. You all ready to become Mrs. De Luca?"

"Can't wait."

"How's the packing going?"

"Pretty good. I'm almost done, then headed to bed."

"Make sure the alarm is armed."

I smiled. "It is." His fear was unfounded. If anything, the last year had proved that no one was interested in harming me, not as Brad De Luca's fiancée. Might that change when I became a wife? An official member of the crime family? I swallowed the bead of nervousness and returned to my place on the floor.

"And you're not trying to move boxes yourself, right? I'm gonna send someone over tomorrow afternoon to pick up that and your furniture."

I rolled my eyes. "I know. You've told me several times. Don't worry, I have no desire to heft my own boxes just for the hell of it."

"Any chance we can get breakfast? I may need a pep talk, reminder of why I'm leaving my life of bachelordom."

I huffed into the phone. "No pep talk, no breakfast. You can wait 'til noon tomorrow like everyone else."

"But we'll talk in the morning, right?"

"Noon. You made it thirty-odd years without talking to me. You'll survive just fine."

He growled, a sound that drove me crazy with desire. "I love you." His voice was husky, and I smiled.

"I love you, too. See you tomorrow."

"Noon."

"Noon." I hung up the phone with a happy sigh.

♥♥♥

Frustrated with my lack of cooperation in the form of personal security, Brad had focused his resources on Fort Knox-ifying my crappy student dwelling. It was a waste of money considering that the threat to my safety would begin after I moved out, my life only endangered upon my induction into the Magiano family. But maybe it was the thought of danger, or the idea that his family would renege on their promise—whatever the reason, I was surrounded by safety measures. Every window in my house had been replaced with security glass. If the windows were opened, cracked, or broken, an alarm would blare and the police and security firm would be alerted. The same went with exterior doors. A triggered alarm could only be ended with a personal code and a call to the security firm. A panic button was now installed next to my bed, allowing the police to be one short pressure point away. I was, with the best security system money could buy, safe.

Security was only effective when protecting an intelligent individual. My safety was comprised in the simplest way possible.

At 10:46 p.m. my car alarm blared. Three high-pitched sirens and then silence. I looked up from my packing and listened, unsure if the noise I heard had belonged to my SUV. Standing, I crawled onto my bed until I was at the bedroom window, pulling open the blinds and looking out onto our front yard. There, illuminated by our lone street light, sat my X5, parked on the curb, no one in sight. I started to back away from the window when something caught my eye. Leaning in closer, I tried, through dirty glass and a dark yard, to examine my car.

"What the …" I whispered, trying to tell what was on the BMW's windows. Some white marking of some type. *Letters.* I let go of the blinds and hopped off the bed, shoving my feet into shoes and heading for the front door. Disarming the alarm, I stepped outside, taking a few steps into the front yard and looking closer, my eyes widening as I got close enough to see the letters in the dark.

S L U T. In letters big enough to scream, the writing angry in its strokes. I glanced around, seeing only the empty street and walked forward, scared to see what was written on the other side. I reached in my back pocket and pulled out my cell.

I heard a sound from behind, out of place enough to make me turn. Then, a wet cloth came across my face, so tight I couldn't breathe, much less scream. I tried to take a breath, my fingers tried to move across the screen of my phone, tried to…

Oblivion.

Chapter 55

Brad hung up the cell. "She's at home."

"And you don't want to go out."

"We did. We went to Bern's after the rehearsal."

"Bern's?" Stevie shot him a look that communicated everything in one simple glare. "The king of pussy goes to a *steakhouse* before tying the knot." He shook his head.

"I've had pussy. I don't feel the need to jeopardize my relationship for subpar ass."

"Then take us out so we can get some. I'll take subpar over none. And your definition of subpar is another man's dream."

Brad took a long drag of his beer. "You have nothing to bitch about. There were plenty of girls at the party we had last month."

The man snorted. "And guys. A joint bachelor party? I don't understand how you guys can let loose and have fun when the other person is there."

Brad laughed. "Yeah. A couple doing things together. Doomed." He leaned back in the couch. "I hate to break it to you, Stevie, but my life as a slut is over."

"And you seem remarkably calm about it," Ben remarked, walking into the room with fresh beers and passing one to each of them before settling into one of the large leather armchairs.

Brad shrugged. "You know Julia. I don't deserve her as it is. This is the happiest I've ever been."

"I'm not saying it doesn't make sense. I'm just surprised that you recognize it." Ben leaned forward, clinked his beer against Brad's. "You hit a home run with her."

Stevie groaned. "This all is great, but let's at least order a stripper. Get a PG-rated lap dance, and then let me take her upstairs."

"The man owns a strip club. He's not going to get excited about some tits bouncing up and down," Ben said dryly.

"Owned a strip club," Brad said, finishing the bottle and setting it on the counter.

Stevie glanced over. "What the hell are you talking about?"

"Didn't seem like something a husband should have. I signed it over to Julia."

Stevie coughed hard, sitting up and setting his beer on the floor. "Holy shit. You really are whipped."

"Don't give me that. You handed Nikki your balls in a velvet sack on your second date."

The man shrugged. "Hey, she handles them better than anyone else." He stood. "That doesn't mean I'm turning down blowjobs from strangers. I guess I just assumed that if Brad-fucking-De Luca ever froze over hell and got remarried, that he'd go out with a bang." He laughed. "Or five or six bangs, given your reputation."

"Sorry," Brad said shortly. "Guess Ben will have to be the new wild man." He leaned forward, clapped the man on the back and stood. "Martha made some carrot cake this afternoon. You guys want some?"

They moved to the kitchen, Stevie bitching the whole way about the unnaturalness of cake at a bachelor party, before pouring a big glass of milk to drink. They drank, ate, smoked cigars on the porch, and then crashed, the two men heading to the guest bedrooms while Brad climbed the stairs to spend his final night as a bachelor, alone in his big bed. He glanced at the clock. 1:35 a.m. Too late to call, but he needed to hear her. Already missed her. He rolled over in the silent dark and tried to fall asleep.

The seven month old BMW X5 4.41 was wrapped in plastic and loaded onto a vehicle transporter, along with other cars of questionable origin. It left town less than two hours after Julia Campbell's capture, traveling north on a busy interstate, headed for Canada.

Chapter 56

WEDDING DAY

I woke up in pure blackness, my senses reengaging one by one, slowly reporting grim details of my surroundings. *Sight.* Pure dark, so complete in its entirety that I felt a wave of claustrophobia hit me. *Sound.* Muffled voices, hard tones filled with anger, hate, and — most terrifying of all — glee. The rustle of fabric against my ear as I twisted my head, the sound informing my brain that I was, in fact, blindfolded. *Smell.* A sickly, sweet scent, coming from the blindfold, almost, but not quite, overriding the dirty, masculine stench that reeked in this room. *Taste.* Wet cloth in my mouth, tugging at my skin, keeping my tongue in place, the horrible aftertaste of vomit in my mouth. *Touch.* Hands bound behind my back with rough, scratchy rope. Ankles spread and secured to chair legs beneath me. Sitting upright, utterly secured, my body recognizing, even without sight, the bruises that covered me.

My brain understood everything about the situation immediately, bursting into reality in one, horrific instance, like stepping into the harsh sun, painful in its strength. I screamed through the cloth, my effort producing only a small sound, and strained every muscle, thrashing my body from side to side, trying to free some small part of my body in at least one minor way. The chair rocked, tipped, and in an agonizingly slow motion, tipped back and crashed to the concrete floor. The impact slammed my head backward, and with one painful crack, my body stilled, all senses instantly snuffed.

◆◆◆

I was taken for a reason. To win a battle, a battle of control and emotions and pride. Step one was to take me. Step two involved making sure I would never be a part of the Magiano family. That step could be accomplished in two ways, one of which was death. The other option's viability would depend on how I reacted to my capture.

I did not react well.

Chapter 57

"Did I miss something?" Becca barged through the doors of Noche with a ferocity that startled half the women in the spa's lobby.

Olivia shot her a look of warning. "Stop yelling. This is the type of place where you whisper."

"Ten, right? I checked my text messages. We were going to meet here at eleven. Look." She thrust her cell out, forcing Olivia's eyes to focus on it. "Hair and makeup appointment at eleven at Noche. From that scary ass assistant of Brad's. Did you get one?"

"Lower your freaking voice," Olivia hissed, sending an apologetic look to the woman to her right. "Yes, I got one. And I talked with Julia last night. She said she'd be here."

"So where is she?" Becca didn't wait for a response, she pressed a button and held the phone to her ear. "I'm calling her again. She hasn't responded to my texts."

Their names were called, and they stood, Becca taking a long look at the clock before following the uniformed attendant through the frosted doors. 10:19 a.m. Julia was late.

As they walked through the quiet hall, Becca's phone buzzed, her eyes catching on the lit screen and reading the message quickly, then passing it to Olivia.

I won't make it to Noche. I need time to think. I'll call you later.

Their eyes met in the dim light, and Becca frowned.

◆◆◆

White uniforms converged on Fleur De Lis like maggots, bits of white weaving with a rapid pace through the stone halls, placing gloved hands on every available surface. Flower arrangements were wheeled in, tablecloths ironed, place cards straightened, then straightened again by nervous fingers. Corsages were pinned, bobby pins placed in curled hair, and wedding programs were unwrapped and placed in the hands of eager ushers. The final moments were completed in an orderly and excited fashion, everything unfolding exactly as to plan. And, an hour before the ceremony was to begin, limos began the slow, precise journey through the front gates. The guests were starting to arrive.

The world ran on appearances, and that day was no exception. Brad disagreed with that mandate, but you had to play the game to win it, so he played along. And, as usual, he seemed predestined to win, the details handled perfectly by Rebecca and the two wedding planners' capable and expensive hands. And, as he glanced through the open doorway off the lobby, everything seemed in place. *Just missing one thing.* He moved into the drawing room, set off to the side of the chapel and scowled, settling into one of the high stools. Lucas walked over with a smile, moving around behind the bar. He poured a shot of whiskey and held it out.

"Bottoms up."

Brad shook his head, sliding his phone in his pocket.

"What's wrong? Pre-wedding jitters?"

The comment earned Lucas a scornful look, and Brad stood and walked to the window. "Can't get ahold of her."

"Julia? She told you — you couldn't see her today."

"I want to talk to her. Hear her voice."

"Brad. The ceremony's in an hour. Then you'll have the rest of your life to talk to her. Relax and take a damn shot."

"I can't just sit here. The waiting is driving me crazy. Let's head outside, Stevie is down there." He stood, shouldering into his tuxedo jacket.

"If I didn't know any better, I'd think you were nervous."

Brad met his eyes. "When it comes to Julia, I'm always nervous."

Chapter 58

"It seems a little early to panic." Olivia's voice rang out in the lavender-tinted room, causing six updo'd heads to turn her way.

"Early?" one of the wedding planners said, her over-plucked eyebrows coming to a point in the middle of her lined forehead.

"It's eleven-thirty," the other planner said anxiously, as if everyone in the room wasn't aware of the hour. "The ceremony starts in thirty minutes. And no one knows where she is. A bride, missing from the wedding ..." She started to breathe quickly, in terse gasps, on the verge of what appeared to be a nervous breakdown.

"She cancelled on us for hair and makeup," Becca said flatly, shooting Olivia a look, their argument already hours in the making.

"Which would make sense if she ..." Olivia shrugged suggestively as the words dropped off.

"If she what?" Becca shot back.

"I'm just saying ..." Olivia said airily, "maybe she changed her mind. Decided she was making a mistake."

"Making a mistake?" The female linebacker, who worked for Brad, stepped forward, her arms crossing in front of her ample chest. "Making a mistake by getting married? Have you *been* in the same room with them? Spoken to either one of them in the last year? They were made for each other; I've never seen two people more perfectly matched. Not to mention this is Brad-*Fucking*-De Luca. Women don't 'change their mind' about Brad, they hunt him down like rabid animals." She snarled the final words, now officially inside of Olivia's bubble, her teeth bared and claws out.

Olivia wilted slightly, glancing away and studying her fresh manicure. "I'm *just* saying that we could give it a little more time. You already drove by her house. She's not home so she's probably on her way here."

"I think we should tell Brad," Martha spoke from her post at the window.

"No," the two planners spoke in unison, panic crossing their faces. One stepped forward. "It's common for brides to flake. It's better that the groom doesn't know. It can taint the ceremony for him, or cause a fight right before the wedding."

The room was silent, her logic making sense. Rebecca nodded. "Brad will lose it if he knows."

"So what do we do?" Julia's mother spoke from her seat in the center of the room, her features tight, mouth pinched.

"We wait. We wait for her to show up. She'll show up," Becca spoke from the doorway, and it was the last words spoken for a while, no one having a better solution to offer.

Chapter 59

Rebecca knew this was bad. This was beyond bad. She ground into nothing the soft napkin, the one with Brad & Julia perfectly printed, just as she'd wished. It seemed ridiculous that she'd ever cared. Why did napkins matter when a bride was missing? And it didn't matter what the bimbo in the other room thought. Julia wasn't flaking out. It was impossible. She wasn't *that* kind of girl. And Brad wasn't the kind of man who got left at the altar. Something was wrong, she could feel it in her gut. She looked at her cell and wondered, for the thirtieth time that day, if she should call Brad.

♦♦♦

Debra Campbell paced, her heels snagging on the carpet when her steps got too hurried.

"Please, dear. Sit."

"I can't sit. Something is wrong. I should have known it earlier. Her not returning our calls this morning?"

"She's always hard to get ahold of by phone." The man stood, stopping his wife's journey with firm hands, pulling her over to a loveseat and pushing her down. "Your blood pressure has to be sky high. Please. Panic isn't helping."

His touch grounded her, as it always had. She took a trembling breath, reached out and gripped his hand. "She wouldn't stand him up, would she?" There was hope in the last word. Hope that her daughter was abandoning this marriage. A humorous development, considering she had been thanking her lucky stars just one day prior. Julia had done well. Her new husband was successful. Adored the ground she walked on. Would do anything to make her happy. But now, there were only two possibilities. Something was terribly wrong, or Julia had cold feet. She prayed for the latter.

Her husband held her gaze steadily, more moisture in his eyes than she had seen in quite some time. "I don't know, Debra. I really don't know."

Down the hall, there was the sound of shouting, and she wiped her eyes. "Let's go back. See if anyone's heard anything."

Chapter 60

She was not responding. They had found her on the floor, still tied to the chair, a pool of blood around her head. One man had panicked, calling the man who shouldn't have been called. And now they stood, in a circle around her body, repeatedly checking for a pulse and untying her limbs. They carried her to a bed, a bed that had already hosted its share of dead bodies, and prayed that hers wouldn't join the ranks. If she was to die, it was only by his order. Now was not the time, and failure was unacceptable.

◆◆◆

In actuality, I never had a chance to walk down that aisle. It was never in the cards, plans made to remove me from the equation long before I ever tried on wedding dresses, long before invitations were sent. I don't think dramatics was their intention. Perhaps they thought that snatching me the night before would be enough advance notice to hold the ceremony—to call guests and cancel the event. As it happened, my absence was not discovered in time, and even then, was suspected to be a case of pre-wedding cold feet.

◆◆◆

"Can we panic now?" Rebecca screamed into Olivia's face, grabbing her shoulders and shaking her roughly, the girl's thin body shaking like wet spaghetti. "It is *time*, the guests are seated, and they are about to start the damn music!"

"Stop yelling at me! It's not my fault she isn't here!"

"Who called her cell last?" one of the wedding planners asked anxiously.

"I did," Julia's mother said, wrapping her sweater tightly around her shoulders. "Her voicemail is full."

The strands of music almost missed their ears, drifting among the room casually, weaving easily between their strained words. The second planner looked up with a stricken look. "Oh my God. They're starting." She fumbled for her sleeve, pushing back the material to reveal a watch face. "Early." She fled the room, her heels clattering down the hallway.

The room sat in silence, the chords of the song changing as it reached its crescendo.

Becca finally spoke. "So ... what do we do?"

The remaining wedding planner spoke. "We go. Just like we planned. It'll take ten minutes to do the procession. We'll just have to pray she shows up."

◆◆◆

"She's breathing," the man spoke rapidly, and the doctor shot him an irritated look.

"I'm well aware of that; I did attend medical school. Please back up and let me examine her."

"I'm just saying, she must have only been out for a few minutes. I think she's just sleeping now. Might still be from the chloroform. If she's breathing then she's not dead, right? And we checked for a pulse—it seems … present."

The doctor bit back a sarcastic response and started his examination. "It means she's not dead *yet*. That could all change quickly depending on what is going on with her brain. At the minimum, we're talking a concussion. What are these?" He ran his fingers lightly over a bandage on her shoulder, blood staining its edges.

"We cut her. With a knife. When we found her on the floor. Some thought she was faking. But she didn't flinch." He chewed at the edge of his cuticle nervously.

The doctor raised his eyebrows but said nothing, moving to the front of her body and lifting her head slightly, his fingers gently probing the wound on the back of her head.

"Best I can tell: she was unconscious when you found her. You're right in that she is sleeping—that can be from her concussion. Her pupils show that she was sedated recently, that she might have just gained consciousness recently before her head trauma. The drugs are still in her system, and could partially account for her state. But head trauma is a messy and unpredictable animal. Normally, I'd do a CT or MRI scan. But I'm assuming that this is a situation where you don't want her to be moved?" He glanced at the men, one giving a silent nod. "Well, I don't want to put any more drugs in her system. From the looks of the wound, and the fact that she is sleeping right now, the impact on her skull was pretty severe. All we can do is wait, and let me talk to her when she wakes up. A concussion can be deadly, but we'll know in a few hours if you'll have another body to deal with." He pulled off his latex gloves and dropped them in the closest trashcan. "I've got to get back to the house. Call me if anything changes."

"Thanks, Doc."

Hands were shaken and the doctor left, leaving the two men alone with her, their eyes meeting above her body, silent communication passing between them.

"The boss is gonna be pissed."

"Not if she pulls through. You still got her phone?"

"Yeah. Lots of calls and texts. Should I respond to any more of them?"

"No. Drive a few miles away and kill it. I'll watch her. Talk to the boss while you're gone. Feel out the situation."

There was a silent power struggle, and then the man spoke, "Okay. I'll be back soon. Call me if she wakes up." He glanced at the girl, then back at the man. "I'll be back soon."

"And I'll be here."

Chapter 61

Brad exhaled, his hands clasped before him, the collar on his tux scratchy. Finally. Fourteen months after she had walked into his office. Thirteen months after she had broken in and stolen his heart. The year-long engagement had dragged on, punctuated by empty nights where she stayed at her house, nights he realized how much he wanted and needed her to be his wife. He felt lost without her—incomplete—like he was missing out on something incredible. She had become, in those twelve months, his best friend as well as soul mate, the power of their relationship terrifying in its perfection. And now, finally, he would have security. Would have the strength of their marriage. A message to his family and to the world that they were, and always would be, together. Musical chords began, the orchestra gradually joining in, bit by bit, until the entire ensemble was participating, their notes rising in a strong crescendo. His heart swelled along with the music, until he thought it would burst, and he smiled despite himself, a break in the dam that they had reached this day safely.

The doors opened and the wedding procession began, Julia's mother entering to the tones of Bach.

Had Brad paid any attention during the procession, he would have noticed the tight faces of the women, their hands clenched around their bouquets, worried glances flitting from one bridesmaid to the next. But he didn't pay attention to them. He stared, fixated on the large arched entrance, and waited. Waited for Lohengrin's March to begin and for the love of his life to appear.

Tones played, and he worked through the processional schedule in his mind, trying to sort through how many more individuals would walk through that arch before Julia. It had to be soon, her mother and bridesmaids having already made the slow walk. His palms sweated as he stared at the space, waited for her to appear. A small blonde appeared, Catalina, his niece, throwing petals into the air with happy abandon, a small tuxedoed boy at her side. The presence of Catalina reminded him that Julia was next, rose petals an indication of her pending arrival.

The music changed, familiar notes beginning, the announcement of the bride. The audience turned as one, a hushed silence falling over the room. He attempted to breathe slowly, attempted a calm veneer, but couldn't stop his mouth, grinning widely. This was one of those moments that defined — one of the few moments in his life where he was certain he was in the right place, at the right time.

The music continued, the audience waited. Waited. Strands floating through the air, the rise and fall of notes sweet and perfect in their promise. There was uneasy movement through the audience, heads turning, voices whispering. Then the notes ended, silence fell, the doorway remained empty, and Brad's world ended.

Silence. It was often the worst and loudest sound in the world.

◆◆◆

The time at which my body chose to wake was an unfortunate one. Or very fortunate, however you chose to view it. It's said that when your brain reawakens, its initial moments are perfectly clear, superhuman in their speed of thought, the brain pure before it is again bogged down by thoughts, worries, and unnecessary details. I awoke to the sound of a zipper, my legs spread, my lower body naked in a cold room. I opened my eyes, looking at a stained tile ceiling and bright fluorescent lights. I felt a hand, the palm calloused and rough, grip my thigh, felt something brush against my mound and I tensed in response, my mind shuddering through recent events as understanding of my situation suddenly came into focus.

I did not move, I did not scream. I waited, my eyes closing, and tried to ignore the events happening below my waist. My mind shuffled the cards of Ben's training, picking up and discarding different defensive strategies. I listened, trying to figure out if anyone else was in the room. But all I could hear was one, his hard breaths, the slick sounds of his hand as he prepared himself for entrance. He seemed to be in a hurry and suddenly reached up, leaning forward as he pulled my shirt up, over my breasts, his free hand roughly gripping a breast in one hand. The change in position, the hand suddenly within my grasp, changed everything, my mind focusing on the golden opportunity that was suddenly presented.

Chapter 62

Brad moved, taking the steps quickly, moving down the aisle, crushing delicate petals in his wake, strides increasing as he passed through the crowd, fixated on and anxious to get through that arch and into the arms of his bride. His mind struggled with the possibilities that were battling for attention—all of the reasons why she hadn't walked down that aisle.

He burst through the opening, entering the ornate lobby, his eyes skimming over the few individuals there, looking for a white dress, then her face, then any sign that would point him to her. A blonde stepped forward, clipboard in hand, a tight face that screamed 'problem.' He focused on her, recognizing her features: one of the overpaid wedding planners Rebecca had insisted on. "Where is she?"

"She … ahh …" Her hands flapped nervously, a clipboard still in one hand, creating a puff of air. He had the urge to grab them, submit them into stillness.

"Where is she?!"

"We don't know. We haven't seen her this morning, and she isn't answering her phone." The calm voice behind him caused him to turn, and he looked to a brunette with a direct stare. *The other planner.* This one seemed to have a hold on her emotions, something he appreciated.

"And no one planned on telling me?"

"We thought it was cold feet. It still could be. It's common, though the brides normally arrive by the start of the wedding."

"It's not that. She wouldn't do that." And she wouldn't. If Julia was having second thoughts, or had decided not to wed, she would have told him. Communication had never been a problem between them, even if they didn't like what the other person had to say. He pulled out his phone and called the police.

Holding the phone away from his mouth, he spoke to the woman. "Get the bridesmaids. Have them call her roommates and find out when they saw her last. And get all of these people out of here."

She nodded and turned, walking off with quick and efficient strides. Stevie walked in and Brad snapped his fingers, catching his attention. Covering the phone with his hand, he communicated everything to Stevie in one determined look. "My father. Find out where he is."

Chapter 63

A. Arm Across. I moved, wrapping my legs around his torso and pulling him tightly to my body, my left hand grabbing his right arm and shoving it across his body. He fell toward me, his eyes meeting mine in surprise.

S. Scoot away. I moved quickly, sliding my body away from him, pushing him down my chest. He swung his free arm upward, but the additional space made him unable to reach my face.

L. Leg over his shoulder. Putting his trapped arm in my other hand I waited until he reached back with his free hand and then I swung my leg over his shoulder, his head now trapped between my legs. He gritted his teeth, glaring at me, struggling to free himself.

Brazilian Jujitsu was developed with one main focus: to allow smaller and weaker practitioners to defeat much larger and stronger opponents, using leverage in ways that couldn't be overcome by strength or size. I had practiced this move for five months, able to easily submit Brad, a man of massive proportions and strength. This man, a hundred and seventy pounds of coward, caught off-guard and unprepared, was a cakewalk.

A. Ankle. I released his hand and grabbed my raised ankle, tucking it under my other leg and tightened my legs, causing a scissoring motion to occur on his neck.

P. Press Head. Pressing down on his head, I squeezed my legs.

The triangle choke did not kill through asphyxiation; instead it restricted blood flow to the head while making breathing difficult, causing the victim to pass out. I held tightly, unable to see his eyes, staring at the top of his head, a head that struggled, his free arm reaching but unable to inflict damage, and knew the minute that unconsciousness hit, his entire body going limp against me. I continued the hold, using the time to look around the room, taking my first assessment of the space. It was a small room, consisting of the bed we now laid on and little more. White linoleum floors, one metal folding chair, a squat counter, trash littering its surface. The door to the room was closed, giving me no clue into what lay behind it or if it was locked. I had two options at this point: release the man, giving myself anywhere between thirty seconds and a minute before he would gain consciousness; or, I could maintain the hold for another four minutes, until his brain starved for oxygen and he died.

I tightened the hold and waited, starting a slow countdown in my head.

◆◆◆

Very few people have held the life of another in their hands. Have had the horrific opportunity of choosing whether someone lived or died. I had no desire to kill this man. Horribly maim and disfigure him, yes. Lock him away in prison, yes. Death was a sentence I was not equipped to give. And four minutes was a long time to contemplate, a long time to calculate the time I would need to escape. But thirty seconds to escape, when facing a closed door, with no idea of what was on the other side — it was not enough time. So my choice was clear. Save him or save myself.

One minute. I looked down; the only part of the man visible was the top of his head. Spiky hair, thin enough that I could see pale skin underneath. I wondered if he had a family. If I was killing an innocent child's father. I closed my eyes, forced myself to breathe, and counted. Listened hard to see if I heard anyone. Four minutes was a long time. I could be putting myself at risk waiting that long. Maybe it'd be smarter to stop. To release him and run like hell. Pray that a clean exit lay on the other side of that door.

Two minutes. My arms were tired. I had a cramp in my right bicep, a cramp that was screaming for attention. I shifted slightly, trying to find a more comfortable position, and second-guess my plan. I was *killing* this man. This was not a movie, or a book. He was dying, the life leaving him with each passing second, and would never wake up again. Would never hug his wife, or kiss his daughter. Would I be able to handle this? Was this one move that would mentally fuck me up for the rest of my life? And how selfish was I that my main concern, while killing someone, was about the physiological impact on myself? I focused on my breathing and told my whiny bicep to man the fuck up. I forced myself to slow my counting, and listen, but could hear nothing from outside the door.

Three minutes. Who did this man work for? Why was I taken? I thought I was safe, a non-issue. I thought Brad's family would stay away, and any slight risk from outsiders would start after my marriage. *I can't do it.* No matter who this man was, what his purpose, I couldn't kill him. Maybe I wasn't mentally strong enough. Maybe I wasn't cruel enough. Three minutes had been long enough. Long enough for him to still live.

I moved before I could second-guess the decision, shoved his weight off my body, his mass hitting the floor with a dull sound. I avoided his face, avoided the slack expression of unconsciousness staring accusingly out at me. I sat up, swinging my legs off the bed, testing the stability of my limbs before standing. My head roared with pain, my throat was dry, and I was still naked from the waist down. I glanced over and saw gray fabric, my pants from last night, bunched in a heap on the floor, purple panties peeking out of the sweats. I yanked the clothing on, rushing to the door and twisting the knob, letting out a moan of relief when it turned. I hesitated, unsure of what lay on the other side, then yanked hard, bursting through the door and into an empty hallway.

Twenty seconds.

I ran, worn linoleum underneath, my eyes picking up and processing items as I moved. I seemed to be underground, the hall artificially lit, the rooms I passed windowless and dark. It was almost empty, my eyes picking up on offices and storage rooms flying past. I saw the sign for a stairwell and flung open the door, headed up the empty stairwell, my bare feet quiet on concrete steps. As I climbed, I thought, trying to plan some sort of strategy if I encountered someone. I had no weapon, no phone, weak arms and legs, exhausted from four minutes of exertion. It was a depressing equation my brain had no solution for.

I reached the first floor landing and said a silent prayer, pressing on the door. I moved through it into a short hallway and was then in an open space, some sort of a showroom, display boards lining faux walls, multiple kitchens and bathrooms back to back, carpet samples and tile choices covering a center open space. I turned, scanning, looking for the one thing I needed: an exit.

Ten seconds. Then I heard it. Salvation and damnation in one moment—a door opening, an electronic chime announcing its movement. *Someone's here.*

I ducked, crawling on all fours until I was in a kitchen, an impressive Viking stove in between me and the door. I waited, holding my breath, listening to the sound of footsteps across the floor, casual and unhurried, the rustle of a plastic bag accompanying them. My lungs bursting, I inhaled slowly, trying to mask the sound with my hands. Then I heard the stairwell door open, banging shut on its return trip. It had taken me less than fifteen seconds to run through those halls and up those stairs. His trip would be slower, leisurely in its steps, but short all the same, meaning I needed to move *now*. I ran, heading for the door, almost weeping when it came into view, my hands slipping as they reached for the bar, yanking hard on the metal. A loud clang sounded through the room, the sound of metal hitting unyielding metal, the door barely budging. *Locked.*

Chapter 64

"Your fiancée is missing, on her wedding day, and you wanna talk to the police chief?" The woman's voice drawled through the phone, skepticism lacing every word.

"Yes. This is Brad De Luca, he will want to take my call."

"I don't care *who* you are—if you and the chief are such close buds, then call his cell. This is a line reserved for *emergencies,* not your girlfriend who decided not to walk down the aisle."

"I did call his cell, and left a message."

She snorted. "Then I guess he *don't* want to take your call."

"Goddammit, this is not a case of a runaway bride. This is foul play. Page. The. Chief."

"Missing. Persons. Require. Twenty-four hours. Unless you got a bloody scene you wanna point us to, you need to call back *after* twenty-four hours have passed. I'll leave a note for the chief with your number. If he wants to call you back before then, he can."

He gritted his teeth, releasing a string of expletives when she ended the call. He turned, seeing his father before him, Stevie by his side. So the man *had* shown up.

"Is there a problem, Brad?"

"Come with me," he said tightly, striding past the pair.

They moved, a staggered group of three, his father taking his time and depending heavily on his cane, his back erect and head up as he walked carefully behind Brad. They moved into a rectory office, Brad closing the door behind his father and waiting until he took a seat to speak.

"I don't care how you do it, I don't care if we kill half the city and bribe every street thug in a ten-mile radius, but you find her NOW. Put a hundred thousand dollar bounty on her alive head."

His father chuckled, his hand caressing the head of his cane. "Suddenly you are a fan of our work? You have mocked us for years, yet now need our help?" He tilted his head shrewdly, his eyes meeting Brad's. "I told you the girl wouldn't last, that she didn't care. And now? What if I say no to your demand?

"You won't."

The air grew hot as the two men regarded each other, one calm and composed, the other a bundle of electric heat. "Don't test me, son."

"Don't test *me*. You have no idea of what I would do for her."

♥♥♥

I pushed and pulled on the doors handle in disbelief, panic flooding like hot liquid through me. *Locked*. I fumbled, my hands finding an upper deadbolt and I flipped it, trying the door again and almost crying with relief when it moved, pulling open, the announcement chime reminding me that I needed to get the fuck outta Dodge.

Daylight. I was instantly relieved and afraid, the sun exposing me in the worst way possible. My bare feet flew down a broken sidewalk, my eyes looking everywhere, alighting on an industrial street, warehouses and closed businesses lining its streets. Saturday. It was, unless I had slept through days, Saturday. Someplace had to be open. What place could I trust?

I was open, exposed, the lone individual on the street, and I searched for a side street, a place to hide. I was suddenly afraid to stop a stranger, should I encounter one, my paranoia not knowing whom to trust. *Escape*. I needed to put distance between my prison and myself. Any moment the door could burst open behind me. Any moment I could be back in that room. From somewhere to my left, I heard an engine roar, the chirp of tires as a sharp corner was turned at too fast of a speed. I ran up the steps of a closed tire store and hid behind a large UPS drop box. The car slowed, a white truck driving past without stopping, my ears telling me what my eyes could not — they had not seen me, or they didn't care about a barefoot girl tucked in an filthy doorway.

I waited until the engine sound faded, then stood, stepping back onto the sidewalk and running as fast as I could, the beat of my feet not catching up with the pounding of my heart.

◆◆◆

The criminal underbelly came to life in a citywide search for Julia Campbell. Her photo was circulated, her plate number scribbled down on the back of receipts and stuffed into dirty pockets, mingling with stale cigarettes and loose change. The price on her head was high, especially for a non-felony action. Find a beautiful brunette and deliver her to De Luca. Piece of cake for the lucky man who stumbled upon her. The fact that she was a future Magiano had no effect. Money was money, and a hundred grand was a universal motivator.

The man came to on a dirty floor, his shoulders shaken roughly, a familiar face in his line of sight. "Wake the fuck up!" He blinked, the urgency in the man's voice letting him know that something was wrong. But what? Something had happened. Something… fuck. He pushed the man off, reaching out—pushing off the floor, trying to stand, trying to stop the spin of the room—but failed. He fell to his knees, held his head, and tried to think.

"Where is she?" the man's hoarse voice broke through his fog.

"I don't know," he gritted out. "Find her."

The man above him straightened, moving quickly to the doorway and out of sight. The man blinked, his senses returning, the fog lifting. He rose slowly and walked forward, gained stability on his legs as he moved out of the room and into the hall. Pulling his cell from his pocket, he took the time to re-zip his pants, buckle his belt, his mind working through what this would mean, the consequences that would occur if she was not found. He glanced in doorways as he walked, unsure of where to go, upstairs or downstairs, every dark room a place where she could be hiding. Then the call was answered and he stopped, his mind and feet coming to a resolute silence. "We have a problem."

He explained the situation, and then waited, making a decision and jogging up the stairwell steps.

The man on the other end spoke. "I'm sending a team. Stay in the building, make sure it is locked, and search every inch of it. Pull the security tapes and find out what happened. Get your head on straight and fucking tell me something other than that she's gone. Call me when you know more."

The call was ended, a dead silence meeting his ears. He stood in the hallway, perspiring despite the cool air. *He shouldn't have touched her. Should have sat in that room, gun in hand, and watched.* He took a few slow steps, moving toward the electrical room, where the security tapes should grant some explanation of recent events. How long he was out, where she had gone. He should be more aware, but his feet felt heavy, sluggish, like lead was in his shoes. The girl could be anywhere. He could be killed next, his steps never making the complete path to the electrical room. He wondered distractedly if this was what the steps of the damned felt like. Because he was certainly the one the blame would come to rest on. And in this organization, as the case with others, blame always came with consequences.

Chapter 65

The inability to do anything was paralyzing, wrapping a fist around Brad's heart and squeezing the life out of it. He had bribed, threatened, and begged every contact he knew, questioned Julia's roommates, friends, and neighbors, searching for anything, any observation or piece of information that might bring her back to him. Late afternoon he had finally spoken to the chief, had gotten them to place a trace on the last signal her phone had sent out. The location had come back on the north side of town, in a residential area that had no connections to anything. They searched and found the phone crushed and tossed on the side of the road, no prints on it. Brad had lost it at the news, punching the closest wall repeatedly until his hand was a mess of blood. He should have overpowered her request, put the damn tracker on her SUV. He had bought the BMW for her; it wouldn't have been that ridiculous to insist that it be traceable. But she had refused, her face strong, eyes fiery, a stubbornness to her posture that he found irresistible. So he had yielded, letting her have her way, a decision that might cost her life.

Their family had too many enemies, the possibilities for who had taken her too great. But the logic behind it was questionable. He had assumed she was safe as his fiancée; he had been slack in protection coverage because it made no sense for another family to cause her harm. Once married to him, as time progressed and different families warred with the Magianos, there would be times when their life would be at greater risk than others. Diminished risk, since he was estranged from the family, but risk all the same. But right now was a time of peace, everyone coloring inside the lines and minding their own business. For a family to make waves and take a woman, a woman on her wedding day, one who was marrying an estranged member of the most powerful crime family in the city … the elements were all wrong.

It could be a random crime, one of thousands that occurred each week in the city. Young, attractive women disappeared every day, most never to resurface, sold in the sex trade or killed and disposed of. Another possibility, one he had fought with, defended against entry to his mind, was that his family was involved. The shepherd eliminating new sheep from entrance to the flock. That should not be a possibility. His father had promised to leave her alone, and had never broken a promise before. In their family, their word was everything. That was why he typically despised the words coming out of his father's mouth. Because they were ugly in their truth, indicative of his father's real and rotten nature. Now, with that history of truth, he refused to believe that his father threw away a lifetime of 'honor' over one twenty-two year old girl.

Then again, Julia had disrespected him. Stood her ground and spoke to him in a manner no one else had dared in over three decades. Anyone who had was now dead. She had been a slap in his face from the moment she had entered his life. They had, with this marriage, forced his acceptance of her. And Dom Magiano didn't like to be forced into anything. So, with all that considered, maybe he had acted. Maybe he had thrown his honor aside for a slice of vengeance. Brad sent a silent prayer upward, making promises he couldn't keep, trying to bribe The One who couldn't be bribed. *Anything to get her back.* Anything.

Chapter 66

My feet tired first, not from the exercise, but from injury. They were raw, dirt caking into cuts from gravel, rough cement, and small pebbles on pavement. I ran on sidewalks when I could, stopping frequently to hide when a car passed. I needed to find a minivan—a minivan driven by an overweight soccer mom with three adorable kids, preferably listening to Christian music. But minivans didn't pass through this part of town. This was the area of truck stops, seedy gas stations, lumberyards, and warehouses. At one point I saw a cab, two blocks over, moving slowly through the streets, its top light off. I hesitated, then let it pass. Paranoia dominated my thoughts, every person, car, and business a trap, designed to catch me and deliver me back to those who wished me harm. To make everything worse, my headache, dull when I had woken, was now a full-fledged jackhammer, the pain causing occasional spots in my vision and a piercing pain when I would lean over to rest. I had vomited twice, the horrible aftertaste residing in my dry mouth, and was thirsty, my throat and body begging for liquid of some sort. I eyed puddles as I passed, their dark pools dotted with oil and waste, cursing the lack of public water fountains in industrial areas. In addition to my head and my feet, my shoulder throbbed, every swing of my arms stretching a muscle that screamed in response.

There was a bandage there, the adhesive on its edges pulling on my skin, and my mind itched with the desire to pull it off, to reveal whatever it was that it hid. But I didn't. I ran, I hid, I ran, and I thirsted.

I headed toward the sound of quiet, heading away from the noise of the highway, hoping to find a residential area, a place of libraries, well-kept homes with flower boxes, supermarkets, and joggers equipped with cell phones. I would call Brad's cell, wary of the police after learning of their corruption. I saw movement, the bumper of a car rolling out of an upcoming side street and immediately veered, my speed increasing as I moved down the side of a building, worried that I wouldn't reach its end before the car passed. Or, that I would turn the corner and run into a group of thugs, trading one danger for another. I held my breath as I sprinted around the corner, hearing the rumble of engine as the car traveled down the street, my feet disappearing from sight just in time. Then I skidded to a stop as my eyes raced frantically over the scene before me.

Two vehicles. *Alarming.* I would have preferred an empty lot, no strangers. In this area, every individual was a potential foe, my mind not trusting anyone. I searched frantically for any sign of the car's owners. I listened to the street behind me, and ducked behind the first car, my eyes flitting over and then focusing on a green hose, coiled on the

floor beside a parking bay. *Water.* The hose glowed,
like a spotlight was focused on it, and everything
else faded to gray. I crawled behind the second car,
a green truck jacked up on off-road tires, neon
yellow shocks blocking my view of the building. I
exhaled slowly, listening for danger, then ran, loose
gravel kicked up by my raw bare feet, a few hitting
the truck behind me. *Water.* My sole focus followed
that hose, the nozzle mounted on the side of the
building and my hands reached for it greedily,
turning the handle rapidly and hearing the perfect,
orgasmic sound of water flowing from its end. I
grabbed it, pressing it directly against my open
mouth, grains of dirt mixing with the initial flow,
the hot water pouring down my throat in a
powerful stream, too much for me to take, and I
lifted my mouth briefly, gulping in air and fighting
a cough, swallowing the water and pausing before
lowering my mouth to the hose. This time I was
more careful, sipping from the stream, the liquid
turning cool, tasting better than it ever had, my
starved body drinking it like it would never stop, a
need that would never be fulfilled.

I finally stopped, my hand stumbling over the wall
until it reached the handle and turned, the hose
going limp in my hand. My stomach was physically
engorged, a round ball of liquid, and I felt sleepy,
my mind turning on me, becoming a drugged
machine that performed at half-speed. I crawled, on
my hands and knees, finding a space between the
dumpster and a fence, and laid down, not minding

the unyielding feel of parking lot beneath my body. At that moment, with my belly full and the weight of my body no longer carried by my feet, I was beyond content. Encased in a dumpster shield of privacy, I felt safe and secure enough to briefly close my eyes and rest.

Chapter 67

"What do you think is really going on?" Becca played with a string on her dress, sitting on the back porch of Brad De Luca's house. Olivia leaned against a porch column, staring out on the back yard, which was a picture of romance, white flowers and candles floating through the lit pool, dusk falling gently over the space.

"I've told you what I think. I think she changed her mind. It's the right decision."

"Fuck off, O. Stop being a bitch and push your opinion of their relationship to the side." Becca's tone was strong, and Olivia glanced up in surprise.

"Jesus, what's gotten your panties in a twist?"

"She's *missing*, Olivia. The police found her phone smashed into bits, she's been gone since last night, and you don't even seem to care!"

Olivia said nothing, bumping the column with her shoe. "So what are you saying, Becca? You think she's dead? You think someone else sent you that text?"

"I don't know what to think. I just know she wouldn't disappear like this. Her missing the makeup appointment was one thing. But this long? And the smashed phone? She wanted to marry Brad; I know she did. Julia's not flaky and she wouldn't scare her parents like this, you know that."

"But who would have taken her? Luke?"

"Are you kidding me? The worst thing he'd do is hug her to death. Brad asked me about him earlier. I can't see him doing this. Showing up at the wedding, yes. But he doesn't even know where she lives. She'd just yell at him, and he'd leave her alone."

"Yeah," Olivia said quietly. "But why would anyone else hurt her?"

"I don't know? She's young, she's hot, she's about to be loaded? Maybe it's someone with an issue with Brad. Someone he lost a case to."

"It's easier for me to think she just got cold feet, Becca. I don't want to think about anything else." Olivia pushed away from the column, stepping into the house and closing the door behind her.

◆◆◆

There were several times in a man's life when his world changed. Often this change happened without incident or recognition—a chance meeting of a woman who ended up becoming his wife, a new job that led to a change in destiny. With Brad, his life-changing moments were very clear.

The morning that his mother left, leaving behind nothing but a short note and the scent of her perfume.
The moment he walked out of his father's colossal mansion, separating himself from his family—The Family.
The moment that, at the possibility of losing Julia, he realized that he loved her, and found true happiness for the first time in his life.

And now. Now, the moment where she was lost, and his world might forever end. He would not survive without her, that fact was certain in his mind. If she were to leave him, yes, he would survive knowing she was happy. But if she were killed, snatched while fighting and screaming for his help … well, he would never forgive himself.

He gripped his phone tightly in his hand, willing it to ring, willing her to be safe, willing the brave, strong woman who had his fragile heart tightly in her capable hands to return to him.

◆◆◆

In a Holiday Inn, two miles from Brad, the Campbells resorted to the only thing they knew. Prayer. They prayed, they argued, they prayed some more.

Then, with no clear idea what to do, they got in the car and headed north. Made a few wrong turns, checked their phones incessantly, then finally arrived. Pulled their car into Brad's driveway and parked. Martha opened the door before they could knock.

"Come on in. I've been cooking, don't know what else to do. Brad also asked me to prepare the guest room. He's not worth speaking to at the moment, but I'll do everything I can to make you comfortable." She held open the door, gesturing for them to come in, and bit back tears when Julia's mom threw herself into her arms.

Chapter 68

The two men watched the surveillance tape, fast-forwarding grainy footage, jerky movements zipping by in black-and-white detail. Hunched together in the small electronics closet, the hum of machinery on all sides, the air grew hot quickly. The two men didn't move, didn't wipe the sweat as it ran down their faces. They stared, intent on their task, their eyes glued to the small screen before them.

"Stop. Play from there."

The footage showed a hallway, a man closing a door and walking away from the camera, his steps relaxed and unhurried.

"That's me. That's when I left to ditch the phone. I'm pulling out my cell right there."

"Okay. Keep watching."

They sat in complete silence, the clock in the bottom of the video counting slowly through the minutes, neither man moving an inch. Thirteen minutes passed, then they stiffened, watching the doorknob twitch, then still. Then the door swung open, and a girl burst into view. They watched in silence as she ran down the hall, out of view of the cam.

"Switch screens."

Fingers clicked, screens flickered, and they watched in silence as the upper showroom revealed the close encounter, the girl hiding while the man strolled by. Then, her escape through the front doors.

"Fuck. Better call the boss. He ain't gonna be pleased about this."

"No shit, man. No shit."

◆◆◆

Dom Magiano sat alone in his bedroom, in a chair by the window. He stared, unmoving, at the trees, their palms swaying in the breeze. When the call came, his hand was already on the receiver, and he lifted it to his ear without speaking.

The voice's subdued tone came through the line with specks of frustration dotting the words. "We don't know where she is."

His face tightened. He cleared his throat. "How is that possible? You lost her?"

"We're working on it."

"You're proving why you have never gained status in this town. Track her down before she is found. My son has half the town out looking." He hung up the phone without waiting for a response, leaning back in the chair and closing his eyes, waiting for the peace of sleep, peace that would not come for quite some time. The open window brought a blast of warmth, gentle fingers of heat that washed over his tired skin, doing nothing to loosen the stress lodged in the deep lines of his face.

◆◆◆

Night fell and the search for Julia Campbell continued, police reluctantly joining the hunt. Brad paced, an emotional storm on the edge of destruction. Martha cooked dishes no one would eat, and Stevie and Ben watched silently. News channels picked up the story on the police scanner, and the phone rang incessantly, until the point that Brad ripped it out of the wall. Then they appeared, white decaled vans, cheery faces plastered over their sides, inching down the street until they lined both sides of it. Curtains moved, neighbors watched, and everyone held their breath.

At ten o'clock, the girls left, Olivia driving her and Becca in circles through town, scanning the streets for Julia, silence and tension filling her Jeep. The Campbells returned to the hotel, watching the evening news and sat together, hands gripped, heads bowed, and hoped for a miracle.

Fourteen miles away, another group, men of a hardened nature, set up a three-mile perimeter around the showroom, bringing in dogs and starting an organized block by block search, intent on my recapture, the blood of their cohort setting fire to their hunt. Just inside that perimeter, I woke to mosquitoes, the sting of their bites prickling the skin on my arms and neck. I sat up, slapping my forearm and glanced around, my eyes adjusting to the darkness. I peeked around the edge of the dumpster. An empty parking lot, street lights illuminating spots of the bare asphalt. I stood, and my legs and back instantly screamed in protest.

In the distance, I heard a dog bark, and the tire crunch of a nearby car. The sound kicked my adrenaline back into gear. *How long I had been asleep?* I eased around the edge of the dumpster, glancing around quickly, my feet starting a silent bitch-fest, their raw bottoms readjusting to the rough gravel/pavement combination. I sent a silent prayer upward, thankful for the dark shadows that the dusk granted, then took off running, heading farther in the direction of quiet.

Chapter 69

Running had always helped me to clear my mind. Thoughts seemed to fall into place best when my body was occupied. I settled into a rhythm, trying to conserve energy, breathing shallowly and attempting to ignore the pain signals my body was shooting to my brain. My head, thankfully, had lost its piercing pain, settling into a dull throb that was somewhat bearable. I ran — redirecting any intelligent thought to try and figure out what the hell was going on.

I could see no reason to kidnap me. Was I being held for ransom? The wedding held off until Brad paid some exorbitant amount? I had so little information to go on. When I had first waked up, tied to a chair and blindfolded, I had heard men talking. Multiple men. They had been waiting for something. For me to wake up? I had probably knocked myself out in my attempt to escape from the chair, the wound on the back of my skull evidence to support that. Then I had reawakened, with that man on top of me … was that why I was taken? To be raped by a stranger? That seemed even less likely.

I took a deep breath, lengthening my strides in an attempt to change the muscles worked. Twice I had to hide, headlights reflecting off nearby items, warning me in advance of approaching cars. I used that time to breathe, crouched into a tiny ball, comfortable in the darkness, my confidence increasing the farther I ran. The streets were changing, becoming more commercial in nature. I passed a few homeless men, their eyes watching me closely, one reaching out for me as I passed, his fingers grasping empty air, my steps moving me away from him. I cut over one street, avoiding the main road and taking a side street, the hum of traffic giving me a burst of confidence. My eyes examined the back of closed business, doctor's offices, accounting firms, an auto parts store. I was moving closer to suburbia, the sidewalk less cracked, gravel transitioning to landscaped area. Everything closed. Then, ahead, I saw the glow of lights. A pharmacy, its bright red sign visible from the back road. I came to a stop, trying to make a decision.

It was the first place worth stopping at, the first commercial business I had come to, where the public moved freely in and out, where I could walk in and ask to use a phone. But wouldn't that also make it the first place they would look for me? Maybe I should continue, put another mile between them and me. I exhaled deeply, my throat dry, starving again for liquid. The pharmacy would have something for my feet. Maybe even shoes, not that I had any money to pay for it. But they might cover me until Brad arrived.

I walked, studying the store as I approached from the back. My body yearned to burst inside, dramatically collapse on the floor, and have all matters of liquids, ointments, and comfort thrust upon me with helpful, eager hands. But something felt off, so I picked up the pace and continued running. Ahead I saw decorative lighting and prayed for a residential street.

Given the distance I had run, the odds were finally in my favor. A ten-minute jog past the pharmacy delivered me into suburbia. It was practically Wisteria Lane, minivans and manicured lawns on either side as I stood in the middle of a gravel-free road. I nearly wept, running forward and sinking to my knees on soft grass, the purr of a sprinkler treating me with a spray of cool water. I stumbled to my feet, running with the sprinkler's movement, the glorious arch of liquid cooling my overheated body, water running down my face, my tongue outstretched. I slowed to a walk, the cushion of grass heaven to my abused feet, and then sank to the grass, lying on my back and waiting for the curtain of water to make its sweep over me once again.

Peace. Safety. A splash of cool water, the taste of it somewhat metallic. The tick of a sprinkler head as it moved on. A moment of glorious relaxation, the plush grass beneath me, the tickle of blades against my arms. The lull of sleep interrupted by a new blast of water, as the arc made its way back around.

The sprinkler was on its third sweep when the yard was flooded with light, painful fluorescent beams that caused my eyes to squeeze tight in an automatic reflex. I sat up, the sprinkler choosing that moment to hit me full force in the face, a pelt of water that had me momentarily blinded and coughing, the water catching me unprepared in my throat. I staggered to my feet, my hand wiping my face, my eyes blinking widely as my contacts attempted to find their place on my eyeballs. I held up my hands and froze when a commanding voice spoke from the directions of the lights.

"You've come to the wrong neighborhood if you want to get drunk and cause trouble. You've got sixty seconds to get off my lawn and out of this area, or I'm calling the cops." It was a woman's voice, strong and throaty, and I stepped forward, my contacts finally cooperating, my vision coming into focus. Steely blue eyes framed by a mess of red curls with a look that let me know my sixty seconds had begun.

"Please," I whispered. "Please. I need to use a phone." I sank to my knees before her, clasping my hands together and staring into her eyes, the dramatic pose entirely fitting, given the circumstances.

She surveyed me, her eyes traveling over my wet t-shirt, pajamas, and bare feet. She glanced out at the street, then back to me, studying my eyes intently. "You drunk?"

I shook my head. "No."

She pointed to a swing on the front porch. "You can use my phone, but stay on the porch." She started to head inside, and I stood, a smile crossing my face.

"Ma'am?" I called out, trying to catch her before the door swung behind her. She turned, eyeing me with a question in her glance.

"Do you mind turning the porch light off? I won't do anything wrong, I swear." I glanced over my shoulder, hating the bright lights that illuminated me on the dark street, a beacon to anyone on the hunt.

She gave me another long look, reached a hand over and flipped a switch, darkness settling back over the yard. I breathed a sigh of relief, waiting until the door shut before I moved to the swing.

If there was a heaven, it was something like that moment. I felt, for the first time since leaving my home, safe. Crickets chirped softly, the sprinkler purred before me, and a soft breeze danced gently on my wet skin. I glanced down, noting some red stains on the wet of my shirt and reached over, gingerly fingering the bandage on my shoulder, then carefully moved my hands to the back of my head, my fingers coming away red, the skin sore. I sighed, leaning back in the darkness and pushed lightly with my toe, starting the swing's movement.

The front door opened and the woman appeared, a bottle of water and a phone in hand. "Here," she said tartly, handing out both. "I watched you from the window. You don't have to drink from the sprinkler. I'm pretty sure that water isn't fit for consumption."

I smiled gratefully, setting the water down and using the cordless phone with both hands, my fingers shaking in their eagerness. I dialed Brad's cell, pressing the numbers deliberately, then held the trembling phone to my ear, biting my lower lip to keep the tears at bay.

Chapter 70

The moment I heard his voice, the tremor in it, the knowledge that he was as close to breaking as I was, my dam broke. I sobbed, unable to speak, my words unintelligible in the flood of tears that wouldn't stop coming.

His voice broke, saying my name repeatedly, asking me over and over if I was okay.

"Yes," I gasped, hiccupping on the word. "I'm okay. I need you to come get me."

Behind his voice I heard the slam of a door, the roar of his car.

"Where? Where are you?"

I sniffed, a loud, phlegm-filled sob, and looked at the woman before me, her eyes watching with a mixture of concern and curiosity. I move the receiver away from my mouth. "What's your address?"

She gave it to me, waiting as I repeated it to Brad, then offered a few reference points, which I also passed on.

"I know the area. I can be there in ten minutes. Julia, baby, I love you so much."

"I love you, too. I'll talk to you when you get here." I hung up, passing the phone to the woman, smiling through my tears. "Thank you," I whispered.

"You okay?"

I nodded tightly, trying to keep my emotions contained, a wave of happiness and relief spilling into me, and I smiled, tears running down my face. "Yeah," I whispered. "I'm good."

She didn't ask me anything else, just sat next to me on the swing. We sat there in the dark, my eyes fixed on the street, my ears listening for the sound of Brad's engine. I wondered, for a quick moment, if I should have called the police instead. But all I had thought of during my run was Brad. He would know whom to call; he would know what to do. Who was safe, and who was our foe. The swing rocked, the crickets chirped, and my tears fell, a constant flood down already-wet cheeks. Then I heard the sound, a squeak of tires on a turn, the acceleration of a heavy foot on the gas, and his car flew into view, my feet already in motion, flying down the steps, across the grass and into his arms, my face burying in his neck, sobs wracking my body. His hands ran over me, checking me for injuries, and he pulled away when he found my shoulder, then head wound, my body flinching at his touch. The concern in his eyes tugged at my heart.

"What happened? Do you need a doctor?"

"I'm fine. Don't worry about it. I want to go home."

His face grimaced, smiling in a way that broke my heart, and pulled me to him again. "Of course, baby. Let's go."

His strong arms. They lifted underneath my thighs and hugged my wet body to his. Unnecessary, not needed for the five steps to his car, yet he carried me. His neck smelled of sweat and cologne, the sharp rub of his jaw telling me that he had shaved. For the wedding. My heart broke for a brief moment. Then, we bent as one and he settled me, soft as a baby, into the passenger seat, his mouth brushing over my lips gently. Dark brown eyes, wetter than I've ever seen them, vulnerability mixed with a shot of relief, doused with love, met mine, and we did nothing but stare at each other for a moment. Then he shut the door softly, and I watched him, through tinted glass, take a few steps back into the yard, speaking to the woman with the red hair. He pulled out his wallet, they had a few minutes of discussion, then he handed her something. I leaned back in the seat, reclining it slightly, and closed my eyes.

I had barely taken a breath when he was in the car, his hand sweeping over my face, my eyes opening to find his concerned gaze on me. "Is everything okay? Your eyes just closed. I'm calling a doctor."

I laughed weakly. "I'm tired. Please drive. I want to get the hell outta here."

He obliged, putting the car into drive and holding my hand gently. "Just relax, baby."

I did, closing my eyes, and felt instantly drugged, my entire body sinking, the hum of the car hypnotic, my entire self happy to surrender to his care.

♥♥♥

Brad called Martha as he drove, trying his best not to jostle Julia's sleeping body as he navigated home. She answered on the first ring.

"It's me. I have her. She looks bad, like she hasn't eaten in days. Can you fix her a plate, and have someone prepare the bedroom? I can't remember much of the last twenty-four hours, but feel like I may have broken a few things up there." He glanced over, studying Julia's profile, wanting to wake her up just so he could look into her eyes.

Martha's voice calmed him, her strength giving him something to hold on to. He answered her questions as best he could, the lack of information difficult to accept on both their parts. He ended the call with a promise to be home soon, and asked her to call Julia's parents and to get a doctor over to the house.

He caressed the hand he held, it's limp grip reminding him of all the possibilities that could have occurred. The fact that she was here. The fact that she had returned in one piece, a miracle. He vowed to spend the rest of his life earning it.

Chapter 71

Movement. Jostling. Brad's arms. Once again being carried. My eyes opened to find him watching me. "I'm sorry," he whispered. "I didn't want to wake you."

"It's okay."

He carried me through the bedroom door, moving toward the bed, which had been turned down, extra pillows added. I stopped him with a hand. "Don't put me on the bed."

"What? You're exhausted."

"I'm also disgusting. And I want, more than anything, a shower." I grinned weakly at him and he turned, carrying me into the bathroom and setting me gently on my feet. I fought a wince when my feet hit the floor, his eyes catching the tell anyway, focusing on my feet, his face flaring with concern.

"What is that from?"

"My feet are a little raw … they got scraped up a bit."

He said nothing, a tic in his jaw giving away his anger, and he moved to the shower, turning knobs and pressing buttons until the bathroom started to fill with hot steam. He stripped, my eyes traveling over his gorgeous body, loving the curve and bend of muscles as he moved, his dick hanging between his thighs, sexual even when relaxed.

He studied my clothes, then opened a drawer, pulling out a set of scissors. "Hands out," he instructed.

I obeyed without asking, too tired to put up a fight. He moved carefully, sliding the scissors open and cutting my tee-shirt off, his eyes examining my bare chest, an eyebrow raising.

"I didn't have a bra on when I was taken," I said quietly, aware of his thought process.

He nodded, kneeling before me, gently cutting fabric until my sweats and panties fell away.

"I didn't want to try and pull your clothes over your feet or your head." he said softly, offering his hand and leading me to the shower.

He stopped, just before the entrance, his hand tightening on my arm, a pained question in his eyes. "I don't want to ruin evidence." He said tightly. "Did anyone… did they—"

I stopped him quickly, with a firm shake of my head, seeing where his question was going, the raw fear in his eyes. "No. Nothing like that."

I could see the relief, it poured through every muscle in his body as he exhaled, his hands gently pulling me closer and brushing his lips against my forehead. Then he let me move, and I stepped in delicately, moving quicker when I felt the hot water, the gentle rhythm massaging my skin as it cleansed. I moaned at the sensation, Brad running a loofah gently over me, creating a path of bubbles that disappeared quickly beneath the torrent of water, suds of soap pooling at my feet. I stood limp, letting him wash me, his hands gentle as they ran over and across my body. He examined my shoulder bandage, leaving it alone and washing around it. Then he turned off the water, wrapping me in two hot towels and carrying me to the bedroom. Someone had laid out my robe, a monogrammed piece Brad had given to me for Christmas, and I slid into the fluffiness of it, climbing carefully into bed and settling back into the stacks of pillows.

He sat on the bed next to me, his brown eyes full of concern. "Martha has been cooking all day, hoping you'd return. Do you feel up to eating something?"

I grinned at the thought of food. "I'm starving. Is she still up? What's she got?"

"What do I got?" A loud voice came from the direction of the door, no delicate or dainty treatment in her voice, and I turned to see Martha, wiping her hands on her apron, her full face smiling broadly. "Girl, you had me worried sick!" She maneuvered through the door, meeting my eyes with a face-splitting grin. "I got chicken and rice soup, or pot roast, or chicken salad, or lasagna. If none of those sound good, I'm happy to make you something else." She moved to the side of the bed, her wide hips easily bumping Brad out of the way, her arms wrapping around me in a hug that made me wince.

"They all sound good. I'm starving. I'll take the pot roast if there's enough."

"There's plenty; all the food's been going to waste, everyone too worried to eat." Her eyes softened. "We're so happy you're home. I spoke to your parents and friends. I told them you needed rest tonight, but I won't be able to hold them off for too long. They'll be by in the morning." She studied me. "Your parents, I know they'd sleep a lot better if they heard your voice."

I nodded. "I'll call them now. Thanks, Martha."

Brad brought me the house phone, my fingers slowly pushing the digits, trying to figure out how, what to say when they answered. But it turned out nothing was needed. My mother's sobs, my father's gruff exclamation of love… we all cried like babies, then they told me they loved me. Told me they'd be by in the morning, if I felt up to it. I told them I would and hung up the phone.

Martha then brought the food on a tray, the smell floating upstairs in a delicious announcement, my stomach audibly moaning at the scent. Brad let me eat in peace, watching me intently, like I was tissue paper and might crumble before him. He spoke the moment my fork hit the plate, when I settled back against the soft pillows with a content sigh.

"Julia, I know you are tired, but we need to punish whoever did this to you. If you could tell me what you know—"

I held up a hand, and he instantly quieted. "Brad, I'll give you what I know about where I was kept. But I don't know anything else. I was drugged or passed out for most of the time. I didn't hear or see anything that clued me in to who they were or what they wanted." The memory of *his* hands, pushing apart my thighs, popped into my mind, but I dismissed it, knowing the effect it would have on Brad, wanting to keep his mind clear as I gave him this information.

I spoke, telling about the downstairs room I was kept, the developer showroom, the street it sat on, storefront names I could remember, street names that had stuck in my mind. I spoke, even as the doctor entered and began his examine, my voice cracking when he inspected my head wound, my skin goosebumping when he pulled back the covers and checked every limb. Brad's eyes flickered, from the doctor to my face, listening intently, his eyes giving away the processing that was occurring behind them. When my words began to slur, my head nodding, he stopped me.

"Sleep. We can talk more in the morning. That helps." He placed a gentle kiss on my forehead and stood, tugging the blankets up around me and removing some extra pillows.

I nodded, closing my eyes as he moved to the side with the doctor, their voices lowered to whispered growls, my mind already falling down through layers of sleep until I hit the bottom and all was dark, deep sleep taking over my body. Downstairs, unbeknownst to me, a small army was assembling.

Chapter 72

As a half moon rose over the city, casting its dusky glow equally over all areas, oblivious to zip code, property values, or social standing, dark activity bred. In the large kitchen of Brad De Luca, police officers converged, pouring over a map of the city, pinpointing possible locations while loading up on armor and ammo. Their numbers doubled a normal response, Brad hiring every moonlighting cop available, wanting every presence possible, every warm body that carried a badge to be concentrated on bringing down Julia's captors. Two hours after the first officer walked into their house, the FBI arrived, and the house swelled to capacity. Plans were discussed, egos clashed, and Martha's food disappeared, bit by bit, into the mouths of men. Then they disbursed, headed for three possible targets, a sea of black disappearing into the night.

In another part of the city, the security video was burned to a disk, carried to an upstairs office and played for a larger audience, the men watching in silence as the girl opened that door, ran down that hallway, and disappeared from their building. Options were discussed, risks were weighed, and a call was made. Then, cleanup began, starting with the room where she had been kept. The smell of bleach soon filled the air, urgency in the men's movements, every moment until she was found a desperate race in cover-up. The three-mile perimeter was widened, and word of her escape spread.

Dom Magiano sat on his back porch, cloaked in darkness, listening to the rustle of palm leaves as a cool breeze swept across his skin. He was tired, flaccid muscles limp around old bones, his chest rasping as he inhaled the thick air. The day weighed on him, nothing going as planned, the look on his son's face haunting him. It was not the first time he had disappointed his son. Disappointment was good for children; it taught them to value that which was taken or withheld from them. But this fight he had taken on, this lesson he had strived to teach his son … maybe it was not worth the effort. He certainly hadn't expected her to escape, to fight a grown man in doing so. It should have been simple. An exercise in intimidation, one that would have sent her on her way, a way in the opposite direction of his son. Instead, it ended in failure. He was getting old, unsure of how many fights he had left. Better to save the energy and expel it against a worthy adversary. She was not worth his energy. And, given the recent news from his youngest son, the report of his daughter-in-law's cancer … Julia might be needed for grandchildren. They would need to start immediately; he wanted to see new young heirs before he passed.

◆◆◆

While the city moved, Brad sat in a chair by the bed and watched her sleep. His phone, set to vibrate, lay on the dresser next to him, a ticking time bomb, the police instructed to call the moment they discovered anything. They had wanted to question her, the police and FBI insistent, their faces growing red at his refusal. But she had been through enough. She needed sleep, and he didn't want her to say anything until he knew the full story, liability constantly lurking, like a dormant plague, waiting to infect if given the slightest opening. In the morning, when she woke, they could talk. Then, with an attorney present, she could give the police her statement.

Hours ago, with his kitchen full of black uniforms, he had second-guessed his actions, the call to involve them in this situation. Every face he saw, every cop he paid, he silently examined with distrust. There was corruption in the police department, his family being one of the major parties responsible. But they had been his best chance, the source he felt most comfortable using. He hadn't wanted to further involve his family, the nagging possibility of their hand in her kidnapping rendering that a risky move.

She shifted in her sleep, a sigh settling over her body, and he stood, his hand in his pockets, moving closer until he stood over her. There he stayed, his eyes memorizing her features, her breath, the flush of her skin as she slept. His enormous relief at her return was foreshadowed by his panic, his concern that something else could happen. The horrific thing about having everything that he ever wanted was the constant fear that it would all disappear.

Chapter 73

I woke to a heart-warming familiar scene. Brad's bed, sunlight streaming through breaks in the curtains, the clatter of pans, and smells of bacon. I rolled over, stretching, wincing as my feet brushed against the sheets, my head welcoming me to the day with a dull roar of pressure. I was naked, the robe tangled around me, my arms freed from it at some point in the night, and I moved it aside, pushing back the covers and walking to the closet, grabbing a long nightshirt and pulling it over my head.

Brad met me on the stairs, his critical eyes on my bare feet, a frown settling over his features, and I spoke before he could.

"I'm done being babied. I ran for miles on these feet … I can walk myself downstairs."

"You should be in bed. I'll have Martha bring up food."

"Move. I need normality right now. Don't think I can't kick your ass." He grinned at my tone, jogging up a few steps and planting a kiss on my lips.

"Fine. I'm glad to see your spark back. Breakfast is ready if you are hungry."

I shoved him gently over and moved down the stairs, a smile spreading over my face. *I am alive. I am home. I am with Brad.* I left the stairwell, moving into the kitchen, surprised to see a strange face seated at the table.

"Good morning," I said uncertainly, giving Martha a hug and accepting the plate she directed me to.

Brad spoke. "Julia, this is Doctor Barnes. You met him last night. He's just here for a follow-up examination. He's also signed confidentiality papers, so please continue to speak freely in front of him."

"May I eat first?" I eyed my plate—bacon, sausage, hash browns, and eggs dancing yummy in front of me.

"Of course," the doctor spoke, pulling a chair out for me. "Observation is part of the exam, so if you don't mind, I'll watch you closely."

I blushed. "That's fine."

Brad sat across from me, his face serious. "The police want to question you this morning. Before they do, I'd like to walk through with you what happened. An attorney will be with you during the questioning, but it'll help if you go through it with me a few times first."

I shrugged, shoveling food into my mouth with a fork, too hungry to care about the matter of appearances. "Okay. But I won't be much help."

"Start from the beginning."

I did, starting from the moment I heard my vehicle's alarm, explaining the cloth over my mouth, waking in the chair, my subsequent blackout. The doctor interrupted a few times, asking about my body's response — how I had felt upon waking each time. I tried to answer as truthfully as possible, much of my memories vague, my head aching as I pushed it. He re-examined the back of my head, the wound, his touch eliciting a cry from me that had Brad shooting to his feet.

"This wound indicates a strong impact; she must have fallen back onto concrete. She's lucky … her concussion could have killed her. We'll need to keep her under close observation for a few days, and I'd like to get a CT and MRI this afternoon, if the police are done with her by then."

Brad nodded, his eyes on me. "Then what happened? When you woke up the second time?"

I hesitated, his eyes catching on and sharpening in response. I saw his hands clench and I frowned. "I can't tell you this if you are going to freak out about it."

"Tell me," he gritted out.

"I woke up, untied, on a bed of some sorts — a thin one. A man was in between my legs, and my sweats and panties were off." Brad swore, pain on his face, and I reached out to him. "Like I said last night - nothing happened, Brad. Let me talk." He nodded, his eyes on mine. "I waited and tried not to move, tried to pretend to be asleep, or unconscious, or whatever it was that I had been. When I saw an opening, I took it."

"Took what? What do you mean?"

"I put him in a triangle chokehold. Like Ben taught me." I looked down, moving my food on my plate.

"You're shitting me." His voice held a mixture of pride and dismay, and I looked up to find him running a hand over his mouth, his eyes dark.

"No. I held it — " My voice broke, my eyes staying on Brad, watching the flicker in his as I spoke. "For a long time, but not too long, after he passed out. I counted. Three minutes."

"Three minutes," he said quietly. "That's it?"

"Yes. Then I ran. I ran, and I hid, and I ran again. I stopped once, behind a building, and slept between a dumpster and a fence for a bit … until dark. Then I ran again, and I got to the house that you picked me up from."

"Three minutes," Brad repeated, frowning slightly, a question in his eyes, his knowledge not as great in the area of jujitsu as my own.

"Four minutes is terminal. Just three minutes… he'd have regained consciousness."

Brad's eyes darkened across the table.

Chapter 74

The day passed in a blur of questions, medical tests, family, and friends. My wedding dress hung in the corner of the room, a constant indicator of the wedding that never occurred. The money wasted stuck like a forgotten burr, poking and scraping with every reminder—the mountain of wrapped gifts piled in a corner of the guest room, the useless Post-It note stuck to a corner of the fridge, with reception times and a reminder to pull passports from the safe. Our honeymoon also picked at my conscience, despite my unwilling part in my disappearance, all this—the police, the doctor, the haunted look in Brad's eyes—was a burden brought on by my actions. If only I had stayed inside the house, ignored my car alarm and the words painted on the windows and doors. But the guilt was soon washed away in the overwhelming current of love and celebration that filled the home. Mother shone, Dad's eyes twinkled, and Olivia was the beaming best friend of a year prior. We ate every casserole Martha had baked, demolished the groom's cake, and I had some vintage bubbly, obeying the doctor's stern orders to limit it to one glass. Brad's hand never left my skin, his arm around me, his mouth making frequent trips to my forehead, my cheek, my lips. I saw fear in his eyes when he looked at me, a protective, raw emotion that both comforted and chilled me, the dark look so vulnerable in its whatmighthavebeen caress. Then he stood, heralding them all out, glaring at anyone who dared to object—'doctor's orders' his reprimand of choice.

And we had two hours—two hours of peace, our bodies molded together on the bed, his hand trailing lightly through my hair until I slept. Then, Martha's knock reawakened us, and I dressed for the police.

More questions. So many questions. So many I had already answered. The officers questioned me until my voice was hoarse, and Brad held up a hand, giving them one hard look that ended all questions. Then they took a turn, speaking instead of interrogating, updating me on everything that had happened in the last twelve hours.

I didn't know what my kidnappers had planned, but my escape certainly put a kink in their plans. An hour after I returned home, police raided the showroom, finding nothing helpful in their search of the downstairs. The gurney I had laid on? Almost been raped on? Gone. That room had been empty, the smell of bleach strong. The electronics room, which held the security system was also clean, all footage gone, the system's history wiped. The police tracked down the owner of the building at 3:15 a.m. and questioned him. He said the downstairs of the building was leased, and provided, bleary-eyed and irritated, copies of a lease agreement. The police looked up the renter, which turned out to be a bogus corporation with no ties to anything. Dead ends leading to dead ends.

I told the police everything. That I choked him until he passed out, then pushed him off me and ran. I had been unnecessarily prepped by Brad and performed well, his head imperceptibly nodding as I ran through the liability-safe lines of our script.

I was exhausted by the time they left, and sat in Brad's lap on the sofa in the den, the memory of two weeks ago, our fuck on this couch, seeming light years away. "I want to turn the theatre room back into a theatre," I said, my voice muffled slightly by his neck.

"You don't want to train with Ben anymore?" he asked, surprise in his tone. "I thought, with everything that happened …"

"I just want things to go back to normal. In a few months I might start training again. It's too soon right now. I want to go back to using that room for mindless entertainment."

He nodded. "On that note, I have a suggestion."

"About the theatre room?"

"No. About something else entirely."

I turned in his lap, facing him head on, and raised an eyebrow questioningly, his eyes glued to mine as he started to speak.

Chapter 75

Two days later, we wed in a small ceremony in our backyard. It happened at dusk, the pool littered with small flowers and candles, the glow reflecting in delicate patterns off our skin. We were a party of few, the invitees kept to my parents, Martha, and our close friends. Rebecca handled the details, and Martha fed us like kings at the conclusion of the nuptials. I would never forget the look in Brad's eyes, love shining unabashed as he spoke words that have tied together souls for centuries. His love was terrifying in its entirety, an uncontrollable wave that fiercely dominated normal levels of emotion. I worried I was unable to compete, my own love inferior in its selfish humanity.

"You won't understand," he whispered later that night. "Unless you come close to losing me, you will never understand the black hole that my soul became when I thought you were gone. I hope you never understand the depth of love you have for me, I hope your heart is never pushed off that cliff. Just know that I am forever yours. You may crush my heart, and I will ask you for more. I just need to know you are happy and safe. Nothing else will ever matter to me."

He moved above me, his mouth coursing over mine, soft kisses gently caressing my soul, kisses that traveled, down my neck, his body sliding lower, his fingers unbuttoning my nightshirt as my legs wrapped around him. Then, he was at the top of my panties, his bare mouth skimming the line of skin before satin, his kisses continuing lower, until I felt the heat of his mouth through the fabric, teasing my skin, his tongue swiping over my silk-covered sex. I moaned, arching into his mouth, his hands moving underneath me until they gripped the muscles of my ass, lifting me fully into his mouth, the hot air of his breath tickling my inner thighs. The barrier of my panties stretched out my buildup, my frustration growing along with my orgasm, heightening the arc when it came, a quivering explosion of pleasure, his audible moan of arousal incredibly hot to my ears.

Then we christened a bed that we had christened a hundred times before, but this time, as husband and wife, the fucking sweeter, the kisses slower, the look of love in his eyes more intense.

I fell asleep wrapped in his arms, a strong frame of protection that I never wanted to leave. "I'm so sorry," he whispered into my neck, my eyes already heavy with the edges of sleep.

"For what?" I said groggily.

"For not finding you. For not being there. I should have rescued you."

I smiled, my words finding surface before I was captured by the pull of sleep. "You rescued me the moment I met you. My life began on that day."

He pulled me tighter to him, and I fell. The final step. I fell into sleep, into life, into love. It felt as if I had finished a journey, grown and changed by the experience. I had arrived to the place where I was, where I was born to be who I was born to be, with whom I was born for. No matter what the future brought, whether it was danger, or sexual heat that burned me alive, or a weary game of checkers in a nursing home, I wanted it, with every inch of my body. I embraced our future and our ability to spend every last minute of it next to this man. My husband. My mate. My soul's recognition in another.

Epilogue

I am fairly certain it was my father. My own flesh and blood who put her life in danger. I had my suspicions before, and have dug since. Dug as far as I can dig considering I can't use any of my family's connections. There is no real way for me to communicate how I feel about his possible involvement. About the idea that he would destroy my life for ... fuck ... I don't even know why. A personal vendetta? For some fucked up version of pride? What kind of father puts a hit out on his son's fiancée? It might not have started as a hit, but he knew what would happen. He saw her strength at Maria's house. He knew when he ordered her taken that it would mean her killed.

If it *was* him. If it wasn't him ... well, that is the small possibility that walks with such large steps.

I know my family has no connection to the warehouse—that the men in our organization who would handle this were otherwise occupied, their alibis verified in undisputable ways. But my father is too smart for that. He would have set up a wall of separation for a task such as this, would have covered his ass six ways to Sunday.

I have no choice. Damn the chances of his innocence. There is no good reason for him to be in my life anyway. I don't need family. I have her. And now she is my wife. Protected. I have amped up security, and we are looking at a new house, one with a private gate and enough protection for the Queen of England. But I will never stop worrying. I have seen a glimpse of life without her, and it is hell.

So I have cut all ties. Again. Like I did at seventeen, and again at twenty-nine. I will miss my sister, but the rest of them can go to hell. No holidays, no birthdays. Definitely no weddings. I will never be able to hear a wedding march and not think of waiting for her. Waiting for her at the end of that aisle, my heart bursting, and her not appearing. Listening to the song end and the silence that followed.

We are taking off for two months. Taking a honeymoon that gives us one week in Key West and then seven in the Bahamas. Rebecca found us a house with a boat right on the ocean, close enough to Atlantis for fun, but quiet and secluded enough that we can fuck like rabbits and no one can hear. I plan to get her naked, tan from head to toe, and please her endlessly. Take the boat out and fish, dive. Catch lobster and bring them back. Eat, fuck, and sleep late.

The Bahamian house is for sale. If it is like its pictures, if it makes her eyes light up and her mouth curve, I will buy it. I will buy it and spend two months showing her the life that could be forever.

I don't need the courthouse. I don't need the fight. I don't need my family. I sure as hell don't need a town full of exes. Saffire brings in seven figures a year; we can live like kings without working. Assuming my fabulous wife doesn't mind sharing the earnings of her company. And if she wants that law degree, we can spend nine months a year at the university of her choosing. Let her study until her eyes cramp, and debate until her voice is hoarse. Fuck, I'll hang a shingle in Nassau if that's what she wants. Or Miami. Or Colorado. Anywhere. I am untied. I have no bearings. She is my sun, and everything else is bullshit. I love so few people in my life. I need only one. *Her.*

I hope she never knows how vulnerable I am. It is terrifying to me. I hate it—hate how much I love her. I never planned for this. I wanted a companion, and instead turned over my entire heart. I hope she is not too young. I hope she doesn't crush me.

The End

(Please continue on for a link for additional content)

Author's Note

As sad as it was for me to finish Brad and Julia's love story, I understand that some readers might want a little more of a HEA than is provided in the final chapter of this book. If you want a more complete happily-ever-after, please visit this link for a bonus chapter:
www.alessandratorre.com/bradandjuliaHEA

Thank you all for going on this journey with me. My writing career started with Brad and Julia, and I will miss them both terribly. I appreciate all of your support during the best 18 months of my life. I love you all!

If you are interested in more of my books, please visit one of my sites below or consider signing up for my monthly newsletter at:
www.alessandratorre.com/extras/newsletter

@ReadAlessandra
pinterest.com/ATorreAuthor
facebook.com/AlessandraTorre0/

This book would not be possible without my fabulous agent, Maura Kye-Casella, my kickass editor, Madison Seidler, and the constant support of the readers.

A special 'thank you' is owed to my facebook group Torreville – you guys keep me laughing, writing, and inspired. Any fans interested in a daily update on my writing, please feel free to join us there. Also, Keelie, Vicky, Bip, Elaine, Wendy, Sandra, and Shannon – you ladies are my rock. Thanks for all the support.

Printed in Great Britain
by Amazon

34685172R00255